"There must be somethi[ng]...ings," Sanger said as he turned toward the frames leaning against the wall. "Or among the books, perhaps. Assuming they aren't too badly mildewed."

"Even if they weren't musty, I don't believe they are quite the sort of book one admits to owning," said Lady Helena in a fascinated tone. She'd opened a volume and stared, wide-eyed, at one of the many pictures.

Sanger glanced over Helena's shoulder to discover exactly what she was contemplating with such an odd combination of horror and amusement. "My God in Heaven!" he exclaimed, seeing the book she held in her hands and instantly snatching it away. "*You* shouldn't be looking at that!"

Helena tried to get it back. "Perhaps," she said, "I should be shocked into a fainting fit, but you forget I was raised by my grandmother who doesn't allow missishness. Besides, I frequented the stables from an early age, and no one worried about what I might or might not learn there."

"This is different," Sanger insisted. "You should not even know such illustrations exist, let alone look at them." He turned to look at the paintings. They weren't large and they needed cleaning. The one he picked up, however, was a delightfully intriguing study of woman's head and shoulders. She was turned sideways and looked back over one shoulder with an expression of mischief that made one smile just to see it.

"Who do you suppose did this?" he asked. "It's rather incredibly well done, I'd say." He glanced from the painting to Lady Helena and back. "And something of a coincidence, is it not? This reminds me of you, Lady Helena, when you are in a teasing mood."

"Do you think so?" she asked, surprised.

Sanger raised his eyes and met Lady Helena's gaze. "I think I'd like to keep this. In memory of a very special day and even more special, the lady of whom it will remind me."

His look was somewhat heated and Lady Helena felt herself blush. "That is very likely the nicest compliment I've ever been paid."

A Lady's
Proposal

Jeanne Savery

Zebra Books
Kensington Publishing Corp.
http://www.zebrabooks.com

ZEBRA BOOKS are published by

Kensington Publishing Corp.
850 Third Avenue
New York, NY 10022

First Printing: September, 1998
10 9 8 7 6 5 4 3 2 1

Printed in the United States of America

One

Appalled, Simon Mansanger, the very new Earl of Sanger, stared at the woman standing next to him. "But Lady Helena, I thought you understood!"

"That you were merely flirting? I suppose I did." A sad-dog look flitted across Lady Hel's expressive features. On any other face the expression would have caused dismay. On Lady Helena Woodhall's face it merely led one to chuckle. It was very difficult for her ladyship's countenance to be anything but lovely even when she wished it otherwise.

Actually, her beauty had been her bane for several years now. *More* than several, actually. For something near a decade. Still more precisely, ever since age sixteen when Lady Hel's beauty burst forth much as a rose opens overnight.

She'd been a girl merely approaching marriageable age, but her face brought suitors from far and wide. Of course, the suitors didn't object that she'd fortune as well as face. A very large fortune. More wealth than any young lady had a right to, or so thought many a rapscallion living beyond his means. Such men made Lady Hel's life miserable in their attempts to wed her and relieve her of the burden of it. They'd put her off marriage forever or so she'd thought.

Recently she'd discovered a good reason for the right kind of husband. But, upon deciding she'd found the man, perhaps she'd erred. Lady Hel clutched the balustrade that edged the terrace at the back of her host's country manor and stared over the formal Italian-style garden spread out below her. *It has been a long time,* she mused, *since I miscalculated quite so badly. How,* she wondered, *did I do so now?*

"I'm sorry," she said, as the sound of his low-pitched voice penetrated her abstraction. "I was thinking and didn't hear you."

"I said," repeated Sanger, his tone apologetic, "that I couldn't afford to marry where there is no fortune."

Lady Hel blinked. *She'd* miscalculated, had she? *Someone* had erred, but was it herself? Surely Sanger knew she'd bring him something approaching twenty thousand pounds a year? On the other hand, he was new to the *ton* and perhaps he did not? In fact, he'd pretty well made it clear he did not!

"So . . . if there *were* a fortune?" she asked. Her smile was not so sparkling as was usual, thanks to a certain tense wariness.

The tall man, his hair a pale blond, sighed so softly she almost missed it. She glanced up and was bemused by the muscle in the side of his jaw which twitched, and then again and then still a third time before he controlled his emotions.

"Well?" she encouraged.

"Well?" he repeated. *"Not* well. I'd be named a fortune hunter and—" His voice approached a growl. "—I'll be damne- . . . er—" He dropped a sideways look her way. "—I'll be *dashed* if I'll allow anyone to say that of me!"

Lady Hel's hands tightened around the rough stone. "Are you suggesting you'll not wed at all?"

"In the near future? *Absolutely impossible.*" With less heat, he explained. "The estate produces barely enough to cover the mortgage payments each quarter. There is nothing left to make improvements and I'll not ask a lady to live under the appalling conditions to be found at

Sanger-Monkton. You cannot imagine how shocked I was when I discov- . . ." He shook his head, a tight smile appearing and disappearing. He bowed. "Such matters cannot possibly be of interest to you, my lady."

Could they not? she wondered. Ah well . . . Another man who thought that because her face was easy to look upon, her head must be full of cotton wool.

Sanger continued more earnestly. "My lady, I must apologize for giving you the wrong impression, allowing you to . . ."

"Oh, don't act the fool, Sanger," she interrupted. "You know you gave no wrong impressions. This absurd situation is wholly of my making."

She smiled at his wry expression which arched one of his thick brows in a way she envied.

"I am too impetuous, I suppose . . . You see," she continued, "I am honest with you, am I not? It is unfortunate, that honesty," she mused, staring out toward where a group of children played. "If I were the unscrupulous sort of lady who would do anything to trap myself a husband, I'd now resort to the vapors and threats of swooning and would soon have you on your knees insisting I marry you out of hand."

He chuckled. "It is good, then, that you are not out to trap a husband. But you would not have to, would you? I have wondered, actually—" He hesitated, obviously considering whether he should continue. "—just why you are unwed. You are overly impetuous. *My* fault is a curiosity which forces me to ask impertinent questions."

"It is quite simple. Until very recently I've not wished it."

"But you do now?"

She glanced sideways from the corners of her eyes. "Do I? I wonder . . ."

Her lips compressed, she mentally totted up the accidents which had plagued her in recent weeks. Accidents which had quickly become less and less accidental-seeming.

Trailing fingers of fear whispered up her spine, chilling her . . . Had it been *fear* which led her to settle on Sanger as a possible solution? Sanger, new to the *ton,* a military man cited for bravery? Ah! But then there were those broad shoulders and honest brown eyes. They had made the notion a happy one and less than difficult to swallow, had they not?

"I thought I did," she said and forced a teasing note, an impish smile. "Perhaps it is as well I shocked the truth from you, my lord, or you might have agreed and then where would we be?"

Sanger bowed gravely. "I have enjoyed our flirtation, my lady. I was flattered that you, the loveliest woman at this ridiculous house party, should choose me as your current gallant."

"Perhaps I was bored," she said, covering a feigned yawn with one fine-boned, long-fingered hand.

"Bored?" He pulled her fingers away from her face. "I have heard that the Lady Hel is exceedingly unfashionable and never admits to boredom."

"Then perhaps—" Her irritation at the embarrassing path her proposal led them down made her speak a trifle tartly. "—it was my way of escaping boredom at this . . . *ridiculous* . . . party. A good word for it. It is ridiculous. Ludicrous, even. Lady Trewes has no more notion of how to achieve an interesting collection of guests than that pup there . . ."

Lady Helena gestured to where a half grown border collie played with the Treweses' children and their young guests. Instinctively, the dog attempted to herd the youngsters together. That they persisted in straying from a properly cohesive flock obviously distressed the young animal.

Several people with well-filled nurseries had been invited to visit, their children providing company for the

Treweses' offspring. The children, their hostess placidly explained to anyone who would listen, would entertain one another and stay out of the way of the adults.

At least, that was the theory.

Lady Beth, the Treweses' eldest daughter, had other notions. Now she cast a glance toward Lady Helena. Obviously Beth recognized her. Even from this distance Hel could see that the girl blushed rosily, merely because she'd been caught enjoying a romp with the younger children. However embarrassed she might be, Lady Beth hurried toward the terrace in a determined manner.

"You'd best make your escape, my lord," suggested Lady Helena. "Lady Beth is at that stage of existence where she is neither the one thing or the other. She will ruffle her half-formed feathers or pluck a few of mine. Or—" Helena eyed him. "—perhaps even yours. It would be best for all of us if you took yourself off."

He slanted a glance her way. "Have you no more use for me, now you know I'll not wed you?" he teased.

"Blunt indeed, my lord." She cast a sideways teasing look back. "I must think about that, must I not? Now, do go . . . please? I told Lady Beth I'd show her a trick for dealing with that fly-away hair and I think she means to demand my help this very instant."

"You'll not ride then?"

Faint color tinged Lady Hel's cheeks. "I'd forgotten my promise to her when I agreed to ride with you." She glanced up, "You will forgive me and . . . go?"

"You are very kind to her," he said, ignoring her suggestion.

Giving up any further attempt to protect him, Lady Hel's vision clouded. "I remember so well when I was that age. I'd have given a great deal to have had someone take an interest. A certain sort of interest . . . I had preceptors aplenty, but not the one sort I wanted, you see."

"As I said, kind."

"Lady Helena, Lady Helena," cried the girl as she panted up the flight of shallow steps to their level, the pup at her heels, "can we do it now?"

"Lady Beth," said Lady Helena, giving Sanger another of those sideways looks which said as loudly as words, *you see?* "You have, I presume, met Lord Sanger?"

"Yes, my lady." Lady Beth's plump cheeks reddened again and she dipped a hurried curtsy in Sanger's general direction. "Please," she pleaded, raising glowing eyes, which, big and dark brown, looked very like those of the pup nudging at the girl's legs, attempting to return her to the children's group.

"Be still Sir!" ordered Lady Helena. "Sit!"

The dog blinked and instantly sat, thumping its tail in doggy apology against the irregular-shaped flags flooring the terrace. It appeared he was not truly chagrined, however. The animal's tongue hung out one side of his mouth, with an expression very much like a grin on his face.

"Lady Beth," continued Lady Helena, "you are interrup- . . ."

The chit interrupted again. "It is *hours* yet until Mama will put out the luncheon and—" Lady Beth stared in what she obviously hoped was wide-eyed innocence at Lady Helena. "—you did promise . . ."

Lady Helena suppressed a sigh. "So I did."

"Well?"

The chit's eyes begged. The pup lifted one paw and gently scraped the front of Helena's gown. Lady Hel looked from one to the other.

His voice colored by a touch of humor, Sanger said, "My lady, if you made a previous promise, then I'll not hold you to the one to me that we go riding."

Lady Beth's face suddenly fell into a ludicrous expression of lost hope. "I didn't mean to interrupt."

"Did you not, my dear?" asked Lady Hel, gently scolding. "It was quite impossible that you failed to notice that Lord Sanger and I conversed."

"Oh, yes," admitted the girl with the appalling frankness of the very young, "I did, of course, but Mama says you cannot possibly be seriously interested in Lord Sanger when you've turned down some of the very best matches in the kingdom." The girl continued to stare, wide-eyed and hopeful. "So, you see?"

There was a half innocent, half cynical edge to the comment. Lady Helena couldn't decide whether to box the chit's ears for impertinence or to find the mother who had allowed the daughter to overhear such gossip and box *hers*. She counted to ten.

"Perhaps, Lady Helena," said his lordship speaking over the chit's head, "I'll change my mind—" Lord Sanger's quirky brow climbed his forehead, his twinkling eyes inviting her to laugh. "—if only to confound our hostess. Do you think it a good plan? Of course, you must promise to let me off the hook as soon as the furor dies down."

"Don't tempt me," said Lady Hel in the driest of tones. "At the moment I'm all too likely to take you up on that." Then, surprised he'd trust her, she asked, "But how, my lord, could you be certain I'd keep such a promise?"

"Because," he said gently, "although we've met infrequently previous to this house party, I've found you an honorable woman of many talents and much kindness." He dropped the serious note and, catching Lady Beth's interested gaze, adopted an air of patently false distress. "I will now take my ride in solitary melancholy. You see what you drive me to, Lady Beth? Why—" He continued in a still more broadly melodramatic fashion. "—perhaps I'll succumb to the depths of lost hope and you'll wonder where I've gotten to. You'll find me, my neck broken, where my horse, more sensible than I, refused a regular rasper. I, having lost all judgment and with no care that I live or die, will have foolishly attempted an impossible jump . . . and have paid the price."

He looked at the sky, his sad expression totally unbelievable.

Unless one were fourteen, exceedingly deep in hero worship of the same woman, to say nothing of newly conscious of Romance with a capital *R* . . .

Lady Beth pulled her lower lip between her teeth, biting it. "If you go riding with him—" Beth drew in a martyred breath. "—then his Lordship would not despair. I will find you later, Lady Helena. I am very sorry to have disturbed you and . . ."

"And you, my dear, are a regular jaw-me-dead," Lady Hel interrupted, inelegantly. "Lord Sanger is bamming you and is merely being difficult. We will go to my room immediately. Until later, my lord." She turned away, and Beth, instantly restored to the best of good humor, went tripping along beside her, words of apology and explanation falling all over each other.

Sanger half leaned, half sat against the balustrade and watched as they entered the house by the French doors to the garden room. He rubbed his chin between thumb and finger. It had been a very strange conversation, he mused.

Had the lady really proposed marriage? Or had she proposed something else and he, green to the ways of the *haut ton,* not caught her drift? A revealing muscle jumped in Sanger's jaw at that intriguing thought, but relaxed as he decided her words had been much too explicit for any such misunderstanding.

Seemingly idly, she'd asked questions concerning his plans for the immediate future. He, thinking she was interested in his sudden and unexpected rise to an earldom, said he hadn't had time to know if he were coming or going. He'd explained that he'd accepted Lady Trewes's invitation so he'd be close to Sanger-Monkton, which was, in its current state, uninhabitable.

She'd asked if it had occurred to him a wife would be helpful—at which he mumbled something about not thinking of marriage yet.

Then she'd done the unbelievable. She'd insisted he think about it. Think about wedding *her*. And he'd blurted out that bit about flirting and thinking she'd understood. Blast it, she had understood! She'd admitted it.

So why had she done it? Was it true that Lady Hel had turned down several excellent matches? Very likely yes. Where there was *already* a fortune, a man need not look for one in his wife's dowry, so of course a woman as lovely and lively and intelligent as Lady Hel had received offers . . .

"Lord Sanger . . ."

A soft, lisping voice interrupted his thoughts. A much disliked voice. Sanger, frowning slightly, glanced around. The voice's owner took the steps from the garden at a studied pace, fending off the pup with his cane. What an awful man, thought Sanger, eyeing the overly thin but well-muscled figure.

He'd taken Thurmand Woodhall in instant, probably irrational, dislike when the man was introduced to him at Tattersall's sale rooms. While still in town, Sanger had studiously avoided him. Then, to his disgust, he'd arrived at the Treweses' party to find Woodhall was also a guest.

"Mr. Woodhall," Sanger acknowledged him.

"I watched you talking with my cousin," Woodhall said and continued, his tone insinuating . . . something. "A lovely woman, is she not?"

"Lady Helena? Very lovely."

Longer acquaintance hadn't eased Simon's distaste for Woodhall. For reasons he'd been unable to determine, Woodhall had played the role of his boon companion here at the Treweses'. All too often he'd had difficulty ridding himself of the man.

He'd tried to find a reason for his antipathy. Woodhall

was fashionable without going to the extremes of any particular style, was a more than adequate rider, a good shot, played a decent game of piquet, and was good with a cue. Simon, learning all that, still couldn't like the man.

"She will wed. Eventually," added Woodhall, speaking with that faint but irritating lisp. He stared at his fingernails, twisting his fingers this way and that. He glanced up. "I won't envy the man."

"Oh?"

"Ah!" Woodhall smirked. "She's yet to reveal her temper?"

"I've seen nothing of a temper." Sanger's mobile brow arched. "She's been very pleasant."

Woodhall laughed and Simon counted one reason for disliking him. His laugh had an unpleasant shrillness that grated on the ear!

"You would suggest," added Sanger, curious, "that she is not always such good company?"

"Lady Hel, which she is called with reason, can make a man think Hell might be a pleasure after she puts him through his paces."

"She has put you through them, then?"

Woodhall's eyes widened. "Oh no. I'd never act the suitor, you see."

Sanger wondered why the creature exaggerated his attempt to look innocent, looking *too* innocent? "You think I would? You mistake the situation," he continued coldly. "I am in no position to take a wife. The dibs are not in tune, my new title empty of everything but history. And now I must meet my friend, Jack Alton, at the stables." He bowed. "Good morning to you."

All the way along the terrace Simon felt as if something bored into his back right between his shoulders. As he turned the corner he flicked a look toward where Woodhall stood. The man fiddled with the fob hanging from his watch and stared straight out over the gardens. He wasn't looking Simon's way at all. Simon shrugged and strode on.

A crowd of guests, most in riding dress, stood near a paddock where their host showed off his newest purchase from Tattersall's, a magnificent roan a groom had brought down from London in slow stages. Big Red, as he was called, was a high-shouldered gelding, showing an excess of spirit in the tossing head and swishing tail, the impatiently tapping hooves and, finally, a thundering whinny which challenged the world indiscriminately.

"What do you call him?" asked one of the male guests. "Where did you find him, you lucky dog?"

"Who bred that big red devil?" asked another, more specifically questioning the provenance.

"He's quite the most beautiful creature I've ever seen," gushed the lady who was believed by some to be their host's current lady-love. The fact that Lady Trewes seemed to like her appeared to contradict the notion.

Lord Trewes smiled a sly smile. "I'll not tell who bred him," he said. "I want to check those stables every so often to see what is available and I don't wish every man jack of you getting there ahead of me!"

Sanger, standing well beyond the crowd, studied the roan he'd helped train. Trewes, it seemed, had kept his word he'd not reveal Big Red's stable, which was good. And, so far as he could tell from this distance, Red looked in perfect condition. Big Red, bred in the stables Sanger inherited from his father, was the best hope he'd yet had of raising the wind . . .

If, mused Sanger, the nag would only win a few important races he might actually be on the road to solvency. But, until the racehorse proved himself, until his reputation would reflect to Simon's advantage and bring in patrons willing to pay high stud fees and better prices for Red's siblings and cousins, the animal's background was to remain a mystery. The mystery, all in itself, would pique the racing world's curiosity and eventually bring in business!

And in the unlikely event Red did not prove out . . . ?

Simon shrugged slightly. If he didn't, there'd be another and still another and someday he *would* breed a winner. Then the stud fees and the sale of colts for what they were worth, rather than for what he could get because he needed the cash, would begin. He nodded almost as faintly as he'd shrugged. Trewes had had all that explained when he bought Red and had agreed to keep the secret. Having become better acquainted with the man, Simon still had some hope he would!

"Well, Simon, settled it all in your mind, have you?" John Alton laughed and clapped his old friend on the back. John was the only man who knew how much rested on the success of the animal everyone praised.

Simon and John stood shoulder to shoulder, much of a height, but Simon was blond and John nearly as dark-haired as Lady Helena. Alton's features were more amiable than Sanger's and he laughed more often and more freely.

Simon Mansanger envied John Alton that freedom to find humor in anything and everything. Simon's life had, too often, been a trifle too difficult for laughter. And now, he'd a new problem: a title he'd no expectation of inheriting from a distant cousin he'd never met and an estate so mortgaged and so run down it was a millstone around his neck rather than the honeyfall some of his acquaintances thought it must be. The muscle in Simon's jaw jerked again and again as he studied the roan.

"Sanger?" called Trewes. "What do *you* think?" He laughed at what he perceived as a good joke.

"Perfection," said Sanger quietly. "Will you race him?"

"Oh, I think so. Don't you?" Trewes chuckled again.

Simon shrugged, plagued by the suspicion Lord Trewes would, somehow, give away his secret, half meaning to do so. "When you enter him I'll put a monkey on him," he said, forcing a lightness he didn't feel. "I cannot afford five hundred pounds, but I've a feeling about that big-boned look. I think he'll do well. For now however," he added, turning to Alton, "you agreed to ride with me over to Sanger-Monkton, did you not?"

"So we planned." Alton glanced to where a pair of grooms stood. "The hacks are getting restless, too."

Simon nodded. He strolled to where his groom held a neat-looking mare, another high-shouldered rather rangy animal. "Come, Jack. Since you were rash enough to promise me your advice, we've much to do." Sanger mounted and started down the lane knowing his friend would catch up.

Not only did he *wish* to go, he had to. It seemed more and more likely he couldn't trust Trewes to keep his promise, which might make for some difficulty, since he was a guest in the man's home! Unfortunately, until Sanger-Monkton could be put into some sort of shape, he'd not much choice but to stay.

Allie, Lady Hel's gray-haired maid, bustled in carrying freshly ironed gowns half an hour after Lady Hel gave up teaching Lady Beth to fix her hair. Lady Beth, realizing she'd very likely outstayed her welcome, very prettily made her thank-yous, her excuses, and, with a curtsy, departed.

"She forgot she was wearing your combs," said Allie, staring at the closed door beyond which Beth had disappeared.

"Thank you for reminding me! I nearly forgot to inform you that you've been telling me for ages they are much too young for me and that I should be shed of them!" Helena also told Allie she was to go to Lady Beth's room the next morning and teach the maid, Maggie, to do Beth's hair as it was when she left. "Or not exactly as it was! She hasn't caught the trick of it herself, but *you* know."

"Whatever next? Your cousin gave you those combs."

Helena grimaced. "Another good reason to rid myself of them. Allie, what do *you* think of Thurmand Woodhall?"

"What do I think of him? 'Tain't my place to have opinions. Not of him nor any other tonnish man."

"Which doesn't stop you having them. So, tell me."

Allie, never one for holding her tongue when given permission to use it, hesitated no longer. "He's an oily snake in the grass," said the maid. "If you step on him, he'll bite. You leave that man alone, Lady Hel."

"I wonder if I haven't already, er, stepped on him . . ." muttered Helena. She gnawed on her upper lip.

"What's that?" asked Allie sharply.

"Hmm?" asked Lady Hel. "Oh, nothing. Nothing at all . . ." After a moment she added, "I suppose I must change out of this habit."

Lady Helena very much wished she could cry off from the afternoon's planned outing and curl up in the library with a book of travel tales. It occurred to her that Lord Sanger had been reading travel tales when she'd discovered him the previous evening in a nook off the library. She smiled wryly. Something else they had in common? Like riding? Another similarity which might draw them together? Something to add to the scales which had already dropped in his favor toward their marriage?

Where, she wondered, had she gone wrong in her calculations? She'd so carefully balanced the facts of their respective situations, most importantly, his need of fortune and her need of protection. She recalled the long sleepless hours of musing the night before and decided she hadn't erred! Marriage to each other would be the best for both of them.

Sanger might believe he'd not wed until his financial position was sorted out, but—her jaw firmed—Lady Hel concluded that their first skirmish, which she'd lost, had been only the opening battle! She knew, without really analyzing it, merely finding it an intuitive proper solution to her problem, that the way to assure the . . . accidents . . . plaguing her were stopped permanently, was to get herself wed and her fortune out of reach.

Which meant choosing a husband. So she had. And the more she thought on it, the more she liked the notion. She would wed.

But *not* her cousin, blast his eyes for ever suggesting it! Allie was never wrong in her assessments of people, so Thurmand Woodhall was a snake in the grass. And there was no way between Heaven and Earth she'd bring herself to wed a snake, squirmy repulsive things—to say nothing of dangerous. That would be pure hell.

Sanger, on the other hand . . . Lady Hel had thought the man more than a trifle attractive when they were first introduced and nothing since had changed her mind. In fact, she'd had some difficulty keeping him out of her thoughts or, worse perhaps, from invading her dreams. As those dreams became more and more interesting, she'd concluded she didn't wish to banish Lord Sanger.

For the first time in her life it occurred to Lady Hel there just might be a possibility of a tiny bit of Heaven right here on Earth.

"What you grinning like a fool for?" asked Allie.

"Am I? Well, perhaps I am."

"A fool?"

"That, too," agreed her ladyship. "We'll have to wait and see, won't we?"

Two

A black scowl settled on his brow as Simon rode beside Jack up the weedy drive toward the Elizabethan structure which had once been a delightful home. The original E shape was lost when half the front was closed off, forming an inner court. Later, a wing had been added, and then, off that, another, making of it a long, rambling house.

Simon had first seen it early that spring and had instantly fallen in love with the smallish, many-paned windows of the older parts and with the multitude of chimneys. The red brick was softened by vines, primarily ivy but also an ancient wisteria, which at that time had been heavy with blossoms.

Simon recalled that first sight of the house, his excitement as he'd viewed his inheritance, and then the panic turning to apathy when he discovered leaking roofs, broken windows, dry rot, floors and stairs that were a danger to the unwary . . . the list went on and on.

And finally a growing, growling, determination. *The devil take it,* he thought now. *I love that house. I'll find the means to repair it if I have to learn every trade and fix it myself.*

"A comfortable-looking house," said Alton from beside him.

"Looks can be deceiving."

Simon's voice had a clipped edge Alton knew well, a

no-trespassing sign Jack usually managed to evade. "Roof?" he asked.

"And just about everything else," admitted Simon, giving in at once to his friend's concern. "If I'd any sense I'd have it torn down and begun again from the ground up."

"Have you? In this particular case?" Before Simon could respond, Jack added, "If you get past that romantic streak to which you hate to admit and do the sensible thing, it'll be something new, will it not?"

Simon grimaced. Jack knew him far too well for him to deny the poetry in his soul which occasionally rolled off the end of his pen. "I don't suppose I'll ever develop good sense. You've the right of that." Simon pulled up, crossed one leg over the front of his saddle, and sat back easily on his mare, staring at the house. "I love it just the way it is."

"With holes in the roof?" asked a startled Jack Alton.

"I don't mean that. I mean the house itself. I wish . . ."

"You wish you had the wherewithal to restore it."

"Yes."

"So . . . Why—" Jack watched his friend closely. "—don't you have a touch at the heiress?"

"I won't be named a fortune hunter, Jack. Piece by piece, I'll manage. The only thing is, I don't know where to begin."

"Which is why I'm here," said Jack briskly, firming up his decision that, by hook or by crook, he'd see Simon wed to Lady Hel.

After all, it would be for Simon's own good. Knowing Simon, Jack had a sneaking suspicion it would be good for Lady Hel, too. Each, from what Jack had observed, covered an emotionally reserved nature with humor and a surface lightness that would serve them well in a marriage of convenience. Then, too, the flirtation in which they'd been indulging had set their feet on the right path. It shouldn't be too difficult to guide them to the end of it!

"While we start our tour of inspection," said Jack, "tell me what you've done and what resources you've available. If any."

Simon righted himself in the saddle and clucked softly, turning his hack off the lane toward the first farm which could be seen in the near distance. "I sold out, of course, which brought me a sizable sum and sold off as much as I dared of my young stock to raise more. Then—" He sighed at his Quixotic nature which had forced him to what he was certain Jack would consider folly. "—the minute I'd cash in hand, I ordered new roofs for the tenants." Before Jack could tell him there were more important places he might have used those funds, he added, "Lord, Jack, you should see the hovels in which my unlamented and distant cousin allowed them to live! I wouldn't keep a dog in such miserable kennels."

He went on explaining, as well he could, the state of his inheritance. Simon had met Jack, the fourth son of a large gentry family, when he was orphaned and sent to live in his great-uncle's house. About the time Simon's guardian bought him his commission, Jack, who loved the land, talked the aging estate agent responsible for a neighboring peer's property into apprenticing him.

It was not, of course, proper work for the gentry-born John Alton, who had been expected to go into the clergy. But Jack foresaw that, as a cleric, he'd spend decades shivering and half starved, as some vicar's overworked curate. Then later, assuming he ever received any preferment, he'd gain the essentials but never the elegancies of life. By following his plan he was well recommended by his retiring mentor and already had a snug home, a generous salary, and a well-respected position as Lord Hathaway's new agent—even if the position was *not* quite what his mother wished for him!

In any case, when Simon begged aid of his knowledge-able friend, Jack took a short leave from his own work.

"It'll be a challenge," said Jack long before they'd finished their initial tour.

"I warned you nothing has been repaired for decades."

"It also appears not one tenant knows the first thing about modern farming methods, which would increase their harvest and everyone's income."

It also seemed everyone had lost hope anything would ever change for the better and, worst of all, that included the new Lord Sanger. Simon's tenants gave one the impression they expected Simon to behave in exactly the same way as his predecessors had done. Even the new roofs, which were nearly complete, weren't proof Simon meant to do things differently. There wasn't a man jack amongst them, who wasn't exceedingly wary of his new lord.

"But, what can I do, Jack? I don't have the means to promise them the earth. You must tell me how best to spend what little I have."

"It's barely enough to dip a toe into these deep waters," warned Jack.

The warning, though expected, didn't approach the encouraging noises Simon had hoped to hear. "So?" he asked.

"So let me think about it for a day or two. Then we'll see."

"Is it hopeless, Jack?"

"No. But an infusion of real money would be the greatest help."

"Since I've no money . . ."

". . . we'll have to come up with something else," finished Jack, and was more determined than ever to get his friend wed to the heiress. As all the world knew, Lady Hel had more than enough money to do the trick!

Finished with what they meant to do that day, the two men returned to the Mansanger gardens, where they struggled to find a path through overgrown shrubbery to an odd structure they'd spied from a nearby hillside. It turned out to be a half-collapsed pagoda, something else that needed fixing or, in this case, tearing down. Standing on the steps, Simon eyed his home with a hungry expression.

"How," he asked, "could I fall in love with a *house*? I *hurt*, Jack, just seeing what it suffers. I feel its pain. I ache to begin healing it."

"It was once a lovely home, Simon. It will be again."

"But *when*?"

"Simon . . ."

"I know. Money." He sighed.

Jack tugged at the chain to his watch and pulled it from his fob pocket. He flipped open the front of the golden hunter and checked the time. "It's getting late."

"Yes." Simon sighed. "If I remember correctly, an informal ball is on the schedule, is it not?"

"You can dance all the dances with Lady Hel."

"I can do no such thing," scolded Simon, "and really, Jack, you shouldn't call her that."

Jack chuckled. "Simon, I've heard her *grandmother* calls her that. The *ton* gave her her nickname years ago."

Simon ignored the first bit. "Years? You'd say she's over twenty? I'd have guessed less."

Jack blinked. Then he laughed. "I keep forgetting how long you've been out of touch, Simon. Lady Hel came out during the same season as my middle sister. Which means she has, at a guess, as much as a quarter century in her dish."

"All of that?" Simon's mind returned to their hour together on the terrace. Was her odd proposal because of a sudden fear she'd be left on the shelf? "I wonder why she's still unwed," mused Simon.

"You do like her, do you not?" asked Jack softly.

But reading Jack's thought, Simon responded, "It makes no difference whether I do or don't. Besides, you said I should have a touch at the heiress. You can't be suggesting

I set up a harem with both the heiress and the beauty! Besides, I'll not wed until I can support a wife."

Jack stared, astonished. Didn't Simon know Lady Hel was the heiress? A rather impish sense of humor kept Jack from revealing that interesting tidbit. Instead he sighed elaborately. "Ah yes. First you must take years to put the land in order, the increased profits paying off the mortgages. Slowly, of course. Once that is done, you'll restore the house which will take only a decade or two. You'll save your pence until you've enough put away in the four percents, and *then* you'll think about taking a wife. I wonder . . ."

"You wonder?" asked Simon, uncertain whether he wished to laugh at his friend's description of his future or box Jack's ears.

"I wonder if you'll still be capable of siring an heir!"

Boxing won out and a brief and satisfying scuffle left the two men, the tensions of the day forgotten in the skirmish, laughing uproariously as they brushed each other down and set themselves to rights.

"My lord," said Lady Hel.

She curtsied deeply in response to Sanger's request for this dance. He bowed just as deeply and offered his arm. The two took their places in the set just forming.

Lord and Lady Trewes had gathered together enough neighbors that, with their guests, they could form two sets, a comfortable number for their moderately sized ballroom. The musicians, hired all the way from Cheltenham, began playing and, with little or no thought, Lady Hel's feet found their way through the patterns of a Scottish reel.

When the music ended and they'd bowed their final bows she put her fingers on Sanger's arm and, with a pressure so subtle he hardly realized he was led, maneuvered him into the anteroom. He ladled her a cup of punch from the bowl set there. Lady Hel took one sip and, grimacing, set it aside.

"Don't serve yourself, my lord," she whispered, laying her hand on his when he lifted another filled ladle. "It is worse than the orgeat they serve at Almack's and I'd have said that was impossible." No one had entered the anteroom. Perhaps everyone else knew the Trewes served unpalatable punch? "I know where His Lordship keeps his good stuff," she said on a suggestive note. She glanced at him from the corner of her eyes.

Simon grinned. "Is that an invitation, my lady?"

"Merely a suggestion," she said primly. "The dancing left *me* thirsty."

"Lead the way, my lady. The reel is an easy dance for my out-of-practice feet, but an energetic one. I, too, am parched."

Lady Hel glanced around, decided they were unobserved, and exited into the hall.

But they *had* been seen. As they disappeared, a frowning Thurmand Woodhall stepped into the ballroom doorway. Quite obviously he'd the intention of following the truants, but Jack Alton also noted their departure.

Observing Lady Hel and Simon together in the dance had reinforced Jack's opinion the two were a perfect match. He meant to do what he could during his necessarily brief stay to see all was set in train for their wedding! And, he was not about to let Lady Hel's cousin, or whatever he was, interfere. Not when Simon had such an excellent opportunity for getting to know the lady.

Jack deftly intercepted the man. "Mr. Woodhall!"

Thurmand turned. "Ah. Mr. Alton, is it not?" asked Woodhall coldly. "You wished to speak with me?"

"I wonder if you've met Miss Harris," said Jack, pointing discreetly toward a rather plain young woman sitting beside a palm. He urged Thurmand toward her. "Would it not be a good deed if we all do our best to make her evening a pleasant one? Come along now. It will be quite painless, I assure you. She is a surprisingly good dancer; so you'll not find it a burden to dance with her. I will introduce you. Miss Harris . . ."

Woodhall's pride allowed no one to say his manners were not the best. He was, therefore, despite wishing to be elsewhere, forced to ask Miss Harris for the next dance. Acting the perfect, if monosyllabic, gentleman, Woodhall remained at her side while one set finished, and he stood up with her for the next.

Miss Harris, who loved dancing, put up with his boorish ways until she was able to leave him with as unconvincing a comment on the pleasure of the dance as was his own. Not that he noticed. He was far too preoccupied by his need to track down his cousin and Simon Mansanger, who had not yet returned to the ballroom.

If Lord Sanger thought to restore Sanger-Monkton with the Woodhall fortune, he could think again.

Simon looked around the small paneled room. "How did you discover this private room, Lady Helena?"

"I, too, am cursed with a curious nature, my lord," she said, reminding him of his admission of the fault earlier that day. "I've a habit of poking my nose where it doesn't belong," she added.

She fiddled with the carving beside the fireplace. She didn't immediately find that for which she searched and Simon heard a few softly murmured words Lady Helena shouldn't have known, and *certainly* shouldn't have used . . . and then a hidden door swung open.

"Aha!" Holding a half-filled decanter, she turned, triumphant, to discover Simon grinning at her. She cocked her head. "You seem well entertained, my lord. It is merely a burgundy and not the brandy I rather hoped I'd find."

"Entertained? Not that exactly . . . Intrigued, perhaps? Yes, I believe I am intrigued. My lady," he said, adopting a mock-scolding manner, *"where* did you learn your vocabulary?"

"My . . ." A rosy tinge to her complexion improved her already excellent looks. "Did I swear?" she asked self-consciously.

Her expression set Simon to chuckling. "Fluently," he said when be could speak. "I'd some of the scummiest of Viscount Wellington's enlisted men under my command in the Peninsula. I assure you, you could hold your own with any of them."

"You exaggerate, I hope. But, the thing is, I spent—" She tipped her head. "—or perhaps one would say I *misspent* much of my youth in my father's stables. With his connivance, of course, or I couldn't have managed it. He was hunting-wild, you see. The head groom was an excellent man, except for his temper. He never bothered to remember my tender ears when he was angry."

"You ride to thc hunt then?" asked Simon. Simon loved horses, but he didn't hunt. Not that he didn't raise hunters in the stables inherited from his father. While in the army, Simon spent his every long leave there. Then, later, a still longer convalescence when he'd taken a ball in his thigh which wouldn't heal properly. His head groom's fomentations had done more good than anything the doctors had done to him, drawing out the poisons and, finally, a piece of something unidentifiable which the ball had pushed into his flesh . . . But that was a year or so in the past and this was now.

"Sometimes," said Lady Helena, "I think I like horses better than I like people, but, to answer your question, I don't hunt. I've never liked the vicious end when the dogs are allowed to get at the poor beast." She shrugged, dropping the subject on that rueful note.

Helena poured each of them a glass of the wine and

brought his to him. When he took it, she raised hers. "To us."

"To *us?*" he asked, startled.

She blinked, then smiled. "I forgot I'd asked you to wed me. Very well, if you do not care for my toast, you do the honors."

He grinned. "To us," he said and drank. "I am overly sensitive, am I not, when all you meant was a conventional toast. Jack Alton would tell you I am either far too sensitive or I miss things which are right in front of my nose, utterly oblivious to something which should be clear as glass. There seems no middle ground with me."

Lady Hel, having evidence of that in his unawareness that she was an heiress, suppressed a smile. "I see. Well, here's a toast you may drink to with impunity. To the success of your current venture." She drank.

"My venture, as you call it, will need all the help it can get," he said, dryly. "Have you ever seen an estate which has been impoverished not merely through neglect but by the constant draining of its resources?"

"I'd heard rumors Sanger-Monkton was in a bad way, but I am sorry to have it confirmed." Sipping their wine, they remained companionably silent for a few moments. Then, after eyeing him once or twice and assessing his mood, Lady Helena mused, "I have also heard tales of a truly wonderful house." She poured them each a further glass, pleased when Sanger expressed an interest in how she'd heard of it. "My grandmother visited Sanger-Monkton both before and after her marriage. She enjoyed herself immensely. When I informed her where I'd be these weeks she recalled it was nearby and told me I must see it."

"I'll take you over the house if you don't fear dirt or the possibility you'll fall through a floor or—" He grinned a quick teasing grin. "—seeing a ghost or two or three?"

"Ghosts? Ah!" Animation enlivened Lady Helena's features. "There is no way you'll keep me away now. I have always had a secret yen to observe a real ghost. Truly? There are ghosts?"

Simon suppressed a desire to grin and solemnly informed her, "I haven't a notion, my lady. But having gone through the house it is my considered opinion that if there are *not* there *should be.*"

She chuckled. "When may I see it?"

"I'll be there tomorrow." He grimaced slightly. "Very likely I'll be there every day for the foreseeable future. Perhaps you could suggest to Lady Trewes that she arrange a picnic and you all join Jack and myself at midday?"

Lady Hel pouted. "Well . . . no."

"No?" Sanger's brow arched. "But you . . . ?"

"I did not say," she interrupted, "that I wished the whole party tramping though your home and frightening away my specters." She wondered at her instant negative reaction to a picnic-party. Arranging tête-à-têtes with eligible gentlemen was *not* her way!

Lord Sanger, wishing to protect her reputation, frowned. "I do not see how we can manage, then."

"Very simply," she said smugly. "I come myself. With a picnic sufficient for four."

"Four?" asked Simon. *Ah,* he thought, *Lady Helena means to include a chaperon.*

She promptly dispatched the notion. "You, Alton, my groom, and me."

"Lady Helena," he asked, "does propriety allow you such freedom? Do you think you should?"

"You are scolding me, are you not?" Her face revealed her surprise. After considering for a moment, she added, "I cannot decide whether I find it nice that you care enough to do so or whether I am angry with you for presuming to set me straight!"

"I would not have you endanger your reputation merely because you wish to see a nonexistent ghost."

"Don't be stuffy, my lord. Besides, my little eccentricities are widely known. One is that, in the country, I often ride alone with only my groom for company. I have done so for four or five years now. Everyone is aware of my shocking behavior and it is such old news no one thinks a thing of it—assuming *you* don't give away my destination, of course."

"You can trust your groom not to reveal such an interesting tidbit as that you've trysted with two unmarried men in an out-of-the-way place?"

"Still so stern," she said. She sighed. "My lord, if you wish to recall your invitation . . . ?"

He didn't respond and she sighed again.

"Do you?" she asked bluntly, meeting his eyes and holding his gaze.

"I don't want to," he said, a muscle jumping at the side of his jaw, "but I wonder if I should." He was rather surprised at just how much he didn't wish to call back the invitation!

"My lord, you may do so with my good will and it will make not a jot of difference. I'll simply surprise you. Tomorrow? About midday, at Sanger-Monkton? *You've* nothing to do with my decision and may feel properly pure of heart since you cannot be at fault if I come to grief." She raised her glass in triumph and drank off her wine. "Now, my lord, by reason of that propriety of which you spoke, I believe we must return to the ballroom."

"Good Lord yes," he said, startled into realizing how long they'd been closeted alone together. "You will have been missed."

"Very likely both of us will." She scowled. "It is a great bore that other people cannot keep their noses out of my business."

"It does cause you concern, does it not?" he asked when she glared at nothing at all.

"Not at all. I merely do not understand people's interest in other's people's doings. But I ceased worrying about such things when I turned down my third really excellent match and my grandmother washed her hands of me!''

"She can't have done so.''

Lady Helena looked at him, a question in her eyes.

"Or perhaps it is that she forgave you?'' When she still looked perplexed, he explained, "You informed her you'd be visiting the Treweses and she told you stories of my nearby home?''

She went through the door he held open for her. "Oh! As to that, we've always been on the best of good terms, my lord. I didn't mean to imply otherwise . . . blast!''

"Bla- . . . ? Oh—'' Simon suppressed a grimace. "Good evening, Mr. Woodhall.''

"Thurmand, why do you glower in that very odd fashion?'' asked Lady Hel.

"I am, as usual, cousin, worried about you.''

"You, cousin, really must not concern yourself. In the first place you have no need and in the second you've no right.''

In icy tones, he retorted, "We bear the same name, cousin. I do not care to hear it the subject of gossip, as it is whenever you're off on one of your starts.''

"Starts?'' asked Simon, passing an interested glance between them.

"You have been in the military and out of the country, I believe,'' said Woodhall to Simon. "You will not have heard of my cousin's penchant for getting herself into difficulties.''

Simon noted that, suddenly, the man's lisp was not in evidence.

"I have never in my life been in any trouble,'' said Lady Hel, "which *you* have not made for me!'' Her glare matched her cousin's scowl. "Only through *your* machinations does the world hear of my so-called *starts* and when you finish telling a tale, a simple situation, which I have enjoyed immensely and which has harmed no one, including myself, is blown all out of recognition. I wish, Thurmand, you would take your nose elsewhere."

"You have the strangest definition of what constitutes a simple little situation, my dear Helena. What about the time . . ." He stopped when Lady Helena raised her hand. "Yes?" he sneered. "You would prefer that I not reveal the extent of your folly to Lord Sanger?"

"You are a snake, Thurmand Woodhall. You were a snake when we were children and you have not changed." She stalked off down the hall and into the anteroom to the ballroom.

"She is a hellion," said Thurmand, a trifle fervently . . . for him. "Why, I could tell you . . ."

"Excuse me," interrupted Simon, whose dislike of the man had just grown to new heights. "I am promised to Lady Trewes for this next dance and it would not do to miss it." He bowed.

As excuses went, this one was inspired. Thurmand was forced to accept it or be insulting to his hostess. Thwarted in his desire to tell tales, he bowed and moved aside.

Once again Simon felt as if something bored into his back. A snake, Lady Helena had called him. A slithery, slimy, nasty snake. Simon's poetic mind carried the image further and, for a moment, wondered if, like the snake was purported to be, Woodhall was evil, carrying venom which could be fatal?

Simon scolded himself for overly dramatic daydreaming and hurried his pace so as to find his partner before the next set began. They took their places only just in time.

"You've checked the tack, Rod?" asked Lady Helena, hiding her anxiety even from her much-trusted groom. Her eyes wandered restlessly around the stable yard.

"Yes, my lady," said Roderick Cole grimly. "Nor, my lady, I haven't taken my glims off the creature since I saddled

her. There hasn't been a soul near her. We won't be having
any *accidents* like when the girth broke and we found her
bit was roughed up."

At his tone Helena looked straight at Rod, catching and
holding his eyes. "You are absolutely certain it was no accident?"

The groom's lips compressed. "Couldn't have been.
And why you refuse to tell your lady grandma'am, I don't
know. Or about the time the carriage . . ."

Lady Helena waved him to silence, refusing to listen to
more. She would not tell her grandmother of the ordeals
which had recently plagued her. She had long experienced
her grandmother's partiality for Thurmand, how the old
woman always believed the worse of herself when Thurmand told one of his tales.

And finally, she reminded herself, again, she'd no proof
her cousin was involved. Still . . . whenever she thought of
the accidents, she also thought of Thurmand!

"Never you mind, Rod. We've no business worrying her
about a situation she can do nothing to correct. Assuming
there *is* a situation and it isn't all in our heads!"

Lady Helena indicated she wished his help mounting
and they rode down a side lane in a direction which would
not take them to Sanger-Monkton.

"Are we going anywhere in particular?" asked Roderick
once they were well beyond the stable yard.

"Sanger-Monkton."

"This isn't the right direction," warned the groom, pulling up and waiting until she did as well.

"Rod, I may not give six pence for what the world says
of me, but I don't go out of my way to give it reason for
talk." She continued in the direction she'd originally
taken. "We'll ride a bit and then you can guide me there."

Over an hour later they trotted up Lord Sanger's ill-kept
drive. As they rounded the curve the house was revealed
in all its glory and Lady Hel pulled up. Sanger-Monkton!

Her grandmother had not, it seemed, exaggerated. It was a welcoming house, charming and somehow beckoning, somehow expressing delight that you were coming to visit.

"Which is all nonsense, of course, but"—Lady Hel grinned at her ridiculous thoughts—"delightful nonsense, nevertheless."

"My lady?" When she didn't respond, her groom realized she'd been talking to herself again. "Needs a flock of sheep," he muttered.

The sun was high and hot. Lady Helena squinted out over what had once been a lawn. It had been long neglected however. There were even volunteer trees sprouting in the rough, flower-starred, grass. Actually, some of the trees were a good ten years old judged Lady Helena. Perhaps older.

"Sheep," she repeated. "An excellent notion. I wonder if Sanger has thought of it. In case he has not I'll contrive to mention it."

Already craving the house for her own, she walked her horse toward it. How could she get it? And the man, too, of course. She'd been rather surprised by how much she liked the new Lord Sanger, by the depth of her disappointment when he'd turned her proposal down. There was a strength to him, an integrity she admired, a confidence that enhanced good, if not outstanding, features and—

Lady Helena felt her skin heat.

—a form men would envy and women find attractive. Perhaps best of all, he didn't pander to her slightest wish!

Blast and bedamned to the stubborn man! By all that was holy, he *would* wed her! Her jaw firmed. Now, how was she to go about it? Ah! Too late for plotting now.

Sanger awaited her. His lordship and his friend stood on the overgrown flags paving the area before the entry to Sanger Monkton. Lady Helena pulled up and he strode forward to lift her down.

"You may tether the horses near ours over there,"

Sanger told the groom, pointing to where his and Jack Alton's animals grazed.

"And then join us here, Rod," added Lady Helena. "Don't forget the saddlebags." She turned to look at the house and couldn't repress an exclamation of dismay.

"I warned you," said Sanger softly.

"So you did. I suppose I didn't believe you. How could anyone have allowed this lovely house to deteriorate so? It is criminal! Someone should have long ago *demanded* they do the right thing by it!" Lady Hel felt a pang, an ache at the damage neglect had caused. "Oh, I cannot understand such waste!"

"The late Lord Sanger and his father before him were avid gamblers. They cared only for the turn of a card or—" Sanger sighed. "—anything else on which a bet could be laid."

"Yes, but if the estate were entailed . . ." Her brows arched when he shook his head. "I see. No entail."

"I have been led to understand there was one—" Sanger shrugged. "—but that it was broken in the usual fashion."

Lady Helena's eyes widened in shocked surprise. "You were so foolish as to have signed such an agreement? Oh, surely not."

He frowned. "Sign? I? What agreement?"

"If, as an heir presumptive, you signed nothing, then the entail could not have been broken. Only if all the heirs presumptive put signature to such a document is it legal. And you never did so?"

"My lady, how do you know so much about entails?" asked Alton, curious that a woman would have such information at her fingertips.

"Hmm?" She eyed Sanger, wishing she'd not used the word "foolish." Obviously, it caught him on the raw! "What was that, Mr. Alton? Oh, entails. I spent my formative years with my father who never sent me off when business was in train. And my grandmother, who had a goodly hand in rearing me, comes from a generation which did not believe that ignorance is bliss!"

"It is a refreshing trait," said Jack. "What is more, you are correct. Simon, *did* you sign anything of the sort?"

"No," he said slowly, rubbing his chin, "but if I were unavailable, and I might easily have been, could someone else not have signed it for me?"

"That, too, would have been illegal. I wonder if one could go through the courts and get the *mortgages* declared illegal," mused Jack.

Simon felt hope burgeon and then, fearing to allow it to take root, he glanced at Lady Helena, who wore an interested look. "Jack, we can discuss this another time," he said more sharply then he might have done. "Lady Helena came for a tour of the house, and since you've not yet seen the extent of the damage, you may make another of your unending lists as we go through it. Jack," Sanger explained to Lady Helena, "has been doing his best to discover everything that needs doing around the estate. In that way we may determine where best to begin putting things to rights."

"A flock of sheep for the front lawn," she said promptly, given the opening, and then added the suggestion that the tenants be allowed the wool. "I know you cannot afford to offer them much, but little rights of that sort are often valued by a person's tenants."

Once again Alton gave her a measuring look. He'd already decided she was the right woman for his friend, but that had been in part that they enjoyed each other's company and, still more, that she was an heiress. Now he wondered if she wouldn't be an excellent partner, a *working* partner, in what would be the long job of restoring the estate.

Some things would take years even with her fortune!

"Sheep . . . I like that notion," said Sanger thoughtfully. "My tenants are rather unfriendly." He grimaced and tried

to explain. "It feels rather like I'm in a war where the
natives are hostile, so if you think up any other little per-
quisites to get them on my side, but which would cost me
next to nothing, please feel free to tell me! I was not bred
to this work, Lady Helena and, frankly, I've no good notion
of how to go about it!"

Rod Cole returned with the saddlebags. "Shall I find
the well, my lady, and put the wine in to cool?" he asked.

"The only well that hasn't filled in or become tainted
is around back," said Sanger. "I believe there was some
sort of caretaker, at least for a long time, because there
are a few rooms near the kitchens which are in reasonably
decent shape and that well has good water. There is also
a table there under an arbor where we could have our
lunch once you decide you've had enough of dirt, cobwebs
and the nonexistent ghost. My lady?" He bowed, indicating the open front door. "Shall we . . . ?"

Dirt aplenty. And more cobwebs than I knew existed, thought
Lady Hel as she was led through rooms opening one out
of the next in the Elizabethan fashion. But there was magnificent paneling which had, for the most part, survived
neglect—and what the weather threw at it in rooms with
broken windows. Lady Helena fell more deeply in love with
it all. The more she saw, the more regretful she grew she
couldn't, immediately, set all to rights. Her fingers itched
to be busy.

"Grandmother spoke of playing hunt the slipper and
hide and seek. I see why she said it was the best house for
such frolic she'd ever visited," mused Lady Helena as, with
care, they went up still another short flight of steps.

The halls twisted and turned and the floors of additions
were often at a different level from the part they abutted.
One never knew exactly where one was. At least Lady Hel
didn't. She'd long rued that no good fairy had, at her
christening, given her a good bump of locality! She was

lost long before the tour ended and they once again stood in the hall.

"I believe you've seen everything but the cellars," said Sanger at last.

"But you didn't show me the priest hole," she complained.

"Priest hole? What priest hole?"

"I don't remember one on the architect's plans." Alton frowned over his recollections of when he and Sanger first discussed his inheritance.

"The floor plans are complicated and I suppose I might have missed it, but I'd no notion of such a thing." Simon's lips twitched at the corners into something that faintly echoed the smile in his eyes. "Is this something else your grandmother mentioned?" he asked.

Those eyes, she thought. "Hmm? Oh, yes. I'll spare your blushes and not tell you the use *she* made of it, but she did tell me where to find it. Assuming I can figure it out. She said—" Lady Helena frowned, a deep vertical line appearing between her brows. "—something about the library. Not exactly *in* the library, but near there, you know?"

"I have already said I know nothing of such a thing."

"Blast," said Lady Helena on a rueful note. "What I'm asking, in a sort of round-about way, I suppose, since I always hate to admit I am lost, is that you return me to the library and perhaps, from there, I can remember enough I'll discover your priest hole for you."

"As promptly done as said," said Sanger. He offered his arm, covering her hand with his own when she laid it there.

Three

The library was through three rooms and toward the front of the house. It took up the whole end of that arm of the original E-shaped structure. Although it was one of the larger Elizabethan rooms it still tended toward the coziness for which the architectural style was famous. Few volumes remained on the shelves but the room had possibilities, and Lady Hel knew that once she'd restored it to comfort it was one in which she'd spend a great deal of time.

Once she was married to Sanger, of course.

She put aside plans for refurbishing, set her finger to her lips, and turned in a slow circle. "She said there was a private closet, sort of an anteroom, off the library . . ."

"If that's what she meant by a priest hole; I'm disappointed!" said Sanger, already moving toward a door badly hidden in the paneling.

"You needn't be." Helena grinned. "The priest hole is off *that.*"

He opened it and peered in. "I've not been in here," he said and suggested the others wait while he determined if the floor were safe. It was.

"Now what, my lady?" asked Alton, his arms folded.

Simon held a lamp high and, dismayed, Lady Helena looked around the windowless room. "Well . . . Grandmother said there was carving."

The men chuckled.

"She told me," said Lady Hel with mock solemnity, "that you turn the plum one way and the apple the other and then pull on the pineapple."

Sanger and Alton laughed harder. They glanced at each other, glanced around the room which was overly decorated with such carving, and laughed more uproariously.

"This could take hours," said Sanger, grinning.

"And, frankly," said Alton a trifle sternly, "we don't have hours."

"Oh dear." Lady Helena looked from one to the other. "I'm keeping you from your work?"

Sanger's smile broadened at the innocent look which accompanied her words. "You know you are," he scolded gently, "but," he added when she raised her eyes to see how serious he was, "we've been diligent for days and the pleasure of your company has done us good. Still—" Sanger glanced around the room where nearly every possible surface was covered with carving depicting animals, sheaves of grain, and quantities of fruit pouring from cornucopias. "—discovering the secret might be a trifle more of an indulgence than I should allow myself?" He grinned wryly, that mobile brow well arched.

"You are sorting out larger problems," she said with sympathy. "I understand."

But the longing look Lady Helena cast around the room was so patently obvious that Sanger immediately suggested that once they'd finished their picnic she might like to return and explore on her own.

"Yes! I'd like that. And Rod can help."

"Rod?"

"Roderick Cole. His grandfather was my grandfather's head groom and his father, my father's. Rod is my personal groom."

She didn't try to explain the complicated relationship, which was closer to siblings than mistress and hireling, and yet was *not* that. She didn't know a word or simple phrase that described the loyalty, respect and friendship they felt but included a certain distance between them. The relationship was further complicated by an ease that allowed each to speak their mind to the other. Helena had long ago given up trying to define it to others.

Their luncheon finished, Sanger led Helena and the groom back to the library, and the party split up. Helena watched Sanger step over the low sill and onto the broad terrace beyond the library where Acton held their horses. Silently, she admitted she hated to see him go, that she was beginning to want him around far more than was likely to be good for her. When the men moved out of her sight she sighed.

By then Rod had lit the lamp and carried it into the windowless room. He set it on the table which stood in the center. Once again Lady Helena turned on her foot, looking at the incredible job ahead of her.

"This could take hours."

"Then why bother?" asked the groom.

"I don't know. Except I've no desire to return to the Treweses', of course. Now, do you understand what we're looking for?"

"Plums, apples and pineapples. Just standing in one place, I've already counted nineteen pineapples."

"There appear to be still more apples and an overabundance of grape clusters, but, so far, I've seen nothing I'd call a plum. I think we can ignore the wall between the library and this room. It appears to be no thicker than one would expect. So, where, if one were building a priest hole, *would* one put it?" she muttered, thinking aloud.

"You're asking me?"

"Hmm? I guess I am, Rod."

"Then I'd cut the room in two." He used his hands as he talked, quickly indicating a long narrow room which a chop of his hand shortened. *"And,"* he finished, "I'd guess that means *that* end." He gestured. "See? If you look at this wall, the door into the library isn't centered as is almost every other door in this part of the building. It's as if the wall at that end had moved this way?"

"You are a blooming genius!" exclaimed Lady Helena, admiringly. "Help me move this table closer and we'll begin there."

Rod set himself to shifting the solidly built table, and soon, the lamp giving the best light possible, they studied the wall, searching for plums in particular.

"Are you certain she said a plum?" he asked, doubtfully, half an hour later.

"She was quite particular about it." Lady Helena ran her filthy hand down another set of dusty carvings. They had each started in a corner and now Rod backed away to give Helena room to test the last few bits. She shook her head. "It was an excellent notion, Rod, but doesn't seem to have been correct. Let's move the table and begin there." She pointed to the back wall.

Lady Hel started just around the corner from where she'd first begun hunting.

"Eureka!" she cried only minutes after they'd begun their new search.

"A plum?"

"Very definitely a plum. Now for the others. Ah! This apple wiggles slightly and here are *two* of those ubiquitous pineapples. One appears to be a trifle smoother than the other." She eyed the plum. "Dare I do it or do I not?"

"Should wait for his lordship," cautioned Rod.

"So I should."

Even as she agreed, she was turning the plum and then the apple and, finally, pulling on the pineapple. A section of paneling opened, squealing on long unoiled hinges. The opening, however, was so narrow anyone of any girth at all would have been unable to squeeze through.

"My lady," said Roderick quickly when Helena picked up the lamp, "I wonder if I should go first. The floor . . ."

"I'm much the lighter. I'll go. Slowly. I assure you, at the slightest cracking sound I'll back up!"

Roderick sighed. He'd heard that half-teasing, half-determined tone far too often to waste his breath on argument.

"I wish I'd a broom." She said, brushing at cobwebs.

"I saw one in a room off the back entrance."

Helena, temporarily giving up the fight with several hundred generations of spiders, requested that he get it and waited impatiently for him to return.

"Sure you don't want me to go first?" he asked, holding the old, well worn, country besom.

"I'll do it," she insisted.

She swept away what she could reach, and then, setting the lamp on the floor, stepped into the narrow passage and looked from left to right. To the right she made out a set of rough steps, little more than boards nailed to the wall. They led through dark holes in floor and ceiling. That could be explored on another occasion, she decided the moment it occurred to her she couldn't climb and also hold the lamp. In the other direction the passage went only a few feet, blank walls on all sides, but her grandmother had described a tiny room. The plain wall, she decided, must be a further attempt to fool the priest hunters and, brushing down cobwebs in all directions, she moved toward it.

Rod, inserting himself with difficulty through the opening, watched her. "You are not taking care," he scolded.

"I forgot." But by then she'd arrived where she was certain there should be another door. "It's got to be here. You were correct that the anteroom was shortened, since this passage goes beyond the corner of it, so there must be a space behind this wall." She ran her hands over it. "Why can't I find a way into it?"

"Push."

She pushed.

"Not in the middle." He came farther along the narrow corridor. "Try the end."

She moved more toward the corner and pushed again. With a squeal, the wall moved an inch or so. "How did you know?" She pushed again, but the entry remained open no more than the same tempting couple of inches. "I guess I'll have to get out of your way, Rod, and allow you to try."

Even Rod's muscles got the door open no more than another few inches. It was enough, however, for Helena to see that the room wasn't empty. The lamp shed golden rays over a narrow table piled with dust-shrouded boxes. Leaning against the table legs were several framed paintings. And, although that was all she could see, it was enough to set her heart pounding. Could someone have hidden family treasures in the secret room? Would there be something of value that Sanger could sell, so he could, more quickly, set in motion the plans he and Alton had made?

She set her hand to the door and pulled but it wouldn't budge in that direction either. "Blast."

"Worried someone will find this spot?" asked Rod with a chuckle.

"I suppose I'm being ridiculous, but Lord Sanger needs funds badly." She glared at the stuck door, her hands fisted into her hips. "If there *is* a fortune in there I'd hate to have it stolen at the very last moment!"

"They said they meant to check the old mill," said Rod.

"You are suggesting we might ride that way?" She gave Rod a wry look. "Assuming, *you* know how to find it since I haven't a notion where to look."

Aware of Helena's penchant for getting lost, Rod had explored the neighborhood in his free time. "I think I can find it," he said.

"You ready the horses while I see that we've left no clues to help a thief find the location of the secret panel."

Lady Helena closed the panel in the windowless room and tested that it had locked into place. Glancing around, she noticed footprints in the dusty floor and decided that sweeping the room would confuse any possible thieves.

Sweeping proved a bit of a problem. She'd not much experience of the task and had done very little before the dust set her to sneezing. Sneezing violently, she persevered. She was determined that nothing should happen to what very well might be Lord Sanger's salvation.

Once mounted, Roderick lead the way. Twenty minutes later they saw two men riding at an angle, and he and Lady Helena set mounts to a gallop.

As expected, it was Sanger and Alton, and soon the men were within hailing distance. Lord Sanger pulled his mare to a halt and turned in the saddle. When he saw who was calling, he and Jack trotted back. "I didn't expect to see you again until we returned to the Trewes."

"Yes, well, we found your pr-pr-priest's hole."

"You did, did you. And did you find your ghost?"

Lady Helena looked startled for half a moment. "Lord, I forgot all about ghosts. What I found . . . Sanger, you'd b-b-best come," she finished with a degree of urgency.

Reaching out he brushed a cobweb from her hair, another from her shoulder.

"Please? I th-think you sh-sh-should."

He quirked a brow.

"Truly. I think . . . I hope . . . Well, we c-c-c-ouldn't actually get in, but what I saw through the cr-cr-crack." She compressed her lips, drew in a few long breaths. "I'm st-st-stuttering. I haven't st-stuttered in years." She glanced at Rod and the groom urged his mount nearer.

"What Lady Helena would say," he explained, "is that we may have discovered some sort of treasure trove. We couldn't see much, but there were three or four smallish paintings and a number of carefully sealed boxes."

Sanger turned a quick look on Alton who stared, his mouth open. Simon turned back. "Are you serious? This is no game?"

"I haven't a notion if there is anything of any value," warned Lady Helena, who recovered her poise when his lordship had been told the facts, "but why else would anyone take the trouble to hide everything away?"

"Let's go," said Sanger and heeled his mount, already some way along before everyone else managed to get themselves moving in the proper direction. He stayed ahead of them all the way . . . and then had to wait for Lady Helena to catch up, because he'd no idea how to find the priest hole.

Lady Hel was very impressed by his horse. "That," she said, as she was helped from hers, "is a speedy devil! Where *did* you buy her?" she asked, moving to check out the points of Sanger's mount.

"Never mind that. Come show me . . ." Sanger rubbed his face with his hands. "I apologize. But . . ."

"But if there is anything there of value, you need to know it. I am the one who should apologize." As she spoke, Lady Helena led the way to the library window out which she and Roderick had departed. She pulled, opening the unlocked window, and, raising her habit skirts a trifle indecorously, she stepped over the low frame. "Now, if someone would light the lamp, please?"

The lamp was quickly lit and all crowded into the room beyond the library. Lady Helena showed Lord Sanger how to manipulate the proper carvings. Then she opened the secret door and waved a hand. "We didn't go to the end with the ladder. Turn the other way and you'll see an entrance standing ajar. We could get it no farther opened, which was probably just as well," she finished on a frank note, "since I'd have been tempted to explore without you."

Sanger put his shoulder to the door and it opened another inch but still not widely enough for anyone, even Lady Helena as slim as *she* was, to enter.

"We need tools."

"I wondered, my lord," offered Rod, "if I were to set my feet on the far wall and push with my back if I couldn't get it open."

"Too dangerous. If it were to go all of a sudden, you'd fall and hurt yourself." But Sanger was turning as he spoke, setting his feet to the wall and putting his back to the partly open door. He gripped the door frame with his hands. Then he shoved. The door opened a bit and he slipped down, catching himself.

"Still not enough?" asked Lady Helena from just inside the passage.

"I don't think so. You can come try if you can manage, but I rather doubt it."

Helena squeezed by Lord Sanger and fitted herself into the opening. She squirmed and wiggled and, suddenly, found herself inside. "Oh!"

"Your ghost?" asked Sanger half in jest and half seriously.

"Nothing so interesting. Have Rod hand you that blaste-
. . . er, *blessed* broom. I'll not move one more step until I get the cobwebs out of my way!"

Sanger handed her the besom and heard her manipulating it. Finally she handed it back.

"There is something here behind the door. A chest of some sort."

"Can you move it?"

Helena tried. "It is very heavy, but I think I can." She moved it a fraction of an inch, and then again, and, bit by bit, got it out of the way. She opened the door. "Welcome to your priest hole, Lord Sanger," she said and dipped him a curtsy.

He bowed, but rather perfunctorily, already glancing around. Jack Alton, followed by Rod, squeezed into the narrow room, the four of them uncomfortably filling it. Stacked in piles at the back were over-sized and ancient-looking books. More framed pictures stood against one wall. A wooden chair, the iron-bound chest, and the wax-sealed wooden boxes on the narrow table completed their rough inventory.

Helena's fingers itched to open boxes, lift the lid on the chest, see why the old volumes had been stored there away from the library shelves and what the paintings depicted.

Still, she dared not do so, couldn't even suggest doing so. This was Sanger's. It was his place to look at everything first, to catalog it and to see if there was anything which might retrieve his estate from those who held the mort-gages, pull it back to solvency.

"I . . . I don't know where to begin," said Simon, obviously feeling dazed. "Jack? Have you a fresh notebook?"

Jack chuckled. "Perhaps we might simply count things to begin with. I've already counted seven paintings. Would you count books, Mr. Cole? And perhaps you'd be kind enough to count the boxes, my lady?"

"And me? What am I to do?" asked Sanger, still more than a trifle discombobulated.

"Perhaps you should open the chest," suggested Alton, grinning. "If you *don't*, I believe Lady Helena may do it for you!"

Lady Helena didn't deny it. Nevertheless, as suggested, she began counting boxes, keeping one eye on Sanger, of course, who knelt before the chest. She'd completed her job when he gave up and sat back on his heels.

"I think we'll have to break the lock," he said.

"Weren't there any old and mysterious keys among those you inherited?" asked Lady Hel.

"There could be a barrel of keys lying around this house, but finding the right one might take months. I don't have months, as everyone very unkindly points out to me."

"I'll see if I can locate a lever," offered Rod. "There are, by the way, seven books in each pile and six piles. Don't know if they'll be worth anything though. They smell more'n a little moldy to me." He disappeared on the last words.

Helena said, "I counted sixteen boxes. Sanger?"

He chuckled at her hopeful expression and came to her side. "Pick one."

She chose a medium-sized box and handed it to him. He cut the seals with his penknife and pried at the inset lid to the wooden box. It began to come up and for half a second he hesitated and then lifted it away. The inside was packed with wool and, carefully, he began pulling it out. Gradually the top of a small figure sculpted from ivory appeared, a head and then the body and finally the whole.

"She's beautiful," breathed Helena and reached one finger to touch the figure gently. "At a guess I'd say it's the one called the Lady Venus."

"Another of your grandmother's tales?" asked Simon softly.

Awed by the small graceful carving, Helena spoke slowly, "She described a collection of carvings which, she said, completely changed her taste in statuary." Helena got a mischievous look. "And, from Grandmother's portrait painted in that era, I believe this must be the one everyone said was the image of her. Or perhaps they should have said she was the image of it? Grandmother even has rather oddly set eyes although not quite *this* odd."

Helena reached for the carving and Sanger released it into her reverent hands.

"She once had an Oriental gown made, copied from this one, and a black wig and wore them to a costume ball, shocking everyone out of their wits. Appearing in public uncorseted and wearing something like that silk robe was more than enough even in that more licentious era!" Lady Helena gave the statue to Sanger.

Impulsively he handed it back. "You give this to her. As thanks for telling good stories and for having an even more wonderful granddaughter." He grimaced. "I suppose I should give you something, and I will, but this should be hers, I think."

Roderick returned with an iron bar he'd removed from the kitchen grate and while Helena repacked the statuette, the men set to opening the chest. When they finally managed it Helena was disappointed. Inside was nothing but a massive gray urn. "Why do you suppose that was locked away?" she asked. She studied the shallow relief sculpture which was rather blurred and grimaced. "It's not even pretty."

"I've no notion, but it is here so it must mean something. We'll not turn up our noses at it, until I've discovered why," said Sanger. Without attempting to remove it from the trunk, he closed the lid. "But, since it appears to have no particular commercial value, it can wait."

Instead, they opened the remaining boxes and were awed by the beauty revealed. They were also disappointed there was nothing of greater value, no jewels or a store of gold coin. Jack estimated the whole collection wouldn't bring enough to do more than dip another two or three toes into the deep waters awaiting Sanger. At most his foot!

"I'm sorry," said Helena. "I was so certain I'd discovered something important."

"There may be something valuable among the paintings," said Alton soothingly as he turned toward the frames leaning against the wall. "Or among the books, perhaps. Assuming they aren't too badly mildewed."

"Even if they weren't musty, I don't believe they are quite the sort of book one admits to owning," said Lady

Helena in a fascinated tone. She'd opened a volume and stared, wide-eyed, at one of the many pictures.

Sanger glanced over her shoulder to discover exactly what she was contemplating with such an odd combination of horror and amusement. "My God in Heaven! *You* shouldn't be looking at that!"

He instantly removed the offensive book from her hands.

She tried to get it back. "Perhaps," she said, "I should be shocked into a fainting fit, but you forget I was raised by my grandmother, who doesn't allow missishness. Besides, I frequented the stables from an early age, and no one worried about what I might or might not learn there."

"This is different," he insisted. "You shouldn't even know such illustrations exist, let alone look at them."

When she couldn't make Sanger give her her book back, she asked, "Do you suppose the rest are the same?" She chose another only to have it, too, removed from her hands. "Now Sanger . . ."

"Now, Lady Helena! You *know* you should not."

"But I want to. I don't see how what was pictured could be humanly possible."

"You don't need to understand!" said a harassed Sanger. "Jack, is there a market for this sort of lewd book?"

Jack was looking at another volume. "I suspect there are men who would give the shirt off their backs for such a collection. That is, if it *is* a collection and all of them are anything like this one." He didn't look up from an etching which held him fascinated. "The problem will be—" He turned a page. "—Will you look at that! . . . the problem will be—" He held Lady Helena off when she'd have looked. "—to find someone collecting such trash."

"You should consult Mr. Beal in Threadneedle Street," suggested Lady Helena, resigned. She'd long ago learned to bide her time and had already decided she'd return another day. On a day when there were no men to thwart her! "Beal's an expert in antiquarian books and he likely knows about this sort as well as any other although he'd never admit as much to me, of course."

"I can do that for you when I go through London on my way home," offered Jack. "Should I send out an expert in painting and statuary to give you an evaluation of the other things, as well?" he asked.

Sanger was looking at the paintings. They weren't large, the biggest only twenty by fifteen or thereabouts. They needed cleaning. The one he held, however, was a delightfully intriguing study of a woman's head and shoulders. She was turned sideways and looked back over one shoulder with an expression of mischief that made one smile just to see it.

"Who do you suppose painted this?" he asked. "It's rather incredibly well done, I'd say." He glanced from the painting to Lady Helena and back. "And something of a coincidence, is it not? The Oriental Venus is supposed to have looked like your grandmother. This reminds me of you, Lady Helena, when you are in a teasing mood."

"Do you think so?" she asked surprised. She studied it, frowning. "I wonder why one never sees oneself as others do."

"It isn't so such a resemblance of feature as of a characteristic expression," said Jack, thoughtfully. "And here is another. I don't know the painter, but one of your ancestors, Simon, must have been enamored of the model. This, too, is the same woman . . ." He tipped others out from the wall. "In fact," said Jack, straightening, "they all appear to be of the same model and," he finished sternly, when Lady Helena would have looked, "some of them are *not* to be viewed in mixed company." Once again Alton held her away, his hand gentle but firm on her shoulder.

Helena was beginning to dislike the man's prudishness and wished she'd managed to inspect the trove before she and Rod had gone to find the men.

"I haven't a notion," Alton added, "which of your ancestors had such odd tastes, Simon, but if I were you, I'd clear this out, get what you can for it, and forget it ever existed."

Sanger went back to the first painting and again held it so the lamplight fell on it. "I don't know, Jack. Maybe not quite all of it." He raised his eyes and met Lady Helena's gaze. "I think I'd like to keep this one, at least, in memory of a very special day and even more special, the lady of whom it will remind me."

His look was somewhat heated and Lady Helena felt herself blush. "That," she said solemnly, "is very likely the nicest compliment I've ever been paid."

The men chuckled.

She felt her skin warming still more at their knowing tones and sought a change the subject. "It is getting late," she said. "I'd better return to the Treweses' before someone decides to send out a search party." She cast a longing look around the little room. "If only it were more valuable."

"It will bring in *something*. Perhaps more than I've guessed," added Alton in that soothing-the-little-woman voice she disliked. "I am not a collector, after all, and collectors are odd sorts. Perhaps your Mr. Beal can arrange for a little competition?"

"An excellent notion," she said, liking him again for his intelligence. "I will write you a letter of introduction. Mr. Beal will do his best for a friend of mine and if he knows more than one collector of such things, he will organize an auction."

"It will take time," mused Alton, "but one must balance instant need against maximum profit. I'll be very pleased to have an introduction to your Mr. Beal. Thank you."

As they spoke they left the little room, shutting everything away as they went. Lady Helena, still rather irrationally worried about theft, swept at their tracks in the library, raising another dust storm in the process.

The men fled, coughing, to the terrace where she soon joined them. Sanger eyed the sun, which had moved well beyond the meridian. "It is getting on, Jack. Shall we escort Lady Helena back to our host's home?"

Jack agreed. Besides, they'd seen nearly everything and he had his lists. He'd go to his room and organize his thoughts and set priorities.

They rode quietly for perhaps a quarter mile before Lady Helena raised her fine contralto voice in song. She choose a popular Italian air and soon the men joined in, Jack with a surprisingly deep bass and Simon with a wonderfully clear tenor that complemented Helena's voice very well. They took turns choosing songs and were in the midst of a rollicking round when, suddenly, Lady Helena's mare kicked out, whinnying in a shocked, hurt way, and then, before anyone could react, ran off, completely out of control.

For the first time ever, Helena lost a rein. She leaned forward for it and heard something whistle over her head. Occupied with trying to reach the leather while remaining on her saddle, she barely noticed. Instead she talked soothing nonsense to her mount. When that didn't help, she simply hoped she could ride the horse until, exhausted, it stopped on its own . . . and then she heard the pounding hooves of another horse catching up with her.

Lady Helena glanced over her shoulder. Sanger, of course, as she'd have guessed if she'd not been so dazed. The animal which had easily out-distanced them all once before that day, was nearly up to her. She guessed Sanger's intent and, when he closed with her, released her knee, turned in her saddle and, simultaneously shaking loose from her stirrup, she launched herself at him.

Sanger clutched the armful of woman to his side and slowed the mare. Her arms, tight around his neck, were nearly choking him and he felt her body trembling. He reined in his horse and, using both arms, pulled her up onto his saddle bow and into his embrace.

Somewhere she'd lost her hat and her hair had come down. It flowed over his hands, soft and teasing. She continued to clutch him tightly and he bent his head, nuzzling her neck with his lips and wished they weren't on horseback, were somewhere alone.

But this, he berated himself, *is no time for such thoughts.* One additional fleeting thought snuck under his guard, asking if it ever *would* be the right time.

As well as he was able, Simon ignored his growing interest in her ladyship's person and set himself to soothing her emotions instead. "It's all right now. I've got you. You're safe."

Holding her close he murmured the sort of nonsense into her ear she'd just been telling her hack! Helena decided she found it soothing even if her mount had not. She recovered but found she liked his voice, his breath tickling her ear, liked having his arms around her, liked the feel of him pressed against her body . . . and couldn't bring herself to tell him she no longer needed such pampering. She opened one eye when Roderick pounded past, intent on catching her runaway. Silently, she wished him luck. It had seemed to her the beast would race on into doomsday.

Jack appeared next, a worried expression drawing his forehead into a frown. "Simon . . ."

"I heard," interrupted Sanger, his arms tightening protectively.

"But who would sh- . . . ?"

"I don't know," his lordship again interrupted, "but I mean to find out."

Lady Helena found she was curious about whatever it was they discussed. She reluctantly drew away from Sanger who, just as reluctantly, loosened his hold on her. "Find out what?"

"Eavesdropping, my lady?"

"I suppose I was. Find out what?"

"What idiot was shooting at you," he said, a muscle working in his jaw.

"Shooting . . . *at me?*"Helena's head began to swim and she clutched at his coat.

"You're safe, my lady. He didn't hit you, but I think Cole will find a wound on your mare's flank. There was the second shot . . ."

Helena remembered the funny whistling sound which had passed over her head. "I heard it, I think. I'd leaned forward—" Realization filled her with horror. "I might have been hit!" She shuddered and Lord Sanger drew her close again, tucking her head into his neck, his arms closing tightly around her.

"Who is your enemy, Lady Hel?" asked Alton. "Why would anyone shoot at you?"

She shook her head, rubbing her forehead against Simon's cheek.

"An inheritance, perhaps?" Alton persisted.

It was a new thought. "Thurmand might think he'd inherit, I suppose." There! She'd done it again. They discussed a possible enemy and immediately she thought of Thurmand. "I can't think who else would expect to do so . . ."

"But he's merely your cousin, is he not?"

"My family has dwindled to very few, so he might expect something, I suppose. But my solicitor insisted I write a will the day my father's was read." Alton's expectant silence insisted she say more. "At this particular moment, everything goes to charity."

"Have you never told Mr. Woodhall that?" asked Simon. Lady Helena once again straightened away from Lord

Sanger who was looking down at her half in bemusement and half in horror.

"I never saw the need," she said. She raised her eyes to meet his. "It was my business, after all. Not his."

"I think perhaps it might be wise if you find an opportunity to tell him, my lady," suggested Alton more than a trifle grimly.

"But he has a fortune of his own!" she riposted.

"Does he?" asked Jack in a soft voice.

Lady Helena, turning toward Simon's friend, blinked. "What can you mean?"

"I hear rumors from the City. Woodhall's speculations have been talked about. He hasn't had much luck, it seems. It is possible, is it not, that he's lost enough he feels the pinch?"

Frowning, Helena stared off into the distance. "Do you suppose that's why he pressed me to marry him?"

"He's asked you?"

"More than once. I told him, the last time, to give over. I wanted nothing to do with him."

"It is rather interesting," said Sanger, his voice hard, "that he told *me* he'd *never been your suitor.* And now we find someone is shooting at you." Simon held Lady Helena away so that he could look into her eyes. "My lady, are you, by chance," he asked sternly, "the heiress I've heard is attending this house party?"

"You didn't know?" Her expression was all innocence.

The chagrin expressed in his face was almost laughable. "You know very well I didn't."

She tipped him a look and then stared at nothing in particular. "I'd wondered, of course," she said tongue in cheek.

"I'd have had nothing to do with you if I'd known!"

"Perhaps that is why I didn't tell you," she retorted. "I enjoy your company—as you well know."

He smiled. "Touché. It is your fault, of course, that I

made such a mistake. After all, it is a well-established tra-
dition that heiresses are ugly as sin, which *you* are not!"
He sighed. "I thought it was that little monkey, Lord Humboldt's daughter, and my conclusion was supported by the
fact she is always surrounded by the bucks."

"Merry? Everyone likes Merry. You can't help but like
Merry. Which is why she always has a court around her.
You truly didn't know?" she asked.

"It's my policy to have of nothing to do with heiresses.
Thinking she was one I never learned anything more
about her."

Lady Helena felt his arms tighten around her slightly
and wondered if he knew he did it. Whether he did or
didn't, it was revealing. She leaned into him, enjoying the
feeling of being protected. Lady Helena decided that, assuming she played her cards right, she might overcome
his objections and, very possibly, she'd a chance at the
happiness she'd always believed would elude her.

"Here comes Rod with my horse," she said, a faint sigh
revealing she rather wished he'd not caught the creature!

"Do you feel up to riding?" asked Simon, looking down
at the top of her head.

"Not really," she replied, and hoped it wasn't too blatant
a request that he hold her all the way home.

"Then you shouldn't have to," he replied, satisfied he'd
an excuse to continue holding her.

All the way home.

Four

Once Lady Helena was settled in the care of her maid, Lord Sanger returned to the stables where he found her ladyship's groom in an isolated box, alone with the wounded mare. Rod Cole was grim faced.

"The mare will recover, will she not?" asked Sanger.

"The mare will be fine, but she'll be marked. That—" Rod gestured to the horse's rump. "—will scar."

"And that makes you angry?" asked Sanger.

"It isn't that." Rod shut his mouth with a snap and turned away.

"This isn't the first time her ladyship has been in danger, is it?"

Rod stilled. Dropping the curry comb he'd been using on the mare's mane, he swung back and searched Lord Sanger's face. "Why do you ask?"

"Because I want to help."

"I don't know if you can help. She refuses . . ." Again he turned away.

"If you mean she's refused to believe she's in mortal danger, I think that's changed. Cole, I can't help if I don't know what is happening," continued Sanger. When Rod still didn't speak, he said, "Come now. Loyalty is a very good thing, but you must distinguish her friends from her foes!"

"She doesn't want her grandmother upset."

"Lady Catherine will be exceedingly upset if something happens to Lady Helena," said Sanger, dryly.

Rod nodded, sighing deeply. "Lady Hel will have my guts for garters, but here's the story." Rod proceeded to list the accidents which had plagued his mistress.

Sanger's blood ran cold as he understood just how close Lady Helena had come to death on more than one occasion. And, with the realization, came another. Somewhere, somehow, he'd learned to love this intelligent and sprightly lady who reminded him of the women who followed their military husbands, living rough when necessary, putting up with hard conditions and long treks. Women who, somehow, made homes under the most impossible of conditions for the men in their lives to come to when duty was done. Lady Helena had that independent nature, the courage and resourcefulness, and he almost regretted he couldn't wed her and take her back to Portugal—just to prove he'd judged correctly!

"I'll do what I can," he told Rod. "Mr. Alton and I have come up with a notion which may take the trick all by itself. Still, continue to guard her carefully, Cole. Until we *know* there is no more danger."

That evening Lord Sanger watched for a particular grouping of people. In the salon before dinner, there was no opportunity for his little charade. Since he needed Lady Helena's help, he couldn't act afterward when the women left the table, the men remaining with brandy and cigars. Thurmand Woodhall and Lord Trewes must be near Lady Helena when he went into the act he and Jack had contrived, but, frustratingly, the principal actors refused to cooperate, even when the men left the table and joined the women.

Sanger was wondering how to manipulate the scene when, without his contrivance, the proper constellation occurred naturally. Lord Trewes and Mr. Woodhall were in conversation with Lady Humboldt and Lady Hingly-

Tumpton. Lady Helena was nearby, talking to Lady Merry. Sanger rather rudely excused himself to Lord Humboldt and approached Lord Trewes who was holding forth on his favorite subject: horse racing.

"My lord," said Sanger at the first break in the conversation.

"My lord?" inquired Lord Trewes.

"It has occurred to me that I and my solicitor were remiss. Actually, I believe it was my fault for asking a question at the wrong instant. However it happened, I realized today I need the name of a really good local man, if you'd be so kind."

"For what purpose, my lord?" Lord Trewes held up a hand when Sanger's expression suggested he thought the question impertinent. "I'd name one for a land transfer and quite another if you've become involved in a lawsuit!"

"Nothing so dramatic," said Sanger judging the probing comment more out of curiosity than necessity. He tucked away the knowledge that his host, who would be a near neighbor, was a busybody! On the other hand, he'd intended to introduce the subject of wills, and Trewes's question gave him the opportunity. "I merely wish to draw up a will," he said. "It should have been done when I first learned the details of my inheritance, but, as I said, my solicitor and I were remiss."

The line between Lord Trewes's always angry-looking brows deepened. He shuddered. "Did my wife put you up to this?" he sputtered.

"Your wife?" Sanger blinked and shook his head to clear away his surprise. "Why would your wife . . . ?"

"Oh well, if she's not, then she's not, but—" But Lord Trewes still looked suspicious. "—she's been nagging me and nagging me to make mine. I won't. I'm not ready to put my spoon in the wall!"

"But what has that to do with making a will?" asked Lady Helena.

At the word "will" she'd moved to join the conversation. She'd been warned of Sanger's purpose and, unlike the other, unknowing, actors in the little scene, was perfectly willing to cooperate.

"I," she continued, "made mine the day my father's will was read. It is only sensible, is it not? I was too young to know what to do with my inheritance, of course, but my solicitor said I could change the thing at any time if my circumstances changed. That I have one, he said, would simplify things if something happened to me. My wishes would be known, you see?" She shrugged. "I settled most of my fortune as an endowment for a girl's school my grandmother founded years ago and the rest goes to other charities."

Thurmand Woodhall's attention, which had wandered, came round the instant Lady Hel mentioned her will. At her words his face suffused with blood. When she finished his voice overrode something Lord Trewes would have said. "You couldn't be such a blockhead," he exclaimed, viciously—and, again, no lisp.

"Blockhead, Thurmand?" asked Helena coldly. "In what way am I fool?"

"You can't think to leave your fortune away from the family. At the very least you should leave it to Grandmother."

"I should? *She* didn't think so."

"She knows of this idiocy?"

"She helped me decide on the charities I'd name. It is what she did in her will."

"What she did!" Thurmand's eyes seemed to start from his head. "No. She can't have . . . surley she didn't . . ."

"Oh yes she did," said Helena quietly. "If you'd any expectation of inheriting anything from either of us, you'd better think again."

"Her whole fortune?"

"What remains of it—"

"What remains!" Thurmand shouted, his face red and the whole of his lean frame shaking from strong emotion.

"—was long ago settled just as she wishes. You and I have no need of her money so she, too, left most everything to her school." Lady Helena glanced around. "But, really Thurmand, do you think this is a quite proper discussion? I thought you didn't approve of washing the family linen, dirty or otherwise, before strangers."

Thurmand, realizing how avidly everyone was listening, turned from red to white. He bowed. Half strangling on the words, he apologized to his host: "My lord, I am very sorry to have caused a scene." He turned on his heel and stalked from the room.

Gradually everyone's company manners returned and people talked of other things. Except for the Ladies Humboldt and Hingly-Tumpton, who moved away, avidly discussing the unhappy incident in low voices. Lord Trewes, dejected for his own reasons, snapped out a solicitor's name for Lord Sanger and abruptly removed himself to the other end of the room.

Lord Sanger and Lady Helena were left staring at each other.

"I think you must have been correct," she said softly and a trifle sadly. "Thurmand not only reacted very badly to the news of my will, but quite out of his usual character."

"I'm glad you'd the presence of mind to explain your grandmother's will as well. I've a notion your Thurmand might otherwise have turned his, hmm, attentions toward the dowager."

Lady Helena felt shock sweep through her, weakening her. "But I didn't mean . . . that didn't even occur . . . surely he'd not . . ."

"Your Thurmand acted like an exceedingly desperate man, Lady Helena."

"Do stop calling him my Thurmand, if you please." Crossly, she added, "He was the bane of my existence when we were children and, quite obviously, that hasn't changed."

Lord Sanger took her elbow and lead her out onto the terrace. Once there be turned her gently until she faced him. "Lady Helena, you do realize it is very possible it was he who came near to being your true bane."

She glanced up at him.

"Those shots this afternoon," he said, reminding her of something he feared she'd prefer to forget. "When your horse was creased and you heard another shot pass over your head?"

Lady Helena's color faded and her gaze turned inward, Lord Sanger could have kicked himself for reminding her. But he had to remind her, had to convince her, had to find a way of protecting her.

"Come," he said, grasping her arm firmly.

He was surprised when she leaned on him, giving up her usual independence to a surprising degree. He led her into the house by another route, taking her to Lord Trewes's little hideaway where he settled her into a chair before moving to the wall. Unfortunately, he couldn't find the trick of opening the hidden cupboard where Lord Trewes's good wine was hidden. This evening it was he who used language unbecoming to polite society.

His fumbling gave Lady Hel time to recover. "The top rosette," offered Lady Helena. "Turn it widdershins. Then farther down there is a bird. Turn it the other way." At the prospect of a reviving drink, she was almost back to normal. Lord Sanger brought her a small glass and she sipped. Once. It was a rather heavy port, the one beverage for which she'd never acquired a taste. She grimaced and set it aside.

"I'm sorry," he said, seeing her expression of distaste, "but there is nothing else. I could ring . . ." His concern drew his brows into a frown.

"I'll do quite well without—"

He glanced, undecided, toward the bell pull.

"Truly. I am much better now. Sanger, did I thank you for making it possible to, quite naturally, introduce the fact I've a will?"

"Jack came up with the most important part of the plan. It was his suggestion I pretend to need a will myself so I could ask Lord Trewes for the name of a solicitor as a way of introducing the subject."

"I'll thank him, too."

"Had you no clue Woodhall might be dangerous to you?"

Lady Helena sighed. "At some level I've begun suspecting him, but he's my *cousin.* I can't quite bring myself to accept it even now. Still, avoiding *him* was the reason I accepted the Treweses' invitation. I believed it one of the few places my finical cousin would refuse to visit. Finding him here was something of a shock, but, I convinced myself it was only that he wished to try, still again, to talk me into wedding him." She looked thoughtful. "I wonder if I couldn't *allow* myself to believe the accidents I've been having were dangerous."

"But you *had* begun to wonder?" he asked, insisting she put into words that which she didn't wish to face.

Helena sighed. "Rod insisted there was no way the last problem, which involved my personal tack, could have been an accident and told me to tell Grandmother. When I refused, he swore that if anything more happened he was going to tell the tale himself!"

"Good for him." Simon waited. "So you'd begun to suspect all was not well?" She didn't respond and Simon glowered at her, thinking furiously. She still hadn't said what he wanted her to say, and he searched his mind for ways to make her admit, in so many words, her cousin had tried to murder her.

"I must remember to tell Rod he needn't tell her. Surely now," she continued, "it will be unnecessary to inform

her. Besides—" Lady Helena glanced up at Sanger, a sad
look, one which implied a feeling of helplessness. "—I
don't know if she'd believe Thurmand guilty even if she
believed someone was attempting to harm me. He's her
pet . . . you see?"

Simon caught her hands and pulled her to her feet,
drawing her close and holding her in a warm embrace
with all the gentle affection she needed just then. They
stood, silent, for a long moment.

But the feel of her in his arms was affecting him just as
it had earlier when he'd ridden with her before him. His
hands moved restlessly.

Helena felt them move on her body and snuggled closer.

For a moment Simon wanted nothing more in the world
than to kiss her, touch her, make her his forever. But it
wouldn't do. She'd suffered a shock. It was his duty to ease
her mind, not seduce her! He said, "I'd guess your Thurmand will leave in the morning and surely," he lied, "he'll
not attempt your life again since there is no reas- . . ."

Both looked around as the door swung wide. Lord
Trewes, along with several of his more strait-laced guests,
stared in at them. "Well! I didn't believe it!" exclaimed
their host.

Lady Hingly-Tumpton pushed herself in front of Lord
Trewes and glowered. "How dare you, my lady?" She
pointed a long, thin finger at the two of them. "To allow
yourself to be *alone* with a man not nearly related to you!
And to be found in his *embrace!* It is a *scandal.*"

Sanger set Lady Helena away, putting himself between
the woman with whom he'd been fool enough to fall in
love and the elderly lady whose sensibilities were so deeply
and sincerely outraged.

"We didn't mean to announce it just yet, but Lady
Helena," he said firmly, "has agreed to become my wife."
He hoped no one else heard the gurgle of sound from be-
hind him. "It was quite proper for her," he continued

sweetly, "to go apart to receive an offer, would you not agree?" Again he heard the odd sound and was almost certain Lady Helena was suppressing laughter, of all things. "We were nearly finished with our conversation and almost ready to return to the drawing room when the door opened. However—" He glanced from face to face. "—we were not *quite* finished, so if you would be kind enough to leave us alone for a few more moments . . . ?"

"We will leave the door ajar," said Lady Hingly-Tumpton after a moment's hesitation. "*I* will remain just down the hall. Lady Helena, if you have need of me, you've only to call." She glowered at Sanger, gave the slightest of curtsies, and backed into Lord Trewes.

Though not to blame, he instantly apologized.

Everyone disappeared. Unfortunately, the door remained open.

"Sanger, that wasn't necessary," said Helena softly.

"I think it was. Helena, meaning to soothe you I lied when I said Woodhall was no longer a danger to you. I don't *know* that. You may still be in need of protection and I want to protect you. Only if I'm married to you will I have that right."

She gave him a sideways look. "And if I won't have you sacrificing yourself?"

He stared at her. "Lady Helena . . ."

"You saved my reputation by making your declaration, but—" She fiddled with a ribbon decorating her evening gown. "—are you not . . . unhappy you were forced to do so?"

He bit his lip. "My lady . . ."

"Ah! You don't instantly deny it. It is, perhaps, that you don't know how to tell me you are deeply distressed?" she suggested with that mock sadness she could put on at will. "In that case, of course I will cry off after a suitable period of time."

"I didn't say I was unhappy. Or distressed," said the

harassed Lord Sanger who had assumed it would be his duty to placate Lady Helena and was having difficulty adjusting when he found she was *teasing* him. "Besides, we must wed. You need me. I believe I can keep you safe . . . but . . ." He ran his fingers through his hair.

"It is that you don't wish to marry an heiress," she explained for him, tongue in cheek.

"I've no wish to be known as a fortune hunter!"

She cast a sly look his way. "I suppose we could wed and simply have the patience to prove to all and sundry that it's a love match?" She eyed him, wondering how he'd react to that suggestion, hoping that perhaps he felt more for her than simple duty, that it was more than his overly developed sense of responsibility which had forced him to suggest they actually wed. "After many years of wedded bliss—" Helena's brows arched in wry expression of humor. "—our happiness, our simple joy in each other's company, our—" She shrugged. "—whatever. We would, you see, have proven we're madly in love?" Then she grinned one of those mischievous grins he loved. "Of course there *is* a problem." He frowned. "We'd have to make an effort to be happy."

Speaking more stiffly than he wished, he said, "I'm sure happiness would be no problem if we could get beyond my pride!" He ran his fingers through his hair.

"Ah! I *wondered* if you knew *that* was our real problem," she muttered.

Before Lord Sanger could think up a response to that remark, Lady Hingly-Tumpton appeared in the doorway and stared rudely from one to the other, looking, Sanger thought, for signs they'd been indulging in reprehensible behavior.

"You are taking a very long time," she complained, eying Lord Sanger's mussed hair with a shocked expression.

"We will have to finish our discussion another time," said Helena rising to her feet. She lay her hand on Sanger's arm and squeezed it encouragingly. "Courage, my lord," she whispered.

"Courage?" he murmured.

"Have you no notion what we must now endure? No you haven't," she decided. "Well, come along and let us get the worst of it behind us!"

Sanger wished they'd had more time. They needed to discuss Lady Helena's safety and it would have helped if they could have done so while Lady Helena was still suffering somewhat from the shock of discovering her cousin's feelings about her money. But they'd been interrupted before he'd managed to make her face her danger.

Instead they had to face the company. If he'd had no notion of how it would be, he soon learned. They were surrounded the instant they entered the drawing room and the questions fired their way ranged from Lady Merry's desire to know all the details of their romance—*every one*—to Lady Trewes's demand to know what they meant by it.

"What can *you* mean, Lady Trewes?" asked Sanger, choosing to respond to his hostess.

"She'll rave at me for all eternity!" moaned his hostess.

"She?"

"I'll have given my head for washing to—" Lady Trewes, almost in tears, pointed a trembling at Lady Helena. "—*her* grandmother! Have you met her grandmother? Have you any notion of that foul-mouthed old woman's temper? She'll drop me into boiling oil. She'll roast me on my own kitchen spit." Lady Trewes wrung her hands. "Oh, I don't think I can bear it!"

"Roasting on your own spit?" repeated Lady Helena in mock-shocked tones. "I should think not! But, Lady Trewes, *quite to the contrary*—" Lady Helena spoke loudly, catching her hostess's self-absorbed attention. "—you are more likely to be hailed as a heroine and taken to her bosom." She lowered her voice when certain Lady Trewes attended her. "Perhaps you are unaware my grandmother had given up all hope of marrying me off. Since my engagement was accomplished under your roof, she is more likely to make you her friend for life than to castigate you," Helena finished smoothly, as her hostess appeared to calm down.

Instantly her ladyship bristled up again. "Friend? Me? You mean she'd come *here*? No. She can't come here." She cast a hunted look around the room. "I won't have Lady Catherine here!"

"Of course we will," said Lord Trewes. He'd approached in time to hear his wife's last words and wasn't about to insult a woman who had married two earls and was a dowager countess twice over! Always ready to jump on the main chance, he took his wife's arm in an obviously painful grip. "Lady Catherine Rolandson is welcome in our home at any time, Lady Hel. Do tell her so when you write and, of course, my wife will also write, inviting her."

"I . . . she . . . she . . ." Lady Trewes's skin turned ashy as she glanced at the arm held by her husband. She shut her mouth tightly and said no more.

"You'll tell her she's welcome," ordered Lord Trewes.

"I'll be certain to tell her *your* sentiments," said Lady Hel, speaking to both. The devil in her wondered if Lord Trewes was bright enough to hear exactly what she'd said and, then, too, whether Lady Trewes would catch the hint that Helena would head her grandmother off!

Lord Sanger, who was beginning to know her rather well, easily caught her real meaning. The look of amused understanding which he and Lady Hel exchanged was observed by more than one among the guests and, later, was commented upon at length.

From that moment—and for months afterwards—an argument raged throughout the *ton*. Was it a marriage forced by convention to avoid a scandal, or was it, almost unbelievable, a love match? Those who saw the two together suspected the latter. Everyone else who had ever met Lady Hel, and that included approximately eighty-five percent of the upper ten thousand, were far more inclined to believe it must be the former. At first, the bets written into every betting book in town were against the wedding coming off at all. Later, when it did, they were to the effect the couple would separate—usually with a date before the new year!

Lady Helena wrote her grandmother a long letter requiring several crossed sheets. It included a description of her initial brief meetings with Sanger in London and a history of their renewed acquaintance here at the Treweses'—including a lighthearted version of *her* proposal which was turned down, followed by a more serious report of *his* abrupt and unexpected announcement of their engagement under somewhat stressful circumstances, and the fact they meant to wed as soon as settlements were signed and the banns could be called.

Something less than a week later Lady Catherine rode up to the Treweses' front door in a massive old-fashioned traveling chariot. When her ladyship refused to leave her carriage, Lady Trewes was forced by good manners, however reluctantly, to join her guest there.

"Now," demanded Lady Catherine when she'd assured herself Lady Trewes was settled on the opposite seat, "a round tale if you please. I cannot make heads or tails of my granddaughter's letter, which she crossed and re-crossed, except to learn that she has engaged herself to wed that pauper, Simon Mansanger, the new Lord Sanger. How did such a thing happen?"

"I don't know. I swear to you I haven't a notion," exclaimed the distraught Lady Trewes. "I was convinced she only flirted with him to pass the time. I mean, they did spend a certain amount of time together but, truly, only flirting. I'm quite sure of that, and besides, I've heard the oddest tale that Lord Sanger thought that Lady Merry

Humboldt was the heiress and was avoiding *her* and I've heard another tale that it wasn't Lord Sanger who proposed, but Lady Hel, which would be just like her, would it not?"

At Lady Catherine's glare, which had cowed far more self-assured people than Lady Trewes would ever be, the younger lady instantly contradicted herself.

"Not," said Lady Trewes, "that I believe a word of it, of course. Nor the tale that my husband and Lady Humboldt hunted down Lord Sanger and Lady Hel with that awful Lady Hingly-Tumpton in tow, simply out of spite, and thereby forced the engagement. I mean," she insisted triumphantly, when it was borne in on her that Lady Catherine was looking more and more annoyed, "that anyone looking at the two of them cannot think it anything other than a love match!" She took a big breath and forced herself, albeit in a rather tremulous voice, to add, "But won't you come in and make yourself comfortable? I'll have a room prepared for you at once and . . ."

"Pish and tush. I'm settled with friends. The Cooper-Wainwrights, you know. I'll return there the instant I've had words with my granddaughter. Be so kind as to order her attendance on me at once."

"But I can't!" said Lady Trewes, once again convinced she'd soon find herself spitted over her own kitchen fire. "She isn't here!"

"So—" Lady Catherine's frown deepened. "—where has the blasted chit taken herself off to?"

"Why—" Lady Trewes hesitated, wondering if she dared admit what she suspected, which was that Lady Helena was with Lord Sanger, scandalously alone, at Sanger-Monkton or if she should merely state exactly what she knew. She settled on the safe road since it seemed Lady Catherine was not one who found it entertaining to indulge in titilating gossip, speculating on all the juiciest of possibilities.

"—I believe she went out riding with that odd groom of hers in attendance?"

"Odd?" Lady Caroline's already stiff back straightened still more. "Roderick Cole? What is odd about her groom?"

"Why, so free in his manners! He has actually—" Lady Trewes's eyes widened, expressing her disbelief. "—been heard to argue with Lady Helena!" She tittered in an irritating way, a laugh which disappeared instantly with Lady Catherine's response:

"Excellent. I'm glad to hear he's up to his work. The man is supposed to watch out for her and how could he if he couldn't stand up to her?"

"Oh well, if *you* approve . . ."

"Dolt! I approve or he'd not be in her employ!" Lady Catherine leaned rather heavily on her cane, her exceedingly aristocratic nose pushing closer to Lady Trewes who leaned as far back against the squabs as she could manage. "You are exactly as I'd heard you to be, Lady Trewes. A small-minded woman of no particular intellect. I'll await my granddaughter here." She glared, an expression which had intimidated Prinny himself. "*Alone* if you please. Or even if you *do not.*"

Lady Trewes didn't know whether to be insulted she'd been dismissed or thankful she could escape. Lady Catherine thumped the roof of the carriage with her cane and the door opened.

"My lady?" asked her gorgeously outfitted footman.

"Lady Trewes is just leaving," said Lady Catherine disinterestedly, but with something of the formality she'd have used if sitting in her drawing room rather than a traveling chariot. Then, as soon as Lady Trewes was beyond hearing, she made a further, far more affably spoken, request. "James, be so good as to run around to the stable and leave a message I wish to see Lady Hel the instant she returns. *Before* she changes out of all her dirt. I'm not to be kept waiting one unnecessary instant."

The *necessary* moments were long enough. Word Lady Catherine Rolandson had arrived spread through the ranks of the guests and, one after another, from this window or from behind that shrub, nearly everyone caught a glimpse of the old tartar. Lady Catherine sat strictly upright, her hands crossed on her cane. She remained unmoving, staring straight ahead, for the entire two hours she awaited her granddaughter.

When Lady Helena, accompanied by Sanger and Alton, arrived at the stable and received the message, she exclaimed, "Grandmother! Oh dear. And me not here to receive her." A trifle warily, she added, "*Instantly*, did you say?"

The Treweses' head groom nodded.

"Has she been here long?" was the next, slightly more worried question.

"For the better part of two hours, my lady," said the man, relishing his role of doomsayer.

"So long as that? I'd better run." Lady Hel gathered up her skirts.

"I'll go with you, of course," said Lord Sanger, catching her arm and holding her back.

Lady Helena turned to the groom. "Did the order you received mention Lord Sanger or only myself?"

"Only yourself, my lady."

"Sanger," Lady Hel said earnestly, "believe me. You aren't wanted. You *will* be, but likely not today. Do you feel insulted?"

"Not insulted, of course. Merely worried about how she'll treat you. I'll not have you bullied, my dear."

Lady Hel stared. Then she chuckled, hiding the warming pleasure his caring words instilled in her. She smiled, her eyes sparkling. "I thank you for the thought, Sanger, but if there's to be an argument between us, you would have great difficulty determining whether you wished to protect me from my poor grandmother or quite the reverse." When he looked a question, she added, "I give as good as I get, my lord. Be warned!" With that she turned away and strode off with a stiff spine and a determined gait.

Simon and Jack followed. Simon couldn't take his eyes from the woman walking away from him. "She's amazing," murmured Sanger.

"She's just right for you," said Alton. "Have you forgiven me for divulging to Lord Trewes where I thought the two of you disappeared?"

"I wondered if you'd manipulated that scene. I should lay you out for it." Simon chuckled softly. "After all, Jack, having known Lady Helena for even so short a period of time, you must have realized you couldn't be certain she'd do the proper thing! She might have refused to back up my subterfuge. She'd have been forced into social limbo, kept there by the ostracism of all those *uncaught hypocrites* making up the *ton.*"

"I've observed the way she looks at you, Simon," said Jack rather smugly. "When you aren't looking at her, I mean. I rather thought she wouldn't mind wedding you. And," Jack continued still more smugly, "I knew it was the *only* way you'd ever manage to bring yourself to wed her."

"So I'm to thank you, is that it?"

Jack sobered. "I want you happy, Simon. I'm of the opinion she'll manage the trick."

"You aren't at all interested in the fact I'll have gained a fortune?"

"Now why," asked Jack, pretending innocence, "should I care one way or the other that you gain a fortune? Just by the way of it?"

"Because," said Simon promptly, "you care more for land than you do for people, and the condition of my estate has had you in a fret!"

"Oh well. There is that, of course," agreed Jack, with not the least hint of a blush.

The teasing exchange kept Simon's mind from what might occur between Lady Helena and Lady Catherine, but it couldn't quite erase a niggling fear that, once his fiancée was inside the coach, Lady Catherine might simply order her coachman to drive off! Therefore, once he'd entered the house by a side door, he took the nearby secondary stairs two at a time to the guest-room floor where his suite was situated very nearly directly above the entrance hall. Although he and Jack hadn't hurried their normal pace by very much, their route was considerably shorter than Lady Hel's. When Simon looked out his bedroom window, she was just then arriving at the side of the coach. Her grandmother leaned out her window and all he could see was a perky little hat covering a portion of the elderly lady's white hair.

Unashamedly wishing to eavesdrop, he opened his window—not that he thought he'd hear much from this distance. He hadn't taken into account that Lady Catherine was a trifle hard of hearing and had the overly loud voice of the deaf or that Lady Hel would, without thinking, raise her voice so her grandmother could hear clearly.

"Well?" asked Lady Catherine sharply.

"Yes, I think it is."

"Then you are happy?"

Simon heard a touch of anxiety in that and waited, holding his breath, for Lady Hel's answer. The answer was simple:

"Very."

Some tension inside Simon shattered and he felt lightheaded and very happy himself.

"Then I suppose that's all right." Lady Catherine leaned back into her coach. Her voice was more muted when she added, "You may tell John to drive on, Helena."

Lady Hel chuckled. "That's it, Grandmother?"

The old woman nodded.

"But where are you going?"

"I'm staying with the Cooper-Wainwrights. You and Lord Sanger may visit me there tomorrow. At ten."

"I'll be happy to visit you, Grandmother, but I cannot answer for his lordship."

Lady Catherine snorted, obviously disbelieving Helena's protests. "Of course you can. The man will do exactly as you wish, so you are to decide you'll not call the banns immediately, of course. But I promise not to eat him. There, now. You may be content. John," she said preemptively, her cane thumping the roof of the carriage, "do drive on!"

Lady Hel watched her grandmother's carriage disappear and turned toward the house. A hissing sound brought her head up and she found Lord Sanger grinning down at her. He pointed at her and then at himself and then at his room. She nodded. Going inside, she took the stairs far more quickly than was ladylike. After looking both ways to see that no one was in sight, she entered Lord Sanger's sitting room just as he came from his bedroom.

"I feared she might run off with you," he admitted. He approached, reaching for her, but then, stiffening, drew away. "Behave yourself, Lady Helena," he said with a self-deriding grin. "I am a very weak man and must not be tempted, you know."

Her head tipped to one side, Lady Hel eyed him consideringly. After giving a moment's thought to the meaning behind his words, she said, "You really do fear being called a fortune hunter, do you not?"

"I detest the notion," he agreed, standing with military precision. "I am, however, resigned." After the briefest of pauses he added, "I think."

She chuckled. "I've been courted by so many true fortune hunters I know the type all too well. I've always known you were not of that breed. I have difficulty understanding why anyone else would think it of you, when it is so *obvious* you are not."

"I assure you, it will be the main thought in almost every head."

"I am sorry, Simon, but—" Her eyes glinted. "—I very much fear you will be obliged to put up with it." She wandered around the room, casually picking up trifles and setting them down.

"You've decided, then, that you'll not cry off?" he asked lightly but with far less horror than he'd have felt only days earlier. "After a suitable period of time, of course?"

She turned, stared. *Not at all lightly,* Lady Helena asked, "Will you be very disturbed if I do not?"

"You have asked that before. If it weren't for your fortune I'd not care a jot that Lady Hingly-Tumpton forced the issue, although I still wonder how I'll support you. I've been thinking—" It was his turn to eye her rather closely. "—that perhaps we might tie your fortune up so I will not profit by it." Lord Sanger's words trailed off as he became aware, for the first time, of his bride-to-be's temper. "Lady Helena?"

"You cannot be such an complete and utter idiot!" she said through gritted teeth. "I'll not believe it of you!"

"I do not," said his lordship on a dry note, "care to hear myself labeled an idiot. Complete or otherwise."

"Then do not act like one." She turned, her spine rigid. He put his hands on her shoulders. "I'll not live off your money."

Lady Helena felt a tremor run through her. She wished she dared lean back against him, dared move his hands so that his arms encircled her. She sighed.

"*Something* must be done, my lady, if I'm to live with myself," he said softly and roused her anger all over again.

She ducked from under his hands and swung around, glaring. "We'll have to discuss this when I can think rationally. At the moment I only wish to shake you until your teeth rattle."

Startled, Simon laughed. "Do you think you could?"

"I haven't a notion; I only know I wish to try." An image of herself trying to shake the tall and well-built Lord Sanger filled her mind and she giggled. With the change of mood, she relaxed. "I must change from all my dirt, my lord. I will see you at dinner."

Before he could respond, she whisked herself out his door and, almost, into Lady Hingly-Tumpton's arms.

"Lady Helena! How *dare* you?"

"How dare I almost run you down? Well, I'm sorry, but I didn't know you were there, did I?"

"I meant," intoned the outraged Lady Hingly-Tumpton, "how dare you be in his lordship's rooms?"

"Oh. That. Do have some sense, my lady," said Helena, happy to have someone on whom she could vent some of the irritation sparked by her grandmother's arrival and fanned by Simon's continued idiocy concerning her fortune. "If I were engaged in reprehensible behavior I'd not have stormed out of there in such a way that just anyone might see where I'd been. I'd be feeling a great deal of guilt, would I not, and wishful of hiding my sin?"

Helena didn't await a response from the sputtering moralist. She stalked off toward her room, remembering, just as she entered it, that she'd forgotten to tell Simon they were forbidden to call the banns. Blast her grandmother! *How dare she interfere?* Her fading tantrum exploded again and much to her maid's distress, she tore off three buttons and ripped a bit of very expensive lace in her impatience to rid herself of her habit.

"In a temper are you?" asked her maid, studying whether she could mend the lace.

For a moment Helena stood rigid. Then, seeing the lace her maid held up for her viewing, she slumped. "Allie, I am sorry!" she said. "I've made you all that extra work."

"I don't suppose it'll hurt me. Especially here where I haven't any too much to keep me busy. But do tell," she said a trifle slyly, "if you think it'll be a common thing, falling out with Lord Sanger?"

Helena eyed her maid wondering if she dared ask. She dared. "What makes you conclude I'm angry at Lord Sanger?"

"Because you are never angry unless you feel yourself in the wrong," said Allie promptly, "and the only person about whom you feel strongly right now is His Lordship." Allie shrugged. "So who else might rouse you to behave badly?"

"Actually, Grandmother rather set me off and poor Sanger merely reaped the storm."

"Lady Catherine is here?" asked Allie sharply.

"You must be one of the very few who did not know."

"I've been in the laundry," the maid excused her lapse. "She's staying?"

"Not here. At the Cooper-Wainwrights. Therefore, Allie, her *maid* will not be around to hector you. You may relax."

"So *you* say," said Allie with something close to a pout. "If that Sibby is within ten miles of us, she'll find some way of cutting up my peace! You'll see!"

"You need have nothing to do with Sibby," soothed Helena who had, for years, been required to negotiate the peace between the two maids. "Simon and I are to attend Grandmother tomorrow at ten. We will ride."

"Does Lord Sanger know you'll ride?" asked Allie with pretended innocence.

"You may inform his valet," said Helena.

"Oh yes. I'm sure his lordship will appreciate hearing from his valet that he is to ride!"

Helena blinked. Then she grinned. "Allie, you are my good angel. *Of course* I must tell Sanger myself, but you may inform his valet, nevertheless, so he, too, will know."

"I'll prepare your good habit."

"The blue? I hate that habit."

"But, my lady, it pleases your grandmother, and this old brown one, which you will not give up, does not. Besides, you forget, it needs mending."

"Once again, my guardian angel," sighed Lady Helena.

Her ladyship wandered toward the washbasin. She didn't look forward to introducing Simon to her grandmother. As much as she loved the old woman, she did not blink at the dowager's faults. Speaking with a bluntness abhorred by modern society was one of them.

What might Lady Catherine say to his lordship . . . and how would he react? *Not,* she feared, by saying yes-my-lady and no-my-lady. Simon was not one to be cowed by Lady Catherine's famous frown! But she should not worry about what might never happen. Perhaps Lady Catherine would find Simon as delightful as she did herself!

Lady Helena put her concerns to the back of her mind during dinner and the evening of cards which followed. Unfortunately, whatever she'd managed when distractions abounded, once she'd gone up to bed she couldn't get the nagging misgivings out of her head. Worse, they resulted in a series of annoying nightmares so that she woke bleary-eyed and not in the best of humors.

Then, later, at breakfast, she lost the argument with Simon about whether to ride or drive—which didn't help at all when she was attempting to regain her equanimity!

Five

Sanger was in the stable yard checking Big Red's conditioning when Thurmand Woodhall arrived carrying his bags. Much to Sanger's vexation, the man had *not* departed immediately, as predicted, but, the preceding evening, had plagued Lady Helena at every turn. Whenever the two happened to be within feet of each other, Lady Helena's cousin made snide remarks or, alternatively, roused her contempt with oily cajolery. Simon had drawn his fire whenever possible.

Woodhall, seeing his nemesis, scowled. "You."

Sanger straightened away from the big raw-boned horse. "And you?"

"Think you've fallen into the honey pot, do you not?" sneered Woodhall.

"The honey pot?"

Woodhall waved an impatient hand. "Inheriting the title."

"The world should think twice before calling my inheritance a boon—given its condition," responded Sanger, politely. He hoped the man would soon tire of baiting him.

"Ah! But now, if you are to marry my dear cousin, the dibs will be in tune and sing a jolly song, will they not?" Woodhall's eyes widened when Sanger's lips compressed. "Amazing!" he guessed. "You *didn't* know."

Sanger chided himself for lacking the necessary self-control to prevent Woodhall's learning that, when flirting with her, he'd been ignorant of Lady Helena's wealth.

"When we talked on the terrace, I mean," continued Woodhall, when Sanger withheld comment. "I thought you played a game." Woodhall eyed Sanger who looked back with continued and impenetrable politeness. Angry he could make no mark against it, Woodhall turned sarcastic. "She is, as you've since discovered, the wealthiest heiress currently unwed." Thurmand smirked. "At least, she's the wealthiest with any pretense to good blood. But," he said, as if confiding a secret, "she will *not* wed you. She knows what is due her name! When she gives you your congé, there are cits rich as Croesus in whom you might show an interest. If, that is, you are in the hands of the cent-per-cents and a mere *fortune* will not do you."

"I don't need a fortune," Simon said, goaded.

"Do you not?" The sneer was firmly in place. "You would say that rumor lies?"

Simon swung away, kneeling on one knee to put his hands on Big Red's legs. He recalled how, the day she'd proposed, Helena had asked, in that ridiculously wide-eyed way, whether a fortune would make a difference. How stupid he'd been to think the heiress the Ladies Humboldt and Hingly-Tumpton discussed was Miss Merry. But Miss Merry and Lady Helena had been sitting side by side. Simon recalled how his eyes had been caught by a gleam, an almost blue look, to Lady Hel's shiny black hair, by the pert laughing expression she'd turned up over her shoulder toward Lord Horton, who had been among the men surrounding the two women.

He'd also, he admitted to himself, been attracted by Lady Helena's slender but perfect figure and the clean neat look of her. So, because he'd not otherwise have approached her, and he'd very much wished to do so, he'd allowed himself to assume Miss Merry was the heiress.

How smugly he'd assured himself he'd not allow the

gossips to label him a fortune hunter. What irony they'd do so anyway. What a damnable trick fate had played on him! A muscle in his jaw turned over, turned again. A movement at his side caught his eye and he brought his mind back to the man standing there.

"I should have enlightened you sooner," mused Helena's cousin.

Simon moved around Red, checking another leg.

"One makes these little errors." Woodhall's eyes narrowed. "You will take her, and her fortune, if, in the end, she'll have you, despite her devilish temper, will you not?"

"I have fallen in love with Lady Helena. Deeply in love. If she'll have me, then yes, I will wed her."

Thurmand's smallish eyes narrowed, becoming dark beady dots of hard, dead black. "Not sure I believe your protestations. Cream pot love, more like," he sneered. "But time will tell, will it not? We'll just wait and see."

Simon watched Woodhall stalk toward a gig which awaited him. One of the stable boys was holding the reins. Simon wasn't surprised to discover he liked Lady Helena's cousin even less, although he'd have thought that impossible. *Had* the man shot at her? It was obvious why Lady Helena refused to believe it: despite expensive well-tailored clothing, Woodhall looked more a clerk than a killer!

A couple of hours later Sanger drove his curricle around to the front of the house, a very proud, if rather young, stable boy standing up behind. It had taken something perilously close to an argument to convince Lady Helena they'd drive to see her grandmother.

It occurred to him their wills would often clash over such silly little things and he prayed God that Helena wasn't the sort to carry grudges or one who fell into sulks! But, even if she were, he wasn't about to arrive smelling like the stable for his first introduction to the Lady Catherine.

When he pulled up the pair the boy jumped down and

ran to their heads. "Careful lad," he warned, watching to see that all was well. "They're still fresh . . . ah!" he added, seeing Lady Helena approach, properly gowned in a carriage dress, the smart fawn colored skirts topped by a short pink spencer. "Good morning again," he said. "One moment and I'll help you up."

He leaned forward to tie his reins, but before he could finish and go to her aid, Lady Hel had grasped a hand-hold, put her foot in the iron designed for it and was half up into the medium-high rig. She grasped his quickly extended hand and, moment's later, settled herself beside him. For an instant he wondered if it were worth chiding her for such independence, but, just in time, he recalled he *liked* her willingness to do rather than be done for. It would, therefore, be rather hypocritical to complain.

Instead, he said, "I hope you do not object to an open carriage. Perhaps I should have borrowed . . ."

"I much prefer an open carriage," she interrupted. "Did you ask directions to the Cooper-Wainwrights?"

"You, hmm, *suggested* I do so when we met at breakfast. Did you think I'd forget?" he asked politely.

She gave him one of her sideways looks and, seeing a muscle in his cheek twitch, sighed. "I apologize if I was rather sharp about it. My father always pretended he knew exactly where he was going. We were appalling lost on so many occasions I lost count and now I can never go anywhere without checking, twice, that I know how to get there."

He heard something more than exasperation in her tone. "Do you want to tell me about it?" he asked softly, reaching for her hand and holding it down on the seat between them.

"What? And admit to being badly frightened on more than one occasion?" He nodded and she chuckled, a good warm feeling invading her, starting from their clasped hands and moving up and into her body. "Very well. The worst incident, one I always remember with a shudder, was one of the times he allowed me to go with him into the City. He was late for an appointment with our solicitor and took what he insisted would be a shorter route." She did shudder and his hand tightened.

"Got you into the middle of a London slum, did he?" asked Simon, sympathetically.

Looking straight ahead, Helena spoke in a clipped tone. "Before that day I'd been unaware so many people seemed never to have had a bath in the whole of their lives, wore rags my maids would scorn to use for cleaning and, very likely some who couldn't recall their last meal. But even that wasn't the worst. It was the . . . the look of hopelessness in nearly every eye. It was terrible. And unforgettable." She sighed. "There is so little one person can do."

"Lady Catherine's school?"

Lady Helena turned a surprised look his way. "I'd forgotten you knew of that."

"I am correct, then? But it *is* more than one person, is it not? There is her ladyship, of course, and you. But are there not others involved?"

"Now I'm older and have some control of my funds, I contribute, of course, but the school is well supported by a number of people." She shuddered slightly once again, the memory of being lost in the slum affecting her as it always did. "That day . . . I still thank God my father and I were not pulled down and beaten—" She trembled although her voice remained remarkably steady. "—*or worse. A wealthy man caught in the midst of such poverty, you know?* When we returned home I poured out my horror to Grandmother. She asked if I'd feel better if something were done. Only a dip into the barrel, she warned, but something which would help a few like those I'd seen."

Simon cast her a startled look. "She decided *that quickly?*"

Helena grinned. "Actually, she'd been discussing the

school in a desultory way for some time. Now she took up the project far more seriously. She ordered her solicitor to hunt for a suitable building, got a well-known Quaker to recommend a sensible woman to run it, and involved experts in every aspect of the planning."

Helena felt bereft when Sanger let go her hand to attend to his driving but she continued speaking as if nothing had changed. "Grandmother made me sit in on the meetings, although I was only nine at the time. I actually offered a suggestion one day, to the effect that there be exercise twice a day. I was upset, you see, when I heard them talking about lessons *all day long*. The thought of sitting still for so many hours appalled me. One of the Quaker women listened to me. She said I was a sensible child, that one must feed the soul, the body and the mind, and, with it, one must not neglect healthy exercise."

"Your grandmother sounds a practical woman. You were very likely bored, listening to adults argue about curricula and building renovations and salaries, but you must have learned a great deal about charity in a far more useful fashion than do most children who are merely told about it by their vicar of a Sunday."

"Grandmother," said Lady Helena, "is nothing if she is not practical. She is also a tartar. I just thought," she added airily, "that perhaps I should warn you that one never knows what she'll take it into her head to say. I am very much afraid she'll embarrass you or me or both of us long before this interview is finished."

"Hmm."

"You chuckle, but you haven't a notion how odiously frank she can be." Helena sighed.

"Haven't I? I can guess. After all, you are her granddaughter, are you not?"

"You would say I am overly frank."

"And I as well. So let us be frank together? About your fortune."

Lady Hel lay her hand on his arm. "Sanger? Not now? I don't wish us to be, hmm, *heated* when we arrive."

"Is that another instance of your odious frankness?" he asked, that one mobile brow well arched.

"I suppose it is, but, *frankly,*" she quipped, "I am the soul of tact when set beside Grandmother. You'll see," she finished, darkly.

"Yes, I will, will I not?" He turned between high brick columns. The fancy wrought iron gates stood open between pillars topped by lions sitting on their rumps, their manes covered in gold leaf. "We have arrived, so you are correct we'd not have time for an argument. Hmm. What lovely parkland," he added, slowing his pair to a more decorous pace then he'd held them to on the road.

Lady Hel was glad he had introduced an innocuous topic of conversation. She wanted no hint of controversy between them when they reached her grandmother. When she wished, she deftly used the old divide-and-conquer rule. Helena hadn't a notion whether she wished, but they must present a united front. Just in case.

"Look at that lake, my lady," said Sanger. "Man-made, I'd guess, but situated with such perfection. I like that Grecian temple thing next to it, do not you?"

"Grandmother occasionally reads from Lady Cooper-Wainwright's letters. It took over five years to achieve this natural-looking scene and, as you can see, it will take another fifty to bring it to perfection. Many of those trees, large as they were when transplanted, will require decades to mature."

"I hope I may make such plans before I'm finished," he said, looking around with something approaching jealousy.

As Sanger neared the house, he noted a groom lounging near the divided front steps, stationed there in expectation of their arrival. When he pulled up, the Treweses' boy jumped down and went to the pair's heads. The groom ambled around to where Simon was descending.

"I didn't push them so they shouldn't be overheated, but I didn't like the off gelding's action from about half way up the drive. Help the lad check for a stone or a loose shoe, if you will be so good," he ordered. He went, then, around the carriage to help a suddenly demure Lady Helena to the ground.

"Grandmother may be watching," she explained when he teased her about her sudden lack of independence. "I choose how I set up her back, you see, and something so trivial as obeying silly social strictures such as waiting for your help is *not* of much importance in the scheme of things."

As they strolled up the steps toward a terrace, Simon's brow climbed high. "You feel there *may* be something of more importance before we leave?"

Lady Hel's mouth quirked in a rather self-deriding slant, tacitly acknowledging his hit.

From the terrace, they mounted another flight of stairs, these flanked on each side by more lions and leading to oversized double doors. The doors were flung open and they were bowed in by a butler who motioned forward one of two nearly identical, very tall, footmen.

"Madam will see you in her boudoir," intoned the butler, again bowing.

"She would," muttered Helena.

"Some special meaning attached to where she'll see us?" asked Simon.

"It's where I was called when she wished to scold me, berate me, harangue me, or otherwise intimidate me." Lady Helena turned her self-mocking smile on him and shrugged. "It still works."

He chuckled.

"Don't laugh at me. I always feel ten years old and guilty

as sin when I enter her boudoir—even when I am *not*.
Guilty, I mean. I'm no longer a rebellious ten-year-old!"

"Merely a rebellious . . . twenty or so?"

"Twenty-six and," she added, "no longer at all rebellious."

His eyebrow once again climbed to a sharp arch. He
cast her a look, but forbore commenting. A well-trained
military man, he, too, knew how to pick the important
battles.

They climbed a second flight of stairs and turned down
a long hall before either spoke again. "I agree we are neither of us ten," he said softly, "but are we not guilty?"

"Of what? Of falling in love and wishing to wed?"

"Ah, love." He paused for her to elaborate but she did
not do so. Derisively, he said, "Very prudent of *me*, of
course, but can you say the same for yourself?"

"Don't jeer at a need for which you are not at fault,"
she said, and found they were once again arguing about
her fortune.

"I have told you I do not wish—" That revealing muscle
jumped in his jaw. "—to be named a fortune hunter. Wedding you, I'll not avoid the label."

"I'd thought you said you were resigned." She sighed.
"Sanger, I will not give away my fortune, either literally or
by tying it up. We will need it."

"I can pull the estate together myself."

"Yes. Of course you can. But how long will it take you
to do so?"

"Have you been talking to Jack?" he demanded.

"If you refer to my last comment, then no. But from
yours I'd guess *he* has said much the same thing?"

"Blast his eyes, he has then!"

They turned another corner and started down another
long hallway.

"So?" she asked.

Simon sighed. "Lady Helena . . ." He was forced to stop

when the footman knocked on a door which was instantly opened by a rail-thin maid whose steel gray hair was inadequately hidden beneath a plain white cap. *"Later,"* he whispered out the side of his mouth.

"Good morning, Sibby," said Lady Helena, nodding her agreement that they must postpone further discussion which she'd thought she'd avoided earlier. She'd been overly optimistic. Now, with a faintly anxious expression she lowered her voice and asked, "What sort of mood is it, Sibby?"

"Twitty, Lady Hel. Can't say other than the truth, can I? Very twitty, I fear."

"I feared it." Helena sighed then caught her wits around her again. "Oh. Sibby, this is Lord Sanger, my affianced husband."

"Good morning, Sibby," said Simon. "I apologize if my coming has meant a difficult morning for you with your mistress."

Sibby looked him up and down. "A charmer, Lady Hel. And polite with it. Don't think I'd throw this one back if I were you. I'll tell Lady Catherine you've come."

"Like mistress, like maid," muttered Lady Helena when the maid closed the door in their faces.

Simon chuckled. "I like her."

"So do I. I like my grandmother, too. At least I do when I'm not about to be catechized and embarrassed out of my mind."

Sibby stood back, holding open the door. "She'll see you."

"Well, so I should hope. After telling us to come, it would be outside of enough if she would not!" said Helena, moving forward. "Good morning, Grandmother," she finished with only a touch of bravado. "Sibby tells us you aren't quite up to snuff?"

"I am perfectly well. I am merely fretting myself." She

turned her famous glower on Simon. "Well, young man? Like father, like son, they say, do they not?"

"I am not my father, Lady Catherine. You will say he married my mother for her money and went through it like a hot knife through butter, but, that isn't true. When they wed they were much in love. Besides, in my present circumstances, I'd *not* have proposed to Lady Helena if that ridiculous Lady Hingly-Tumpton hadn't caused a scene. I've far too much respect to say nothing of tender feelings for your granddaughter and don't wish her to face the difficult life I must live for some time."

"Ah? A difficult life? You mean to gamble away Hel's fortune as your father did your mother's? Remembering the behavior of the last two Earls of Sanger, I must assume gambling runs in the family, must I not?"

A muscle jumped in Sanger's jaw. *"I am not a gambler!"* He took a deep breath and continued with less heat. "Lady Catherine, I am an oddity in the Mansanger lineage. I'll bet on a race in which I've a horse running, but that isn't often. And the occasional race is all I gamble on if you discount social evenings playing cards for penny points."

Her ladyship digested that and then remembered to glower. "I've heard a ridiculous tale that you'd no notion my granddaughter was an heiress. Do you expect anyone will believe such an obvious taradiddle?"

Helena made a motion Simon interpreted as a wish to interfere. He reached for her hand and, giving it a gentle squeeze, shook his head at her. She subsided.

Lady Catherine watched the little scene with interest but her glower didn't lighten.

Once certain Lady Helena would remain silent Simon turned back to Lady Catherine. "I've no notion, my lady, whether anyone will believe it or not. It is, however, the truth. Or it was for longer than I care to admit to. Lady Helena and Lord Humboldt's daughter were seated side by side when I overheard that an heiress was one of the guests. When I saw how Miss Merry was always surrounded by young bucks I assumed it was she to whom the comment referred. You may believe it or not as you will."

"But you do not say," said Her Ladyship slyly, "if you had discovered the truth when you proposed."

"I had. It is worse. Before I learned the truth, I'd already refused Lady Helena when *she* proposed to *me*."

Lady Catherine, her hands tightly gripped around her cane, eyed him thoughtfully. "So. That's the truth of it, is it? Hel *did* propose to you? Her writing is atrocious and I wondered if I'd deciphered that correctly!"

"My writing is not that bad! And, yes, I did propose to him," said Helena inserting herself into their conversation and this time warning Simon to be still.

"Why?" barked the old lady, turning her glower on her granddaughter.

"If you must know, I've finally found a man who understands my odd sense of humor. I'm also rather certain he understands and, more important, accepts my independent ways, neither judging them nor wishing to change them. On top of that . . ." Lady Helena bit her lip, her gaze straying.

"On top of that," said Sanger firmly, fearing Lady Helena had thought better of revealing her third and perhaps most important reason for wedding him, "Lady Helena has experienced some rather odd and inexplicable accidents recently. I think she believed I might protect her . . ."

Lady Catherine pushed herself erect. *"Inexplicable,* you say? What has happened? When? And how often?"

"Five incidents altogether," admitted Helena, her look promising Simon retribution for revealing her problem.

"It is why we wish to wed as soon as we can," said Simon. "I can protect her much more easily if we are wed."

"We'll see about that," said the old lady sharply. "Tell me about the accidents."

Helena sighed. "A falling cornice came within inches of hitting me. It frightened me but didn't harm me and I didn't think of it again until much later. There was a dish of mushrooms so bad, I actually wished I *would* expire long before it was over. Three other people were ill so I thought nothing of that occasion until the hostess of that evening told me I'd ruined her reputation. I apologized for becoming so ill, but she waved that away. I asked what she did mean. She explained that a small quantity of mushrooms had been delivered shortly before dinner with a note, purportedly from me, saying they were particularly liked by myself and that I would appreciate it if they were added to the menu."

"The implication being that you sent them. But you had *not?*" asked Lady Catherine, verifying her supposition.

"Of course not. I love mushrooms, but I'd never upset a hostess's menu in such rude fashion!"

"I heard of that case, of course," mused Lady Catherine. "That's two near misses. What else?"

"I was deliberately exposed to smallpox."

"What?"

"A raggedly dressed woman thrust a baby into my arms and ran off. I very quickly discovered the child's illness, but by then it would have been too late, would it not?"

"If I hadn't had you inoculated as a child, then, yes, I suppose you might have contracted the disease and died from it. But what has made you think the woman deliberately tried to infect you? She might merely have despaired for her child and hoped you would have the means of helping it."

"I think not. Rod caught her and got the truth from her. Which he didn't tell me immediately because she didn't know the man who paid her to put the babe in my arms. Without that information there was nothing, really, he could tell me."

"I'll have a few words with your Rod, if you please. He should have informed *me.*"

"Well, you went off to the lake district for a holiday, did you not? It would have been a trifle difficult . . . ?"

"Oh ho! So it is my fault, hmm?" Lady Catherine tapped her cane, twice, against the floor. Her glare, which had faded, returned.

Lady Catherine's glare was matched by Lady Helena's. "Don't blame Rod."

Her Ladyship shrugged in a dainty fashion, implicitly giving way. "What else?" she demanded.

"A girth gave way. I got a lot of aches and pains from that particular accident, but nothing worse. Finally, the pole of a carriage I was driving down Piccadilly broke. I'd have been in grave danger of a trampling at best, except I gained a good hold of the seat and saved myself."

"So." Lady Catherine was silent, staring at nothing at all. "Five accidents."

"You've lost track, Lady Helena," interrupted Sanger, sternly. "You are forgetting the latest attempt on your life."

Lady Catherine looked from Sanger to her granddaughter. "Another?"

Helena grimaced.

"Lord Sanger?" asked Lady Catherine, insistently.

He obeyed her ladyship's unspoken wishes. "Lady Helena, Jack Alton, and I were returning from a ride when a shot furrowed a ridge in her mare's rump. Needless to say, her horse objected. You ride a very fast animal, my lady," he said turning to Helena. "I wondered if mine would catch up to you."

"I've always liked speed," she said quickly, hoping to end the subject. "That mare is a favorite of mine. I trained her myself, you kno- . . ."

"You'll not divert me that way!" he interrupted. "I'm not finished." He held her gaze for a moment, his expression full of understanding, before turning back to the dowager. "One might assume the first shot was a poacher's misfire, but a second whistled over her head. If she hadn't leaned forward at just that moment, reaching for a dropped rein, it is likely she'd have been hit and very possibly killed."

Her Ladyship abruptly settled into her seat and turned a pain-filled look toward Helena. "Why?" Almost an afterthought, she added, "Who?"

"I believe there will be no further attempts, Grandmother," said Lady Helena, seating herself near the old lady who seemed to have shrunk. She put her arm around the fine boned, very slightly hunched, shoulders.

"You say that with a great deal of certainty," said Lady Catherine searching her granddaughter's features. "Why?"

"Grandmother . . ."

Lady Catherine pushed her granddaughter's arm from her shoulder and, rising to her feet, stalked to the windows and stared out them. Finally she turned. Her voice was colored by a fierce note when she asked, "Are the rumors true that Thurmand has lost his fortune?"

"I haven't a notion," said Helena promptly.

"You've heard nothing of the sort?"

"I'd heard not so much as a whisper of such a thing." Her grandmother's glare demanded the full truth and Helena, sighing at her grandmother's perspicacity, added, "Until recently, that is. Someone at the Treweses' mentioned the possibility."

Lady Catherine turned back, once again staring out the window. Lord Sanger moved nearer Lady Helena and offered his hand. She placed her own in it and found the gentle pressure encouraging. It eased her tension.

"You said you thought the danger over," the dowager interrupted Lady Hel's thoughts. "How can you be certain?"

"I . . ."

"Lady Catherine . . ." Sanger continued for her when Helena looked up at him with eyes she didn't know pleaded for help. Independent as she wished to be, he suspected she was likely to kick herself if she realized it! "My lady . . ." he began again and again paused.

"I presume *you've* the answer, Lord Sanger?" The dowager turned, straight-backed, a dauntless old lady, her head held high, and hawkish features sharpened by a determination to hear what must be heard. "You will explain to me why you think my grandson is no longer trying to kill his cousin," she said, her voice harsh.

Sanger was glad Lady Catherine had put the unspeakable into words. He didn't try to deny her comment since he believed it to be true. Instead, he told her what they'd done. ". . . So you see, we allowed him to learn that both you and Lady Helena have wills leaving your fortunes to charity."

Lady Catherine didn't miss the pertinent bit of information. *"Both* of us," she repeated.

"He was . . . not pleased," said Lady Helena.

Lady Catherine winced and turned away. "This interview is not finished, but I would have it done another time. I need . . . time. I'd like to be alone now."

"We understand."

Helena rose to her feet, went to her grandmother and pressed her hand to the old woman's shoulder. There was no response, and Helena's lips compressed, her eyes filling with concern. She returned to Lord Sanger's side and he put his arm around her, hugged her, then led her to the door.

"Tomorrow," said the dowager.

Helena turned, but Lady Catherine still stared out the window. "Yes, Grandmother. Tomorrow."

Sibby met them with a worried look. "She . . . ?"

Helena looked at Simon, turned back to Sibby and sighed. "She's had a bit of a shock."

"That Thurmand?" growled the maid.

"How did you guess?" Helena glanced at the keyhole to the door closing in her grandmother.

"Didn't listen!" Sibby scowled, then grimaced, then grinned. She shrugged. "Didn't have to, you see. Could hear without trying. Besides, the little rodent came a-bothering her a few weeks ago. She wasn't herself for days."

"You didn't . . . ?"

"Listen?" The outraged look Sibby wore faded under Lady Helena's disbelieving stare and the maid's mouth pursed as she attempted to restrain a chuckle. "*Of course* I did," she admitted. "He wanted money. He didn't believe her when she said she hadn't anything she could loan him." Sibby's expression combined a determination to reveal all and the horror she felt at what she must say. "He came within a hair of threatening her," she said on a hushed note.

"To the devil with the slimy toad," muttered Helena.

"Or debtor's prison, *more* like," said Sibby with something which sounded like satisfaction.

"Or the colonies," added Lady Helena, preferring him far away.

"Ah! The antipodes," offered Sibby gleefully. "Oh, he'd like a journey on one of them prison ships, *wouldn't he just?*"

"Or . . ." Lady Helena shook her head. She sighed. "I can't think of anything worse then *that*, Sibby. Not for Thurmand, who must have his bath twice a day and a complete change of clothes if he so much as raises the lightest of sweats!"

"Sibby," said Simon, kindly, but on a warning note, "do you think you could put a word in the ear of the butler that he is to deny her ladyship if Woodhall drops by for a visit? Or, if he insists on seeing her, then perhaps the butler might arrange that she *not* see him alone?"

"And you don't mean with just me there," said the maid.

"You want one of the ladies or a gentleman in attendance?"

"Yes."

"General Porson would help, I think," said Sibby in the manner of one thinking out loud. "And I don't think he'd let *either* of them intimidate him into leaving her side."

"Dear General Porson! Is he here?" Helena brightened. "Just the one, Sibby." She turned to Sanger, "One of Grandmother's cicisbeos."

Lady Catherine called from the other room and Sibby gave the door a harassed look. "Must go to her," she muttered.

"Sibby, I'll talk to the general before we leave and have a word with the butler. But, could you pass on the same order, making it seem as if it comes from *her?*"

"I'll do it as soon as I can," said the maid a trifle grimly.

General Porson listened to Helena's painfully told tale and nodded. "Never liked the pup. Should have bought him a commission when he came down from Cambridge. Don't like Cambridge either," huffed the old gentleman. "Should have sent him to Oxford." He gave Lady Helena a sharp look. "Won't let him bother her." He rose to his feet, a tall distinguished-looking old man. "Just put a word in Hibbard's ear."

"Hibbard is the butler?" asked Lord Sanger. "We have asked Sibby to do that and as if the order came from Lady Catherine."

"Good plan. Won't hurt to do it twice. We'll just see to it now."

The general carried a gold-headed cane, but Simon was glad to see he didn't actually use it. Simon didn't think Woodhall was the sort to pay much attention to someone he considered old and useless.

"Think I'll begin carrying my pistol," mused the general. "Got a little one. Hardly so big as the palm of my hand. Carry it when I travel since you never know, do

you?" The general chuckled softly, a trifle dangerously and
Helena got a hint of the man he'd been when younger
and in the army.

Sanger squeezed Helena's arm when she gave him a
wondering look. "As you say, sir, you never know." They
reached the hall and Sanger motioned to a footman who
approached and nodded when his lordship quietly ordered that his curricle be brought around. "I don't see
Hibbard," he said.

"Here! You!" said the general in a parade-ground voice.

The second footman approached. "Yes, sir?"

"Get Hibbard. Want him."

"Yes, sir."

The footman turned on his heel and disappeared behind the stairs. Very soon, his tread stately, Hibbard appeared. "How can I help you, my lord?" he asked, his nose
very slightly elevated.

"It is I who wish you to help us, Hibbard," said Lady
Helena gently. She looked around, noted the pair of footmen had returned to their posts and, turning back to the
butler, asked, "Is there somewhere where we might talk?
Privately?"

"This way." From his posture, expression, and tone
you'd not have known Hibbard was dying of curiosity. But
it showed in the alacrity with which he opened the door
to the porter's room and, once inside, the way he held the
single available straight-backed chair for Lady Helena. "My
lady?" he asked, his chin at a normal level and his nose
all but quivering.

Helena seated herself. "Hibbard, we've a problem."

"Yes, my lady?"

"My grandmother . . ."

"My lady!"

"It is *for* my grandmother," Helena began again, "that
I must explain. I've a cousin, Thurmand Woodhall. Thurmand has been pestering my grandmother unmercifully.

She has, more than once, turned down his request, but, I am sorry to say, he has become still more importunate. If Mr. Woodhall arrives while Lady Catherine remains here, he is not to be denied, but he is not to be allowed to see my grandmother alone. If you would be so kind as to see that General Porson is sitting with my grandmother *before* you show my cousin in I would appreciate it." Her brows arched, queryingly, and she tipped her head, offering a quizzical look that was half an order and half conspiratorial request.

"Of course, my lady. I will give orders, my lady, to the effect that, upon the arrival of a Mr. Woodhall, *I* am to be informed on the instant and he is to be shown to an empty salon where he is to await the determination that Lady Catherine will receive him. I will, in the first instance, inform General Porson of Mr. Woodhall's arrival and only then will I myself carry the news to her ladyship."

The sonorous tone, rolling off well-turned phrases, was meant to be impressive. And was. Helena wondered where the man had learned the trick of it, but she merely thanked him and rose to her feet indicating the interview was at an end. The man stepped aside and, her hand on the general's arm, Helena swept from the room.

Neither saw Lord Sanger press several large coins he could ill afford into Hibbard's hand.

The curricle stood waiting on the broad sweep of drive below the terrace. "You handled him well, I thought," said Lord Sanger, "telling him enough his curiosity was satisfied, but not actually explaining anything in detail."

"Hibbard? I have observed Grandmother's manner for nearly twenty years so I've learned a point or two more than the devil . . . as the saying goes."

He chuckled. "With me you needn't apologize for your every ill-considered word or phrase, my lady." Before she could either take umbrage or decide to feel complimented, he added, "I like it that you say what is in your mind."

Definitely, a compliment! But she only said, "If that's truly the case, that I should speak my mind, perhaps we could put down the young man riding behind at the Treweses' gates. He can walk back to the stables while you and I take a little drive. I've a few words on my mind which I'd like to get off it! My lord, we've a discussion we must finish."

They remained silent this time until the boy, obviously disgruntled by the thought of the walk ahead of him, trudged off up the Treweses' long drive.

Six

Lady Helena had said she'd words to say, but they were well past the next mile post before she began. "First, I wish to say you handled Grandmother admirably."

"I wonder why I hear a little three-letter word at the end of that," he said, mildly.

"A caveat, you think. Well, there *is*. You should *not* have been so blunt when speaking of Thurmand."

"Why?"

"She is old. She has been ill. She should be protected from such knowledge."

"Hmm. Even if you were old and had been ill, would you wish to be protected?"

"That's different."

He smiled. "Is it, my lady?"

"Drat your lights and liver!" Chagrined at once again using a phrase she should not, she cast him a look and discovered he was amused by her outburst. Well, he'd said she needn't apologize for using words she should not! More quietly, she continued. "You know it is no different. And you would say she has lived so long she'll not be surprised by the evils of this world. But it is *Thurmand,* you see. She dotes on him."

"I suspect she dotes on you, too."

By not responding, Helena tacitly accepted the truth of that.

"While she knows both your strengths, and his, and all your excellent qualities, I doubt she is unaware of the weaknesses. In either of you."

Lady Helena remained silent.

"I have erred," he said, with tongue in cheek and a sideways look. "Although it was perfectly acceptable to suggest Woodhall is a worm, I should not have admitted that *you* are less than perfect?"

Lady Helena threw him a startled glance and then chuckled. "You, my lord, are a great tease." Her smile faded. "Nevertheless, it will hurt her dreadfully to suspect Thurmand of trying to kill me, and that perhaps he would think of killing her, something you need *not* have implied when explaining that we'd . . . we'd . . ."

". . . spiked his guns?" supplied Sanger, helpfully. Before she could either agree or object, he added, "I was to allow her to fret about whether he'd come for her next?"

Shock rocked through Lady Helena. *"Surely* she'd have done no such thing! Such a thought would never have entered her head!" When he didn't instantly agree, she added, "You truly think it would?"

Simon reached for Helena's hand and held it closely. "Helena, she is an intelligent woman. She taught you to face things squarely. She'd not have done so if she did not, herself, do so. Do you truly believe it would *not* have occurred to her?" He paused. *"Frightened* her?"

"He is a snake!" snarled Helena, her face contorted by rage. "I wish Thurmand would go away. I have never before hated anyone. I do not like it. It is not comfortable, Simon!"

"Hate is also a rather useless emotion, a waste of time and energy. But you may be comfortable for the nonce: Woodhall departed this morning. When the gig returned I asked the groom where he'd gone. The lad was watering the horses and saw your cousin board the London stage.

They'd very nearly missed it, you see, thanks to Woodhall's need to taunt me a trifle before they left here.''

"Ah! The London stage," said Helena on a relieved breath . . . then added, "Did he *stay* there?"

Simon chuckled. "I believe the next stop on the waybill is Oxford. He'll be gone for a day or two, at least?" In turn, his smile disappeared. "Or perhaps, as he recommended I do when you jilt me, he has gone to have a touch at a cit's daughter."

"Thurmand?" Lady Helena turned, consternation writ large across her features. She ignored the suggestion she'd jilt anyone, explaining, "Thurmand would have nothing to do with such a one. You've never heard him animadvert on climbing cits and his scorn for men who marry into that class merely to retrieve their fortunes."

"Perhaps not then," agreed Simon. "Have we finished with Thurmand? I find him a dead bore at the best of times and this is not one of them."

"I would never wish to bore you, my lord," she said, but her tone was that of someone replying by rote. "My lord . . ."

"You have called me Simon," he interrupted. "I like it." Then, before she could speak about that which she really wished to say to him, he added, "If you've had your say, I believe I must have mine."

"You mean to tell me," she said quickly, before he could continue, "that I may do as I please with my fortune, *but you'll not use it.*" She sighed loudly, covering her satisfaction that, after all, she'd managed to say exactly what she'd wished to say. She turned a curious look his way from under her lashes, wondering how he'd react to it.

"Exactly. I will not use it," he repeated, biting off the words.

"I will not give it up," she warned.

In turn he sighed. "That was a rather stupid suggestion on my part, was it not? That you do so? I don't suppose

I really wish you to do so. You have enjoyed the elegancies all your life. To suggest you forego them now, to suggest that you dress yourself from clothes purchased in—" He gave it some thought. "—Cranbourne Alley, for instance—"

"Cranbourne Alley!"

"—Ah! That *would* be outside of enough, would it not?"

"Simon Mansanger, you"—she visualized the street where vendors of used clothes lurked, their barrows piled high with raiment old in the last century—"you are . . ."

He chuckled. "I know. A complete hand, correct?"

"I was rather going to say a Bansbury man!" Helena relaxed. "I am glad you've seen the error of your ways Sang—*Simon*. If we are agreed, I will have my solicitor draw up the settlement agreement." Again she gave him that sideways look, wondering if she would get away with her plan to do *for* him what he would not do himself.

At least some part of it.

"Yes. If you wish. Just be certain there is a clause inserted to the effect that if you cry off, all agreements are null and void."

"And a similar clause pertaining to yourself, my lord, hmm, Simon?"

He cast her a startled look. "*I* can't cry off."

Lady Helena sobered. Her heart pounded with the fear he truly did wish to cry off. "That irks you, does it not?" she said. "That you, a gentleman, cannot honorably dissolve our engagement, that you've trapped yourself in an unwanted marriage which you had, previously, deftly avoided?"

"*Not* deftly," he said in a reminiscent tone. "In fact, with a great deal of awkwardness, totally lacking in grace!"

She chuckled. "I managed to surprise you, did I not?"

"Wouldn't any man be startled that a lovely woman proposed to him?"

"I was certain *you* would not, you see."

"Would not?"

"Propose to me."

"A matter of expediency, then?"

"Hmm."

"But Woodhall is no longer a threat," he said suggestively, and in turn, cast her a sideways considering look.

"But my decision was not *only* due to Thurmand. It never was—"

He cast her a sharp hopeful look, which faded as she went on.

"—totally that. You are a man who will not bind me or object too strongly to my hoydenish ways. And you do not bore me. How could I resist?"

Sanger forced a light tone. "Then, too, Sibby warned you you weren't to throw me back," he said, with mock complacency.

"So she did. Have we finished our various discussions?"

"I believe we have."

"Then, as much as I dread returning to the Treweses', I suppose we must do so. Lady Trewes has asked all the ladies to join her in planning a country fête to be held as the grand climax to their house party."

"Such a treat for us all," he said and didn't manage, quite, to hide the sarcasm.

Helena didn't try. "Oh yes. A *great* treat. She has said as much."

Startled, Simon allowed his concentration a moment's lapse and then was forced to set himself to regaining control of his team who had used the opportunity to take the bit. "You cannot mean that," he said when he'd done so. He cast her a quick sideways glance, saw her nod, and added, "Surely she can have said no such thing."

"Those were her exact words. We don't, we were told, spend much time in the country; *some* of us actually have no estate of our own; we will find it amusing, we were assured, to help organize such a day and will enjoy it immensely. It will, and I quote her word for word, be *a great treat.*"

"What it will be is a great deal of work."

"Yes." Helena nodded. "She's a lazy soul, is she not? But," she mused, "I don't suppose she actually, consciously, told herself, *now I have all these ladies here to help me I will put them to work and it will not be so very bad after all.*"

"Actually," he retorted, "I can hear her saying exactly that. Perhaps to Lord Trewes?"

"I refuse to believe she can be so exceedingly smug. Are we not returning?" she asked when they passed the second opportunity where he might have turned his curricle.

"We are meeting Jack at Sanger-Monkton. I asked that he bring a picnic today."

"Hmm. I do believe you sound almost as smug as you accused her ladyship of being!"

"I do believe," he mimicked her, "that that is exactly how I feel!" He dropped his hands and his team picked up speed. "My lady, I am kidnapping you! If you've no desire to admit you spent the whole of the day with me, without so much as your groom in sight, you may drop a hint or two suggesting you remained at the Cooper-Wainwrights' with your grandmother."

When the men left her alone, going off to have a few words with Simon's head tenant, Helena found her way to the priest's hole. She chose a book and seated herself on the floor near the lamp.

Though shocked, she could not control her prurient interest. She studied every suggestive picture. Unfortunately the book was written in Latin and, although she'd learned a bit of the language at the progressive school she'd attended for three years, she'd nowhere nearly enough to translate the text. For the first time, she regretted she'd not applied herself more seriously to her studies.

Still, the pictures gave her a great deal to think about and, when Simon returned to the house to drive her back to the Trewes, she eyed him with curiosity. He, guessing how she'd spent her time, felt heat rushing up his neck.

Then, realizing he'd guessed her thoughts, *Helena* blushed.

From the back of his horse, Jack eyed the two of them and he, too, guessed. Carefully controlling his features, he said, "Simon, I believe we should crate up those books of yours so that, when I leave day after tomorrow, I may take them with me to London. Lady Helena's Mr. Beal will be better able to judge their, hmm, value, if he has them in hand."

"An excellent notion, Jack," said Simon heartily, with a sideways look at his fiancée. "Don't forget the two we have, hmm, borrowed and have in our rooms!"

Helena pouted, wondering why it hadn't occurred to her to borrow one! Then she sighed. Finally she shrugged and set aside her desire to learn more than she already had of things it was better she knew nothing about.

Nevertheless, it was interesting to speculate on whether some of what she'd learned might not be of practical interest. She pictured Simon bare-naked and then herself . . . and then wished she had not. Alone in her room she might dare to think of such things. Here, with Jack Alton looking on and Simon's thigh warm against her own it was, perhaps, a trifle embarrassing!

She put the notion of Simon teaching her the ways of love from her mind, "I must remember to write the letter of introduction for you. If Mr. Beal knows Lord Sanger is my fiancé he's more likely to do his best for him."

"The better he does the better it will be," said Jack.

Simon smiled and changed the subject. "I believe you have missed most of today's planning for the fête, my love," he said, "and, if you've been volunteered by the others to do anything particularly tedious, I will make a habit of kidnapping you. In that way you'll be unavailable to do what is asked of you!"

"If it becomes tedious I will ask Grandmother to get me an invitation to join her at the Cooper-Wainwrights'. She would be happy to oblige me, I believe, since she warned me not to go to the Treweses' in the first place and conniving to get me away would put me under an obligation to her."

"Might she not insist you made your bed and must now lie in it?"

Helena chuckled. "You already know her well, do you not? She might if she were not in need of me, but just now—" Helena abruptly sobered as thoughts of Thurmand were roused. "—I think, she'd like me close."

A muscle jumped in Simon's jaw. "I am selfish," he said abruptly, his hands busy rearranging the reins.

"Selfish?"

"I don't wish you to leave the Treweses' while I must remain there."

"But, Simon, need you stay there?"

His hands stilled. "Surely you do not suggest I, too, come to the Cooper-Wainwrights? That would be outside of enough, total stranger that I am!"

"I'd like that, but it isn't what I had in mind. I've heard tales that our officers in the Peninsula must suffer the most extraordinarily uncomfortable quarters. So you are used to rough living, are you not?" He nodded. "That apartment off the kitchen which was once used by a caretaker could be cleaned and there will be a wife or older daughter among your tenants who would do for you, keeping all neat and simple cooking? I do not believe it would cost you so very much."

"And I, too, could leave the Treweses' . . . ! I will think about it."

What he thought about was whether he could trust Lord Trewes to stay firm to their agreement concerning Big Red! He'd do much better, financially, if that information went out *after* his stables had produced a proven winner. And, although he believed Red to be the one, the roan had yet to prove himself.

Lady Catherine demanded that they wait until after Christmas to wed. Reluctantly, they agreed. Some days later Lady Hel's solicitor arrived, along with a clerk and Sanger's solicitor. After two days' hard work, they left with his lordship's and her ladyship's signatures firmly inked at the bottom of a long involved document full of legalese and many obscurities.

Or at least that is how Sanger described it to Lady Hel.

"*You* would have signed it without reading it," she accused, staring over the heads of his pair which was, once again, taking them to Sanger-Monkton.

"Ah, but if I cannot trust the woman I love, then who can I trust?" he quipped, but there was a hint of seriousness to be heard by a keen ear.

They hit a rut and she grasped the side of his curricle. "You should always read contracts before signing them," she insisted, feeling just a trifle guilty that she'd managed to get her way and slip the wording she wanted past him.

Would he be very angry when he discovered it? Discovered he could *not* trust her—even though what she wished to do was in his best interest?

"More of your grandmother's teaching?" he asked, interrupting her rampant thoughts.

She had to scramble to remember she'd last spoken about the wisdom of reading contracts. "No. That piece of advice is a legacy from my father who only once signed something he'd not read. He learned a harsh lesson and he passed his knowledge on to me."

"A story?" he asked, pulling his horses to a walk.

"Not a very interesting one. Merely that, as a young man, soon after he inherited his title, he believed the lying words of a neighbor he trusted, signed where he was told to sign, and then discovered he could not get himself free of a clause the so-called gentleman had tucked into the body of the thing."

"What was the clause?"

"That not only had he sold the meadow which Father *thought* involved, but he gave a hundred-year lease on the bit of adjoining land which was what the man had wanted in the first place."

"Very underhanded."

"Yes. It includes the rights to a very good trout stream, you see," said Lady Hel. "Now, when we wish to fish in our own waters, we are required by that clause to get permission from a man to whom my father vowed we'd never speak! He extracted the same vow from me."

"Then you can never fish there."

"Who says we can't?"

He turned to discover the mischievous smile he loved hovering around her mouth. "If you," he mused, "are called Lady Hel, just what was your father called?"

"What else but Devil Woodhall!"

Sanger's hands dropped and his horses broke into a trot.

"Ah!" Her smile broadened. "Something else you did not know?"

"I've heard tales of the man, of course. Who has not? I *should* have associated him with you, but the relationship never crossed my mind."

"By the time I was born Father had settled down a great deal, but he was always an eccentric and a bit of a renegade and—" A hint of warning entered her voice. "—since we are to wed, when Grandmother finally decides we may, you must accept that that rubbed off on me."

"I have. I believe I've told you that, for the most part,

I like it in you. Helena, what *you* must accept is that there will be times when I feel I must rein you in, must have your cooperation for some particular reason, and when I do, it is not impossible I will expect you to behave in the conventional fashion you abhor."

"I've already seen that side of you, Simon, and it is the one thing that worries me. You, my lord, were an officer in the king's army far too long. You've developed a bad habit of simply giving orders! If," she continued quickly, "you will only explain *why* you are making some idiotic request of me, I am very likely to fall into line like a good little soldier. Unfortunately, I have never been good at obeying blind orders."

He nodded, recognizing the justice in her demand. "We will both do our best to follow that plan, hmm?"

"Of course."

He also realized, slightly belatedly, that she had only said she was likely to fall in line! "So, *also of course,* when you do *not* accept the logic of my wishes, you will do as you please?"

She sighed deeply and, admitting her chagrin, said, "That is all too likely. I am a rather obstinate soul, Sanger."

He chuckled. "As an instance of one of my more idiotic orders, just how many of those tomes I suggested were *not* suitable for your eyes, did you actually manage to read?"

"I didn't *read* a single one," she said promptly. It was, after all, the literal truth.

For a moment he was silent and then grinned. "How many did you open in order to look at the pictures?"

"Quick of you, Simon," she said.

"So?"

"You insist on the truth, do you not? But it was not at all fair that I not be allowed to see them! Unfortunately—" She sighed. "—I found time to study only one of them before you and Alton packed them up and he took them off to Mr. Beal. Have you, by the way, heard from my book-seller?"

"There was a letter this morning. Beal has written three men concerning the existence of the collection and all have responded that they will drop everything to come inspect them. Once they've looked them over, he'll decide whether to sell them as a set or individually, and will hire a man who will auction off the books in a semi-private sale."

"Semi-private?"

"He knows approximately half a dozen other men who have expressed an interest in that sort of literature. They will be invited to the auction after these three, who are known collectors, have been allowed their inspection."

"Why not advertise the sale in the usual fashion?"

"Because of the content. He'd have far too many poverty-stricken young men, and perhaps some who are not so poor, coming for the wrong reasons."

"How can there be a *right* reason for purchasing books of that nature!"

Sanger threw back his head and laughed. "Believe it or not, that type of literature has been written since time began and ranges from crudity to the best of literary efforts. The rubbishy, humorless, sort is common . . ."

". . . as I know," she interrupted. "You refer to something like the French cartoons with which schoolgirls educate and entertain themselves."

He turned a shocked look her way. "Schoolgirls!"

"Such stuff circulates through most schools, according to my friends. It was certainly available at mine and is all very titillating, but nothing at all like what was in the book I studied."

She cast him one of those speculative looks he'd seen before and, as always, the knowledge that she was wondering what sort of lover he'd be, roused warmth in his neck and ears. In the driest of tones, he suggested, "When we are wed, perhaps we can, hmm, explore the more exotic forms of lovemaking, but in the meantime, I do wish you would not look at me in quite that fashion."

"Quite what fashion?" she asked, perplexed.

"As if," he said, "I were a particularly juicy fig and you were wondering just how to approach me in order to eat me up but, of course, remain within the bounds of good manners as you did so!"

"Hmm. A juicy fig. And—" She turned a sparkling look his way "—eat you up?"

"Helena Woodhall, you will, *this instant,* stop that!"

"Why?"

"Because—" He tried very hard to keep his voice light. "—if you do not, I am likely to tie these horses to the next mile post and carry you off into the woods—" The flippancy with which he'd begun failed halfway through and something a trifle desperate could be heard in his tone at the end. "—and ravish you. You haven't a notion what you are doing to me, Helena."

"Something else which must wait until we are wed?" she asked, tongue in cheek.

"Definitely. Now behave."

"And if I do not?"

"Then I will hand you the reins and get down and walk. Helena, you must not do this to me."

She sighed. It was becoming harder and harder to keep her hands off the man. She'd very much enjoyed being held by him when he carried her home after Thurmand shot at her. Since, on those rare occasions when he pulled her into a quick embrace and an equally unsatisfactory kiss, he always set her aside far too soon.

Far too soon! Long before she'd felt more than a hint of the sensation he could rouse in her. Sensations she very much wished to explore with him.

"I *know,*" he said softly but with emphasis nevertheless. The sympathy she heard brought her head around, to discover he was eyeing her with a soft look that made her blush. "I know *exactly* how you feel." After a moment, and this time he did manage a teasing tone, he added, "Just how soon did your grandmother say we might wed?"

His question reminded her of their argument with Lady Catherine. "She is determined we do things properly! It is ridiculous, given my reputation, but you heard her insist it will merely prove my eccentricity, that we do so in this particular case! I don't believe you were there when she said I would enjoy startling the *haut ton* by following society's dictates in such things." This time Lady Helena's sigh was so exaggerated it drew a chuckle. "You think *I* am stubborn, Simon! Would *you* care to make an attempt at changing her mind?"

"Poor dear. And," he added before she could say anything, "poor me! I believe it would be dangerous to carry out our intention to go to Sanger-Monkton while we both are on the verge of losing control. I must return you to the Treweses', ma belle Hel."

This time her sigh was real. "I suppose it is for the best since it was brought forcibly to my attention just this morning that I had better take a hand, again, at organizing the Treweses' fête. If I don't it will be a complete shambles!"

"Why bother?"

"It is a failing in me. Where I can help, I can never walk away from something which needs doing. Lady Trewes is incapable of managing anything. No sooner does she give an order to someone than she contradicts it or, almost worse, tells another servant to do the same thing."

"You think you can make order from such chaos?"

"I have had a little chat with her housekeeper. In fact, I've had more than one chat with the woman. The poor dear is very generous with her praise of me," said Lady Helena smugly.

"I would think so, but why, in this particular case?"

"After first sorting through what had been ordered, I

told her to bring me all further demands. Between us, we make sense of them. Very often we decide an order is nonsense and ignore it. On other occasions, the *idea* is good, but the suggested means of accomplishing it is senseless so we decide what *should* be done. And then, where needed, I merely give my own orders. We both pretend they come from Lady Trewes, of course. I suspect that, for the very first time, Lord and Lady Trewes will provide a fête day which is not one disaster after another!"

"People will be disappointed."

Helena turned a surprised look his way. "What can you mean?"

"Undoubtedly, the guests each year come anticipating what will happen. If nothing of a humorous or weird nature occurs, they will have nothing about which they may talk for the next few months!"

She chuckled. "Perhaps so, but then again, perhaps this year's effort will be such an exception to the general rule that that in itself will be worthy of comment!"

They arrived back at the Treweses' much in charity with each other. Helena, her conscience nagging her a trifle around the edges, wondered just how long that would last once her solicitor followed the written instructions she'd given him just as he left. When Simon discovered her man of business had found workmen and ordered the delivery of supplies, she feared he'd have conniptions—but Sanger-Monkton's roof must be fixed and as expeditiously as possible!

"What's got you so down in the mouth?" asked Allie as she brushed out Lady Helena's hair.

"Just feeling a trifle . . . wistful?" She sighed. "Ah well. It will be a few days yet, before poor Simon discovers what I mean to do."

"Do?"

Lady Helena didn't respond. Just how would Simon react when he realized how she meant to use the freedom given her by the marriage settlements. Not that he'd *cause* for complaint. He'd agreed she might do exactly as she wished with her income!

But still . . . she worried.

Seven

Lady Helena had a further reprieve from what she guessed would be Sanger's response to her interference at Sanger-Monkton. Simon decided to attend the book auction and left for London before dawn the day the first load of slate arrived. She and Rod stayed at Sanger-Monkton long into the afternoon, discussing the work with the foreman and watching to see that the men were as competent as her solicitor's letter promised they would be.

"It would expedite matters if you hired local men to do the rougher work, would it not?" she asked the foreman.

Not that she'd a hope that it could be completed before Sanger returned, but still . . .

"Noo, then—" The man's Scottish accent was strong. "—a verra good notion, my lady."

"I will send word around." She told him what he might offer for wages.

"I will be verra happy to have help," said the man. "I dinna understand how verra big the job would be!"

"Yes, well, two generations have allowed the place to fall to ruin. I suspect we are lucky it is in no worse condition."

Lady Helena returned the next day and was pleased at the response to her call for help. The foreman beamed at her. "And all good workers, ye understand," he said.

That day she didn't stay long, which was just as well. Returning to the Treweses' she discovered a ragged one-armed man with a ratty little face awaiting her at the stables. He had a message. It was, he'd insisted, to be given directly to herself and with no one listening. He glowered at Rod.

"Wait by the water trough, Rod," she told her hovering groom. "I'll go no farther than that fence." She gestured. One last look at the messenger and she turned on her heel, moving to stand with her back to a post. "Well? You cannot be overheard here."

He looked around carefully, assuring himself it was true. When satisfied he raised his eyes to the sky and spoke in a careful, remembering way. "Jist this. Iffen you want the little missy to survive with honor in-tack you bring this—" He pushed a much-folded sheet of greasy paper at her. "—to the White Heart Inn in Chipping Norton on Friday, the twenty-sixth of August. Leave it in room three." The man grinned an evil grin.

"And?"

The grin faded. "And *what?*"

"And what then happens to the, hmm, missy?"

"Forgot." Again speaking with care, he said, "Ye go away. When ye return there will be word in room three where ye can find the missy."

"And do *you* know where to find this woman? Right now? At this very moment?"

The man shot a wary look around. "I know nothin'," he said.

"You know who gave you the message, do you not?" It had to be her blasted cousin, but Helena wanted that verified. "You don't mean to tell me you don't know where to find *him?*"

Lady Helena rubbed her fingers and thumb together as she'd once seen her father do when hinting he might pay a man for information. She didn't like the greedy way the man eyed her and straightened her back, her eyes narrowing. She caught his wandering gaze with a stern look and held it. Immediately he returned to his former whiny self.

"Don't know . . ."

She rubbed fingers and thumb together again.

He wavered. Sweat popped out on the man's forehead. "Might depend—" His eyes darted here and there. "—you see?"

"I think I see very well." She tried to remember what coins remained in her purse. "Would five pounds get me a round tale?"

"Guineas." Saliva pooled in the corner of his mouth at the prospect of so much money. When she nodded, he said, "Done."

She waited, but he didn't speak. "Well?" she asked.

"Don't see no guineas." He pouted. "No guineas, no tale." He crossed his arms and, while still pouting, attempted a glare.

Funny as his expression was Lady Helena didn't feel like laughing. "I don't carry such sums about my person. I must get it."

"Can't plant my sticks here," he objected. There was a warning in that, although Helena wasn't certain of his meaning. It was clarified somewhat when, his gaze once again skittering all around, he added, "Been here too long already now."

"I will return immediately."

But Lady Helena was unable to keep that promise. The instant she entered the house, her grandmother, who had been on the verge of leaving, demanded she come with her to the Green Salon. "I've been waiting forever, Hel, and I do not like it." Lady Catherine turned on her heel. *"Tout de suite,* Hel!"

Lady Helena heard a footman repeating the French expression, mangling the accent badly. This, another oddity which would normally have struck her funny bone, barely registered.

"Oh, blast!" As the old lady disappeared down the hall, Lady Helena asked the footman to inform Her Ladyship she'd come just as soon as she attended to an errand. *"Tout de suite,"* she finished.

Lifting her skirts slightly, she ran in a totally unladylike fashion up the stairs. She was in luck. Allie was in her room and Hel gave the maid coins to the proper amount and told her to run out to Roderick. If the man waiting for her would tell him what he knew, then he was to give over the coins. If the disgusting little man would *not* Rod was to let him go . . . and follow discreetly, returning when he'd discovered where her blasted cousin was holed up. "At least I believe it must be Thurmand."

"Mr. Woodhall, my lady?" Allie gave her a sharp look. "What is the snake up to now?"

"Kidnapping and—" She unfolded the paper. On it was printed a few numbers. "—extortion it would seem! Ten thousand pounds!" She crushed the paper. "Thurmand has lost his wits," she muttered.

Still . . . if there was truly an innocent young woman involved, and the tale was not a figment of his imagination, then the chit was in danger. Thurmand never threatened what he would not do. The girl, whomever she might be, would, as the message had promised, find herself ruined if the money were not forthcoming.

There is one blessing, at least, thought Lady Helena as she returned to the ground floor more slowly than she'd left it. *It is not someone I know. If it were, then Thurmand would have said, so as to upset me still more.* Helena did her best to put the problem from her mind. Whatever else she did, she must *not* allow her overly perceptive grandmother the least little hint something more had gone amiss.

"I have brought you an invitation to join me at the Cooper-Wainwrights'," said her grandmother in her most imperious manner. "Sir Martin was kind enough to suggest it when he saw that I was a trifle moped."

Helena allowed her eyes to widen. "You, grandmother? Moped? Since when have you ever allowed yourself to be moped?"

Lady Catherine chuckled. "Since it occurred to me I'd like you to join me, of course. It took no more than a day or two of dragging around like a sick cow before he noticed. Sir Martin is, you see, a man sensitive to the needs of others." She smiled. "Occasionally, anyway. For a *man.*"

Sir Martin, the youngest son of a minor gentry family, had made his fortune in India and was knighted for it. A modest and decently pious man, he'd felt obliged to spend some of his wealth on charity. He met Lady Catherine and his future wife, Jane, one of the Yorkshire Coopers, through his efforts to rid himself of some of his wealth in that generous fashion. The dowager had taken one of her fancies to the sensible but green-as-grass man. She promoted the match with Miss Cooper, retaining the both of them as friends once the marriage was accomplished.

Lady Hel, too, liked Lady Jane Cooper-Wainwright who had in *her* dish only a handful of years more than her own quarter-century. Normally, she'd have jumped at the opportunity to visit. Unable to justify such self indulgence at the moment she scrambled for an excuse Lady Catherine would accept.

"Grandmother . . . will you think it very odd in me if I say I cannot come to you yet?" It occurred to Lady Hel that if she were to put her grandmother off, but tell the Treweses of the invitation, no one would think it odd when she departed in order to rescue Thurmand's captive.

Half listening to her grandmother rant about disobedient and disobliging relatives, she planned what she must do first. The money. That would require a jaunt to London. And she must do it without rousing anyone's curiosity or causing the least scandal. After all, *preventing* a scandal was the whole point! All in all, she decided, she'd a rather large problem with which she must cope!

"And *why* must you not leave?" finished her grandmother, huffily.

Luckily Helena heard that last! "I've taken responsibility for the Treweses' fête." Helena described what had been planned.

A fête planned for the very date she was *supposed* to be at Thurmand's benighted inn! *Well,* she decided grimly, *that settles it. I'll have to rescue the chit so I can watch that my plans for the celebration are carried through with no interference from Lady Trewes!*

She continued, "The house party winds down after that so I'll come to you as soon as I have seen to everything."

Lady Helena was actually thinking of the poor girl when she said that, but purely by accident, her words implied she referred to her plans for the fête. And that reminded her of another thing she must do. She must remember to have a word with the housekeeper before she left. The woman must be encouraged to appear to agree to all Lady Trewes's erratic commands, but was to *do* exactly as Lady Helena had ordered. It was the only way they'd avoid chaos!

"Nonsense." Lady Catherine's harsh voice broke into Lady Hel's rambling speech and, more importantly, into her thoughts. "A fête here is Lady Trewes's responsibility."

"So it is, but I cannot bear the mess she'll make of the thing. You would not believe how incompetent the woman is . . ."

Lady Helena soon had her grandmother chuckling and then laughing outright at her tales.

". . . but it is not at all funny!" insisted Helena keeping her face sober with difficulty. "Grandmother, I cannot come to you immediately when I am needed here. You must see that?"

"Have it your way, my dear. Actually, I do see where you, with your capacity to set all straight, cannot allow the situation to go running headlong into disaster. You will come directly after the fête?"

"I will not tell Lady Trewes of your invitation until I feel I've everything in hand. I can soothe any hurt sensibilities, of course, by implying I've no choice but to obey what is, implicitly, an order—" Helena's most impish look appeared. "—at least, if you will allow me tell such a tarradiddle. Lady Trewes, you see, is frightened to death of you and will assume I am, too, so she'll not cavil at my leaving!"

Leaving as soon as she could, of course. Certainly not today, and very likely not tomorrow but . . .

That poor girl!

Nothing better interfere with her leaving the following day.

It occurred to Lady Helena that if she could rescue the chit *before* the date Thurmand set, then she'd not need to get the money her cousin demanded and that meant she'd not have to go to London. She saw her grandmother into her huge carriage and returned to her suite where she found Allie awaiting her.

"Man said it was you or nothing," said Allie.

"And you explained why I could not come?"

"Didn't do a whit of good. Not that the little rat didn't eye the coins with regret, but then he up and loped off down the lane. Rod's following."

"On foot?" demanded Lady Helena.

"Oh no. Rod thought it likely the man had a horse tied up somewhere and took his on a lead."

"He'll be careful the fellow doesn't see him?"

Allie gave her mistress a look filled with exasperation.

Helena chuckled. "Of course he'll take care. I only hope he succeeds in locating my loathsome cousin! Blast Thurmand for the devil he is! How dare he frighten a young woman so? At least I'm pretty certain it must be he." Helena sighed. "Allie, you must pack up my things.

Lady Catherine has invited me to join her at the Cooper-Wainwrights'."

"Join your grandmother?" asked Allie warily.

"I'll have a talk with Sibby," promised Lady Helena, automatically soothing Allie's greatest fear. "I wonder how soon Rod will return," was Helena's next worried thought which, as was not unusual with her, she spoke aloud. "You needn't rush the packing, Allie. I've things to do concerning the fête and must wait for Rod, of course."

"Don't suppose he's got too far to go."

"Hmm. Still, you've a day or so . . ."

Wherever would Thurmand have hidden the girl away? *Would* Rod find where her cousin had gone to ground. *Should* she go first to London and get the money, just to be on the safe side.

. . . or, the thought was like a flash of light in her mind, to *seem* to get the money? In case she was watched?

Or could she avoid the whole problem by writing out a bank draft?

Or would Thurmand not want that for fear she'd cancel the draft in advance? *Could* one deny a signed draft? Although perhaps he meant to take the cash and leave the country from one of the western ports, not returning to London at all, in which case attempting to cash a bad draft would cheat some other bank.

The thoughts went round and round in Helena's head until she felt as if she were going mad. Late the next morning Allie finished her packing. Rod, however, had not yet returned and Lady Helena could not bring herself to order out her carriage. The longer the groom was away, the more worried she became.

Perhaps the messenger had no intention of returning to Thurmand.

Or perhaps he'd seen Rod and was leading him on a wild goose chase?

Dithering, Helena decided to get rid of her fidgets by

taking a ride over to Sanger-Monkton. She'd see how the work on the roof progressed. After all, she should inform the foreman she might be unavailable for some days.

Lord Sanger whistled cheerfully as he drove up the lane to Sanger-Monkton. He slowed as he rounded the curve that revealed his house, pulling up to enjoy the view from where the edifice looked its best. From where one could not actually see the missing slates and broken windows!

But the expected and much-loved view of the serene and welcoming house was, this time, destroyed by the chaos of workmen and litter and ladders and . . .

. . . and Lady Hel watching it all! Sanger froze.

What was happening? Not that it wasn't obvious what was going forward. The slates were being fixed! It appeared the central portion had already been repaired. The men were crawling all over the wing to the right while her dratted ladyship stood below and spoke to a spindle-shanked man with a mop of red hair.

How dare she!

Taking a careful hold on his temper, Sanger set his team in motion. All the happy memories of his time in London slipped from his mind, the auction of his books, the unexpectedly high bidding, the talk with his solicitor, who had looked into the legal aspects of an illegally broken entail . . . it all slid from his mind as if it had never happened.

Lady Helena heard the approaching horses. For half a moment her pleasure at the sight of Lord Sanger could not be suppressed. Then she saw the anger he kept well hidden from most eyes.

And *then* she remembered she must keep secret her need to deal with her cousin. Perhaps it was as well he was angry. A good fight with Sanger might be just the thing!

It might keep him from suspecting what she was really up to when she left the Treweses'!

"A word with you, Lady Helena," he said when he'd pulled up beside her.

He held out his hand demandingly. With no least jot of hesitation, she crawled up into the curricle and he drove off.

"What the devil do you think you are up to?" he snarled. "I cannot afford to fix that roof yet as you know very well!"

"But I can."

Actually, so could he, using the auction money, but he'd other plans for that windfall!

"I have said I'll not use *your* money."

"I am aware." She paused just long enough for him to swell up another notch. Pertly, she added, "You *have*, however, agreed I may use it as I please."

He was silent for a long moment. More quietly, he said, "You had this in mind when your solicitor wrote up the settlements."

It was not a question, but she, remembering that a fight with him was just the thing, readily agreed.

"You tricked me."

"We discussed it." Hurriedly she added another coal to the fire. "You *said* I should do as I willed with my own."

"And you will it that my house be repaired?"

"I thought," she said gently, "that since I must live in it very soon now, it might be for the best?"

"Soon. I wonder . . ."

Helena stared tensely straight ahead. "You would cry off, my lord?" she asked. There was a chill to her tone that was not *anger*, as he might be forgiven for thinking, but *fear*.

"I cannot cry off." He glanced at her and his jaw jutted. "I can, however, if I so will it, *delay* our wedding . . ."

The chill which had appeared in Lady Helena's voice

took on a reality of its own and ran cold fingers up her spine. "For how long?"

"Forever and a day," he spit out, his anger exploding. "You have not behaved well, my lady."

Helena forced her own temper to respond, relieved rather than upset by overt emotion in place of the cold control Sanger had maintained previously. Overly sweetly, she asked, "Because you are a fool and too proud to admit you need help?"

If he were angry, she thought, then he *cared*. But, then it occurred to her to wonder what it was he cared *about*. If it were *merely* his pride . . .

"My blasted pride." He swallowed. Hard. "*False* pride, Jack would say."

"Pride is a very good thing," said Helena gently, forgetting her wish to anger him in a sudden desire to soothe his hurt, "but like anything else it must not be carried to extremes. I've not suggested I interfere in the improvement of your estates, my lord, of your land I mean, and I won't, although the money is there if you want it. But I will very much enjoy setting Sanger-Monkton to rights. I have fallen in love with the house and have despaired at its condition, but, if you *must* find another excuse for my behavior, you may lay it to the fact I've no inclination to live roughly. I have, as you've pointed out, been indulged for a quarter of a century with the elegancies of life." She glanced at him, judging his emotions. "My lord, the prospect of water dripping into my bed every time it rains is not to be thought on!"

"But you will not stop with the roof, will you?" he asked, his temper seeping away.

"If you mean to suggest that I've plans for replacing broken windows and refurbishing the inside with wax and paint and new wallpapers—Oriental designs, do you think?—then, of course. How could you expect otherwise?"

"I believe I understand you, my lady, but that does not

excuse the fact you have begun the project behind my back."

"My dear Lord Sanger," she said, mocking the formality in his tone, "explain to me how I might have begun *except* behind your back!"

A short laugh was startled from him. It had a rather sour sound, but it was a laugh. "Am I such an ogre?" he asked after a moment.

Lady Helena relaxed. "Not an ogre, Simon, but somehow you have it in your head that you and only you are responsible for all the problems facing you. Problems which were caused by people you didn't even know." She blinked at that and, more hesitantly, added, "At least, I assume you did not know them?"

"Cousins from my grandfather's generation. We have had nothing to do with that branch of the family since long before my birth. Or, actually and more likely, they had had nothing to do with us? It had never crossed my mind I was in line to inherit."

"So, now you've been thrown into a situation not of your making, why do you insist on complicating your problems and making the job harder for yourself than it need be?"

"Making it harder for myself . . ." It was his turn to stare at nothing. "You would suggest that if I use your money to set things right, then that would make *everything* all right?"

"Simon, the money is nothing. It is the making of decisions and the long-term seeing they are carried through that is the important thing."

"Strange how money is not at all important to those who have it!"

"But it is *not*. Simon, you must think of it as a tool. Pick it up as you would any other tool and use it!"

"Even though it is yours."

"Then," she said, exasperated, "as you'd do any tool

you needed and did not have, *borrow* it. Blast it, Simon, if you will not take my fortune as a right, which you *could* the instant we wed, then do at least that much. *Borrow* from it!"

Sanger pulled his team up and turned to look at her. "Borrow . . . ?"

"Once you get things set to rights, this estate will, as it once did, produce very well indeed."

"So it will." He stared at nothing in particular. "*So it will.* Lady Hel, has anyone ever told you you are an exceptionally intelligent woman?"

She blinked. "Then you will? Borrow from me?"

"Only what is needed to get the land into production. *Not* to pay off the mortgages—" He was reminded of his talk with his solicitor. "—And speaking of the mortgages . . ."

Sanger told her what he'd learned.

"Then it is possible they can be declared illegal?"

"Even if they are," he warned, "I'll see the man is repaid his principal. He'd no way of knowing fraud was involved and I cannot see my way clear to cheating him of what was his."

"But if you owe no interest, that, too, will be a less onerous burden."

"So it will." He looked around. "Where have we got to?"

"I haven't a notion. And I'll be no help finding our way home . . . oh dear!" Lady Hel giggled. "My lord, I have, so far, kept a secret failing from you."

"A failing?" He cast her a mock-horrified look. "Surely the perfect Lady Hel has no *failings*?"

"A weakness, then."

"Hmm. *I* should not admit you've weaknesses either. So . . . just what is this weakness, Lady Hel?"

"I not only cannot tell you where we are," she responded promptly, "I cannot even help by telling you what direction we face! I get lost faster and more easily than anyone you've ever known." She sobered. "I hate it."

"I would guess you've hated it since your father got you lost in that slum. And perhaps you fear it, having experienced how one can get oneself into difficulties because of it. That is understandable." He pulled to a stop. "So. We must decide what to do now." He set to turning his rig.

"What do you intend?"

"We just passed a cottage. We will ask directions for returning to Sanger-Monkton or, if it is the nearer destination, then to the Treweses'."

"How disarming of you to offer to ask our way which my father would never do. And *just* when I wished to be angry with you," she added, muttering to herself as she recalled her theory a spat would excuse her leaving the Treweses' while keeping her newest problem with Thurmand a secret from him.

This time the look he turned on her was one of utter startlement. "Why on earth would you *wish* to be angry with me?"

Lady Helena realized she had spoken aloud. "I must leave the Treweses'."

"*Must* leave?"

"Grandmother has inveigled an invitation for me to the Cooper-Wainwrights'. I've ordered Allie to pack."

"So," he said a trifle sadly, "you must go, immediately, to the Cooper-Wainwrights'?"

Clasping her hands tightly, Helena bit her lip. She wished she knew how to lie so that it didn't sound like a lie. She gave him a sideways look.

Her silence roused his suspicion. "Lady Hel?"

"Blast your eyes."

"I am to understand, then, that you mean to leave the Treweses' but that you do *not* go to your grandmother?"

"How did you guess?"

"I cannot tell you exactly, but you cannot—" That mobile brow arched. "—hide much from *me,* my dear." He shrugged. "I just knew something is not as it should be. So, my lady, with no more roundaboutation, tell me what has happened."

"Must I?"

"I think you must."

It occurred to Lady Helena that that was exactly what she most wished to do. Why had it not immediately crossed her mind to ask Sanger for his help? Hadn't she just told him it was foolish that he not ask hers? And had she not originally wished to wed him because she thought he'd protect her from Thurmand? And did she not, now, again, need protection from her cousin? Or if not exactly protection, then help in thwarting him?

Perhaps she had become just a trifle *too* independent?

"Come, Lady Hel," he said, wondering what secret she hid now. "You cannot stall forever."

"Once you have gotten directions from that man—" She gestured to where a farmer scythed weeds along the base of a hedge. "—then I will explain it to you and, knowing where we are going, we need not interrupt my story."

"Your mistress has told me about the message from her cousin," Sanger later told Roderick. He'd drawn the groom aside by asking Rod to come look at the knees of one of his team. "She said you were hoping to find Wood-hall's current location. Did you?"

"Followed the little rat to Chipping Norton. He left his hired hack at an inn called the White Hart and then walked along a lane to a rough and tumble cottage just outside the village. I'd have been home sooner, but I wished to discover if the finicky Mr. Woodhall was there, which I could not believe, or if the rat had merely gone back into his own hole."

"And?"

"Woodhall was there, but the chit was not."

"Lady Helena insists the girl be rescued. Have you any notions?"

Rod eyed His Lordship.

Sanger grinned. "You would like to suggest the two of us confront Woodhall and force him to tell?"

"Crossed my mind once or twice while I was waiting," responded Rod somewhat laconically. "Didn't think Lady Hel would approve, but . . ."

Sanger, sobering, interrupted, "Why not?"

"Because of her blessed grandmother, o'course, but . . ."

"I should have known, should I not?" Sanger interrupted yet again. "Lady Hel's attitude toward Lady Catherine has her protecting the old lady whether the dowager wishes it or not."

"Always has tried to protect her, but . . ."

"It is a very good trait in our Lady Hel, but one which sometimes interferes in what one most needs to do . . . ?"

Rod grinned, "True, but . . ."

"Did you remain to see if Woodhall was actually staying in this hovel?"

"Been trying to say," said the exasperated groom. "Followed Woodhall when he left the rat's hole. That's what took so long."

"So?"

"Woodhall has broken into—" Rod bit his lip. "—into a house that, according to what I learned gossiping, has been shut up for months. The, um, owners went on a sea voyage, Greece and Constantinople and such places. They aren't expected back for some time."

"Hmm. I would guess the girl is there as well. You agree?"

Rod nodded.

"Did you see any servants about?"

"Woodhall's man of all work. Don't think there was anyone else."

"I don't know about Woodhall, but if I planned something like this, I'd wish as few people as possible involved. Where is this house?"

"Not so very far from the village."

Sanger rubbed his chin in the way he had. "I wonder if you and I . . . Ah!—" Sanger straightened from where he was pretending to inspect his horse's leg. "My lady."

"You wondered," she asked a trifle sharply, "about, *what*, my lord?"

"Hmm? Oh, whether Rod and I can . . . can care for this tendon, or whether I should—" It occurred to Simon he had not yet told Helena about his stables! "—Ah!"

"Should . . . ah!" repeated Helena. Her eyes narrowed and, crossing her arms, she tapped her foot.

Rod did his best to fade away gracefully.

"Such an *interesting* expression," she added when Simon bit his lip.

"Expression?"

"Consternation, perhaps?" she asked, smiling sweetly—but her eyes glittered.

"Hmm . . . just today you recalled you'd a secret to reveal concerning your penchant for getting lost?"

"Yes. And now you wish to confess to a secret of your own?"

"I didn't say I *wished* to," he denied, eyeing her.

"But you *will*."

"I don't think that was a question."

"It was not."

"Hmm." Sanger glanced around and noted the unhidden appreciation with which various grooms and hangers-on stared. He glared at them and told them to take themselves off. When they'd all passed beyond hearing, he said, "I have seen you admire that roan Trewes purchased just before this house party began."

"Big Red? Yes. I mean to have Rod lay a bet for me when he races."

"I will do it for you, if you wish. When I lay my own. The-horse-is-from-my-stables," he finished in something of a rush.

"Your stables?"

"Hmm." Now the secret was out, he could speak with no further agitation. "My father started them with a stallion he won. Since he died they've been managed by m'father's man. I haven't a notion why my great uncle didn't sell them, but I'm damned glad he did not. They've provided a steady if not large income and, once Red wins his first race, I can finally sell for what my stock is worth and make a great deal more on stud fees."

"When were you going to tell me of this asset?" she asked.

"I suppose I'd have done so when it crossed my mind."

She gave him a cross look.

"It doesn't, you see. I mean, I don't often think of it."

"So what brought it to mind now? The need for an excuse to not tell me what you and Rod were plotting?"

He scowled. "Yes. As a red herring I was about to suggest I call in Jagger to look at this horse. My head groom, that is. Except you didn't know I had a head groom!"

She ran her hands along the tendon and then looked up. "You wish him to look at a horse which has nothing wrong with it."

Sanger's scowl deepened. "I forgot you were practically raised in your father's stables."

"So, I ask again. What were you and Rod plotting?"

"Only that we rescue your maiden in distress." Sanger shrugged.

"Ah. And once you'd rescued her, then what would you do with her?"

"Bring her to you?"

"I doubt her father would approve her being alone with you any more than he'll approve her having been with Thurmand."

That particular problem hadn't occurred to Simon. He might have allowed himself to be constrained by the dictates of propriety to engage himself to Lady Hel, but he wasn't about to have an irate father demand he wed some unknown chit he was merely doing his best to help!

"What would you suggest?" he asked after a moment.

"That I leave, exactly as I'd meant to do. That you inform the Treweses you've decided to move into the caretaker's rooms since there are workmen in the house. You leave. We meet at an agreed upon place and proceed to wherever that fox, Thurmand, has gone to earth, which I assume Rod has discovered since you were laying plans. *Then* you and Rod may rescue the chit, bring her to me in the carriage, and we'll send Rod with a letter to her father explaining that Thurmand thought better of his plot and that the girl has been with me all along and will join me at the Cooper-Wainwrights' for a week or two—he may pass on the fact of that visit to whomever he wishes so as to avoid a scandal."

"What," asked Sanger gently, "if Thurmand has already ruined the girl?"

"He has threatened to do so only if he does not get his way, which means if he doesn't get the money he wants. Not before. She is safe, in that way, for awhile yet."

Sanger rubbed his chin between fingers and thumb, his gaze steady on her face. "I cannot like it that you mean to put yourself anywhere near danger."

"I have faith in you, my lord. You will manage the rescue deftly and dear Thurmand will not know the chit has disappeared until we are far away."

"I hope I prove to deserve your faith," was all he said.

The muscle twisting in his jaw was far more revealing of his concern for her than his quiet words.

Eight

"But . . . it is Chabsley!" Lady Helena stared in dismay at the gates near which Rod pulled the light traveling carriage to a halt. The sun had set, but the long afterglow of a late summer evening remained, making it impossible that Helena not recognize the entrance to the home in which she grew up. "I can't believe Mary finally talked Cousin William into taking a sea voyage!"

"Thought you'd be surprised," said the groom, laconically.

"This is the seat of the Marquess of Chabsley?" asked Lord Sanger.

Lady Helena nodded, dumbstruck that Thurmand would have the nerve.

"Then we've one advantage I'd not hoped to have. You'll know where Woodhall is likely to have put his prisoner."

Helena gave the implied question a moment's thought and suddenly sat up stiffly. "Oh, that poor dear!"

"Where?"

"Most likely he locked her into the rooms last occupied by a long dead cousin. In her latter years the poor woman became obsessed by fire. For her own protection, she was put into a secured apartment on the fourth floor. It was designed to prevent her escaping *and* from setting anything afire, herself or the house."

"Barred windows and all?"

"Yes, and a strong lock on the door. Most likely the key will be in the lock as it has always been. It isn't *that* which bothers me. The rooms were fireproofed with Dutch tiles, the floors and the walls as far up as the woman might reach. There are no carpets or drapery. The poor child will be so dreadfully uncomfortable."

"If discomfort is all she suffers she'll have gotten off lightly," said Sanger grimly. "Fourth floor, you say . . ." He eyed the mansion just visible at the end of a long, formal, well-kept drive. "Where exactly?"

"The west end," she said. "It shouldn't be difficult to reach. There are secondary stairs near a side door."

"Which will be locked," objected Sanger. "We may perhaps leave by that exit, but unless I'm to break a window to get in we need a diversion." Sanger rubbed his chin.

Helena searched her mind, too. "Rod, that shed close to collapse just beyond the carriage house. Remember? I wonder if Cousin William has had it torn down."

"What do you have in mind?" asked Sanger.

"Recalling the old lady made me think of it! She'd have loved to set it afire, you see?"

"It is near other buildings?"

Helena reluctantly nodded, knowing what he'd say.

He did. "It's too dangerous. It might spread, and Rod has said there are no servants. But, still, a fire of some sort might be the answer."

"There's an old hay rick to the other side of the carriage house but not too near it. Never understood why it was there," muttered Rod.

"It's still there?" asked Helena, curiously. "Father got a bee in his bonnet one year when a horrendous winter was predicted. He insisted the hay be moved in near where it would be needed. It wasn't all needed, of course, but he never had what remained removed."

"No wind," said Rod, holding up a wet finger. "Dry as tinder, likely."

"The next question is, is either Woodhall or his man likely to see it?"

"Valet likes a smoke. Sneaks out with one of Mr. Woodhall's cigars when he can manage. Most evenings he *can,*" suggested Rod.

"He'd raise an alarm?"

"Maybe he'd fear my cousin would accuse him of *causing* the fire," suggested Helena. "Knowing Thurmand as I do, I can't imagine he isn't aware of the valet's predilection. He always knows everyone's weaknesses."

"Maybe, but I think it likely the man would worry about Woodhall's carriage which, I presume, is in the carriage house and not overly far away?"

"They'd try to put it out, or watch to see it didn't spread," said Rod.

"Rod, you wait here while Lord Sanger and I see if there is a light in the old lady's rooms. At least—" She cast a horrified look toward the men. "—*surely* Thurmand hasn't left the poor girl with no lamp!"

She and Sanger reconnoitered and verified there was light in the windows of the room of which Helena spoke. They also checked that the hay rick was there. When they returned, the three discussed exactly what each must do.

Lady Hel was irritated when the men insisted she remain with the carriage. The fact she was trusted with it soothed her, however. Hitched to it were four of Sanger's excellent horses, chosen so they'd have a good strengthy team with which to make their escape. The high-spirited creatures were far more restive than more placid and plodding beasts. Someone was needed to keep them under control.

Helena forced down her annoyance that she'd been relegated to the most passive role by reminding herself that the important thing was that the girl be rescued. She resigned herself and handed Sanger a note she'd prepared for the young woman. She hoped it would give the girl confidence and allow him to bring her away without an argument.

And then, once the men disappeared up the lane, she settled down to wait with what patience she could find.

Which wasn't much. She knew they could do nothing until the servant appeared with his cigar, that Rod must set light to the hay rick, and that even then they must hope Thurmand joined his servant before Sanger entered the house. *Then* it would take time for Sanger to reach his goal and convince the young woman, who might be in hysterics or unconscious or heaven only knew what, that she was being rescued and not kidnapped by still another villain, and *then* he must lead her to the carriage.

Helena used a long string of the words she'd learned at Rod's father's knee. Words no young lady of the *ton* should *know*, let alone *use*. When she began repeating herself, she sighed, settled back into the driver's seat and stared straight ahead, fretting.

Would all go as planned? Or would Thurmand refuse to leave the comforts of the manor. Could Sanger remove the young woman and bring her away without rousing suspicion? On that thought a distant shout roused her from her fussing and she turned in the driver's seat to see what she could see.

A golden glow from beyond the carriage house told her where the fire had been set and she made a note to remember to congratulate Rod for making such an excellent job of it. But even as she silently congratulated her absent groom, she wondered if the shout would bring Thurmand out.

Barely breathing, straining every sense, finally Helena heard her cousin's angry voice giving his man orders. And then, in mid-tirade, sudden silence. Finally, a single expletive she'd never before heard.

She sighed. Thurmand, she guessed, was suspicious of

the convenient fire and would be running back to the house. Where, she wondered, was Rod? What was he doing now he'd completed his task? Why hadn't he returned?

If Helena had fretted while waiting for the fire, she now found herself much more upset, deeply concerned something would go wrong and that they wouldn't manage to bring away the girl. Worse. What if Thurmand had a gun? What if he shot Simon?

Thurman shoot Simon? Oh no, not Simon. Grasping the reins tightly, she stared wildly toward the orange glow. Thurmand must not shoot him. He . . . She . . . *Oh, lordy, lordy. How foolish of me!* Helena stared wildly toward the orange glow. *I love him.*

When had it happened? How had it happened? And what was she to do? Helena gasped as she acknowledged the pain she'd feel if something were to happen to Simon. But even if he returned to her, safe, what then?

Simon made no pretense of loving her. Oh, he liked her well enough. He enjoyed her company and even appeared to be attracted to her person, but *he didn't love her.*

Living with him, loving him, unloved by him, would be hell. Helena swallowed. Hard. She'd a new problem now: How to hide from Simon that she'd been so idiotic as to fall in love with him. Oh, the irony of that! When she'd suggested they pretend to the world they were in love so he need not worry the *ton* label him a fortune hunter!

But what should she do? It occurred to her, she had never been particularly good at hiding her emotions. She vowed that this time she'd manage. Somehow she'd manage.

A shot interrupted her thoughts. Also the sound of running footsteps. Helena threaded the reins through her fingers as she'd been taught and waited. Rod appeared. Behind him, carrying a complaining bundle of femininity over his shoulder, was Sanger. Her beloved.

"Get her into the carriage," called Helena in a soft but carrying voice. "I'll get us away."

Rod, aware Helena had been well taught, didn't argue. He opened the door, waited for Sanger to dump his bundle inside and crawl in after. Then the groom had only a moment to slam the door and swing up behind as Helena cracked the whip and set the team in motion.

Lady Hel let the team have their heads for a good mile when, with difficulty, she slowed them to a more reasonable pace. Another mile passed and she pulled the team to a stop, her arms aching with the effort to control their unrelenting strength and stubborn desire for headlong flight.

"Rod, come take them. I must join poor Simon inside before that chit expires from hysterics or *he* does!" She clambered down as she spoke, and Rod opened the carriage door for her. He climbed onto the driver's seat and set the restive team in motion.

Helena, once inside the carriage, very nearly laughed. When she'd halted the carriage, the poor girl had tried to climb out a window. Simon was doing his best to restrain her without hurting her.

"Miss . . . Oh dear, I haven't a clue to your name, but I am Lady Helena Woodhall and I have organized your rescue from my cousin. If only you will seat yourself before you hurt yourself, I would much appreciate it. I've a plan, you see."

At the sound of a female voice, the girl let herself be drawn back into the carriage. Lady Helena took the chit's trembling hand and patted it. "Such a terrible time as you've had, my dear."

It took Helena some little effort to reassure the poor child that she was indeed safe . . . for child it was! Barely sixteen, Helena learned later. Her father's only offspring, Miss Stoner was her father's heir. Thurmand would sneer and say that she was only a cit so what difference did her feelings make one way or another? Since his pockets were to let, he'd *use* her, callously, to raise the wind with never a care that he hurt her.

"Now, my dear Miss Stoner," said Lady Hel when she'd managed to dry the girl's tears and get a few important details from her. Her name, for instance. "I've a letter for your father which I'd like you to read, please?"

Simon had lit a lamp when Helena thought perhaps light might help the girl relax. She could *see* her captors were respectable people. In the dim light it took Miss Stoner time and no little effort to read Lady Helena's letter to her father, her mouth moving as she spelled out letters and words.

Helena took the letter back and, realizing the girl had very likely not taken in a bit of the meaning as she'd struggled to make out the words, read it aloud.

"My dear sir. I am Lady Helena Woodhall. You do not know me, but I have rescued your daughter and believe all scandal may be averted if you will allow her to remain for a week or so in my company and that of my grandmother, the dowager Lady Catherine Rolandson. We may be found at the Cooper-Wainwright estate just east of Chipping Norton north of Oxford. I do not know if a ransom was demanded of you as well as from me, but, if so, it will be unnecessary to pay it. In fact, it was because I'd no intention of paying, I thought it best to remove your child from where she was held.

If you think it proper for her to remain in my grandmother's care for a period while everyone learns where she is, then it would be helpful if you were to send on her trunks and her maid so she may be properly gowned. If you send a portmanteau filled with the bare essentials with Roderick Cole who delivers this note, she need not appear even once in a borrowed gown! Believe me, your servant in all things, Lady Helena Woodhall."

Lady Hel paused. "It is, perhaps, rather wordy, but I thought perhaps that in itself would soothe your father's fears?"

"Papa will be frantic," said the child. "I am so sorry I behaved badly when Lord Sanger rescued me, but that other man . . ." She paled.

"He said things to you a gentleman should not say," suggested Lady Hel, and added still another reason to dislike her cousin to an already long list.

"I didn't quite understand all he said, but he told me if my father didn't pay the ransom he'd give me to a woman who would not be at all kind to me and she would give me to gentlemen who would be less kind, and—" She turned her eyes briefly in Sanger's direction, "—I guess I thought perhaps Lord Sanger . . . well, I did not know him, did I . . . that he was one of those gentlemen?" She looked shyly up into Helena's face.

"I will have Thurmand's lights and liver!" snarled Helena, shocking her young protégé all over again. "How dare he . . ."

Simon reached across and laid his fingers across Helena's lips. "I think we have nearly arrived to where we left Rod's horse, Lady Hel. Fold and seal your letter so that it will be ready when he is."

"Poor Rod. He'll get no sleep tonight I fear!"

"No. He'll be in London in something under five hours, I'd guess, but then he must find Miss Stoner's father and convince him of the truth of what you say and then he'll likely be required to lead the gentleman to you at the Cooper-Wainwrights'."

"I didn't think it through, did I?" asked Lady Hel. "Of course, Mr. Stoner will wish to see that his daughter is safe."

Rod pulled the team to a stop. The letter was given into his hands and he cantered off down one arm of the crossroads while Simon, taking the reins, turned the carriage the other way.

Once Simon was safely beyond hearing, Helena encouraged Miss Stoner to tell all her tale which was much as

Helena had guessed. Thurmand had managed to meet the girl when she was shopping. He rapidly insinuated himself into her affections and convinced her their only hope was to elope.

Romantic that she was, Miss Stoner agreed to it. Tears filling her eyes all over again, she insisted she had been an evil ungrateful wretch to have done something so sinful, something she *knew* was so very wrong. The tears dripped down the child's cheeks and she threw herself into Helena's unready arms.

Holding her awkwardly, Helena did her best to convince the child she was not the most wicked creature on God's earth.

"*That* mark of distinction is very likely reserved for Thurmand!"

That roused a weak chuckle and Miss Stoner raised her head. Ruefully, Helena wished she'd thought to blow out the lamp. If she'd done so she couldn't see Miss Stoner's face and might imagine what she pleased.

Instead, Lady Hel was chagrined to note that, although Miss Stoner had indulged her emotions for the whole of several days, or so she said, she still radiated glowing perfection. It was, thought Lady Hel, quite unfair. Even the mildest of temper tantrums would put spots of high color on her own cheeks and tears left her nose red and running and her eyes bloodshot and rimmed with more red. Definitely unfair!

Ah well, Lady Helena thought, no one ever promised life would be fair.

She patted her new protégé's back when the girl laid her head trustingly on Helena's shoulder. It was no surprise, shortly thereafter, when Lady Helena discovered Miss Stoner had fallen asleep. Miss Stoner, it seemed, believed Helena's advanced years made her a properly maternal figure! Helena didn't look forward to the rest of the journey to the Cooper-Wainwrights'. She'd be uncomfortably stiff at the end of it, and very likely her arm would have fallen asleep long before they reached their destination.

Even less did she look forward to their arrival at such an unconscionable hour for visitors!

Miss Stoner went to sleep in Helena's bed, Helena napping on the chaise longue. The girl awakened early, bright-eyed and already well recovered from the horror of finding herself kidnapped and in Thurmand's power. She'd strained Lady Helena's patience to the limit before Allie informed them that Sibby had come with orders that Helena go instantly to her grandmother and explain the ridiculous tale going around that a total stranger had arrived in the night in Lady Helena's company, driven by Lord Sanger and at an odd, in fact, *incredible* hour.

Lady Hel left Miss Stoner with Allie and went to explain the situation. She attempted to slide over Thurmand's role, but her grandmother would not allow it and did not stop demanding answers until assured she'd a round tale of it.

"So. Since he couldn't marry it and couldn't inherit it, he decided to get the money he needed some *other* way. Why not marry this chit?"

Helena shrugged. Again her grandmother demanded answers. Finally, thoroughly exasperated and hoping Miss Stoner would not be too insulted if she ever heard of it, Helena said, "You know Thurmand is overly proud of his blue blood. He'd never dilute it with Miss Stoner's."

Lady Catherine sighed loudly. "No, I didn't know, but if that is the way of it, I suppose it is time I told Thurmand the truth."

Lady Hel folded her arms. "The *truth*?"

This time Lady Helena demanded answers from her

grandmother who was very nearly as reluctant to give them as Lady Hel had been to open her budget and give hers!

"Thurmand isn't a Woodhall at all," the dowager finally admitted. "Close your mouth! You've surely heard the tales. His mother—"

Lady Catherine, who could speak in overly blunt terms when describing the hottest scandal, was quite obviously embarrassed when scandal was so close to home. Two dots of color marred her cheeks.

"—is nothing but a slut. To give you the word with no bark on it, Thurmand is the son of a favored footman."

It was not uncommon for unhappily married women to indulge in affairs, but not, usually, before they'd provided an heir of the blood. Even then dallying with a servant was rare indeed.

"Are you quite certain of that?"

"Quite. Her husband set her aside six months before she became enceinte. And then he was fool enough to die in that carriage accident before the boy was born. The family allowed the mother the fiction Thurmand was her husband's son but only after she signed a witnessed statement that he is *not*. That sealed document is in the hands of the family solicitor, of course. There is no question whatsoever that he could, under any circumstances, be in line for the title."

There was a great deal of arrogance in that last statement and a clue to where Thurmand had acquired his pride in his supposed bloodlines. Lady Helena gave fleeting thought to how her cousin . . . well, *not* her cousin! But, as to how he'd feel upon learning the truth. It would be a blow. One from which he might never recover.

"I will inform him," continued Lady Catherine, "that the family will repudiate him if he falls into scandal. It might be best if he were to leave England. Permanently."

"He evidently has no means of supporting himself," objected Lady Helena although she couldn't imagine why she cared.

"I wish William had not gone off on that ridiculous sea voyage of his!" said Lady Catherine fretfully.

"Why?"

"He could arrange an annuity for Thurmand. One which would be paid only so long as he remains out of England."

"I will provide the annuity if only to get him away!"

"Perhaps you could do so initially," mused Lady Catherine. "I will make William take it over when he returns."

"You feel it is the place of the current marquess to see that Thurmand is paid off?" Lady Helena thought of William's nip-cheese character. He'd even left Chabsley without so much as a caretaker in residence, only to save a few pence! "I wonder if William will agree."

"William will do as he's told," said the dowager. She drew in a deep breath. "And now," she added, "I suppose I must meet the chit."

"I suppose you must. She is quite ladylike. You'll have no need to feel shame for her behavior. If it is, perhaps, a trifle lively, her age will excuse that."

The meeting between dowager marchioness and city-bred heiress went off as well as could be expected. Miss Stoner was quite in awe of the dowager and Helena thought that that might not be a bad thing. It would keep the child in line while she herself returned to the Treweses' to check on how badly Her Ladyship, in less than twenty-four hours, had mangled Lady Helena's plans for her fête.

Lady Hel had grown quite possessive of the Treweses' fête!

Mr. Stoner arrived sooner than Lady Helena had thought possible so she was not yet returned to greet him. He had, of course, heard of Lady Hel. Who had not?

And he was not certain he wished his daughter to have anything to do with such a hellion as Devil Woodhall's daughter was said to be. On the other hand, if her ladyship actually *had* rescued his beloved daughter, then perhaps rumor lied?

Mr. Stoner suffered immensely when his only child did not return home. He suffered more, but in a protective silence, when the insultingly polite letter arrived requesting a ransom for his daughter and, in the most horrifyingly genteel terms, describing what fate would be perpetrated on the person of the young and innocent girl if ransom were *not* paid as specified.

And then Rod Cole arrived with the letter from Lady Helena. Hopeful and despairing by turns, Mr. Stoner organized a fast trip into the country. Later Rod was to tell Lady Hel how surprised he'd been at the speed with which Mr. Stoner insisted on traveling and how impressed by the horses the man, a mere cit after all, kept stabled along the main roads.

As a result, they arrived at the Cooper-Wainwrights' just in time to join the remnants of the house party at the luncheon table where all had gathered even if they didn't wish to eat. Miss Stoner, seeing her father anxiously searching the faces seated around the table, rose to her feet and ran to him. He held her close, tears unashamedly running down his cheeks.

"You're all right?" he asked softly when he could speak.

"I'm very well, Papa," she responded and then, with a soft "oh" and rosy cheeks, disentangled herself. Very properly she managed to introduce her father to those assembled for luncheon and then led him to a chair which had been placed, at Hibbard's direction, next her own.

With extraneous guests around, to say nothing of servants, the situation could not be discussed, but the instant they finished eating, Lady Catherine tactfully led father and daughter to a comfortable parlor at the back of the house where she left them, telling them she would return shortly.

When she did, Mr. Stoner said, "When the villain's letter came, I instantly set about a story my daughter was visiting in the country and went about collecting the required ransom, which I don't mind admitting was *not* an easy thing when such a huge amount was involved. Then I waited. You'll understand how hard that was, my lady, awaiting the day I was to deliver the ransom and, if the villain's letter did not lie, discover how to regain my untouched and still innocent daughter! I didn't know what to think when Cole arrived bearing the letter from Lady Hel."

"Thurmand is *Lady Helena's* cousin," said Lady Catherine just a trifle frostily. It was all right for the *ton* to give her granddaughter the nickname, but a cit? Still, Lady Catherine knew the gentleman deserved a round tale and, when he admitted to wondering how a stranger had become ensnared in the plot she explained, "Not long ago the villain wished to wed Helena and she turned him down. I believe he demanded money from her as well as from you as a form of revenge."

"Well, now," said Mr. Stoner, "I'll admit I did wonder if it was all a nasty prank whereby some members of the *ton* had amused themselves for a few days?"

Lady Catherine, knowing Lady Hel's reputation, swallowed that insult, although with difficulty. "I would have thought the recent announcement of her engagement to a former army officer who was cited in dispatches for bravery might have alleviated those concerns, Mr. Stoner."

His cheeks reddened but he didn't back down. Silently, he managed to imply that the *ton* was the *ton* and it was impossible for such as he to understand its ways. Only seeing his daughter with his own eyes and hearing her tale from her own lips returned him to the peace he craved. But he had seen her, was convinced she was well and was, himself, ready to return to London.

"I must see your granddaughter before I go," said Mr. Stoner, rather choked up. "I can never in the whole of my life thank her for what she did."

"Hmm."

"My lady?"

"Oh, I don't think you need thank her." Lady Catherine raised her quizzing glass and studied Mr. Stoner. Speaking rather laconically, she added, "After all, Hel had decided she'd not pay the ransom. Given that, she had to do something. It would have been dishonorable to allow the proposed consequences of that decision, would it not?"

"You would say she acted only from a sense of honor and not from kindness and generosity?" he asked a trifle stiffly.

"She is generous!" insisted Miss Stoner and then, coloring up, begged pardon for interrupting, "But I cannot allow you to say unkind things about her ladyship. Not when she has been all that is Christian."

Lady Catherine turned the glass on her young guest. When the chit was suitably cowed, she dropped it and turned back to the father. "Honor demanded we aid your daughter. The man who stole her away is—" Lady Catherine found it very hard to continue. "—a connection."

"You would say you felt responsible?"

"I knew nothing about it until it was done," said Lady Catherine. "I would prefer to have continued in ignorance."

The dowager spoke the last lightly, but something in her expression warned Mr. Stoner she meant exactly what she said and that she, too, was suffering, if in a different fashion. For a moment he remained silent. Then, he said, "I see. Would you prefer it if I were to take my daughter and disappear?"

"That would not do. Her reputation must be seen to. She will remain here a week, which will answer any possible gossip."

Mr. Stoner nodded. "I have brought her maid with a portmanteau, but her trunks follow. There was no time to pack properly. And, I've a further request, my lady. Though I understand that it is no longer proper to bring an entourage of servants when one attends a house party, I cannot leave her without a personal footman ordered to protect her from any future attempts."

Lady Catherine stiffened. Then she saw the worried expression in Mr. Stoner's eyes. "I understand that you would feel happier if a man you trusted were watching over her. I should not, I suppose feel insulted that you would think we'd be derelict in caring for her."

"I mean no insult."

It was Lady Catherine's turn to nod. "I sent a groom with word of your arrival to my granddaughter. She should return soon. For now, I will leave you and Miss Stoner to speak in privacy. You will, of course, remain the night."

"It is necessary that I return to London. I'll wait only until I have thanked your granddaughter and be on my way."

"A trip from and returning to London in one day? No thank you! It will be the middle of the night before you can return!"

"It is necessary," repeated Mr. Stoner but with a small smile and a twinkle in his eye.

The door burst open and a whirlwind rushed in. "Mr. Stoner!" spoke Lady Hel. "And I not here to greet you! Do forgive me."

Mr. Stoner blinked, took the hand offered him and shook it. And then he held it staring down into Lady Hel's interested gaze.

"Mr. Stoner?" she asked, gently retrieving her hand.

"You are not at all what I expected," he said. She grimaced. "Which is a terribly unsuitable thing to say! My lady, I wish to thank you."

"No!" Speaking quickly, she continued, "It was necessary for my own sake that I rescue your daughter. You will say no more." She turned quickly. "Miss Stoner, are you to stay with us? Will you be here to enjoy the Treweses' fête? With any luck it will be a delightful day. Luck and a bit of conniving—" She cast a mischievous smile Mr. Stoner's way. "—is necessary to assure that Lady Trewes does not ruin all! Mr. Stoner, will you not also remain for a few days? Since his house party is breaking up, Sir Martin says he'd welcome another man about the place. He feels nearly surrounded by women, you see—" She tipped her head a trifle to the side when he shook his. "—No? Ah, that is too bad. Poor Sir Martin. Ah well, we will take very good care of your daughter, sir."

Mr. Stoner turned to Lady Catherine. "Is it always so difficult to get a word in edgewise?"

"No. She only talks a lot and so very fast when she hopes to avoid embarrassment," said Lady Catherine with the hint of a smile.

"I've no wish to embarrass her," he said sternly, "but I must thank her."

"I do not know how you may do that."

"I've no intention of offering her money, but I wondered if she had a favorite charity?"

"Made in your daughter's name, Mr. Stoner, she would be pleased to have a donation given to the First London Charter Day School. If you would hire some of the young people trained there, it would be an even greater boon. The school trains clerks and servants, for instance, but perhaps it would be better if you were to discuss that with the director."

"I will see the school and the director as the second thing I do when I return to London."

"The first will be to sleep?"

He smiled. "The first will be to find my head clerk and discover what exactly has happened to my business while

I've been inattentive. There will be no money for that donation if I allow my business to fail."

Lady Hel asked a pertinent question. Helena and Mr. Stoner were deep in a discussion of import duties when Lady Catherine, bored to tears, quietly excused herself.

Miss Stoner, her eyes growing bigger and bigger, tried to follow the discussion between her heroine and her father. When they reached a point where she felt it would not be too impolite to insert a question, she asked Lady Helena how she had learned so much about something women usually knew nothing about.

Mr. Stoner looked astounded. "By all that's holy, my daughter is correct. I quite forgot I was talking to a woman!"

Briefly, Lady Hel explained her unusual upbringing and her continued interest in things women didn't often study. "I am more drawn to Parliamentary doings, naturally, than to commerce. The practical end of all this—" A hand wafting through the air indicated she meant the subject they'd been discussing. "—has never come much in my way. I've found our talk not only stimulating and interesting, but very informative. Thank you."

Color surged into Mr. Stoner's ears. "You have nothing to thank me for! On the contrary," he insisted.

Lady Helena raised a hand and covered a fabricated yawn. "Do not, my good sir, become a dead bore," she said in a languid voice, her eyelids lowered half over her eyes. "It would spoil my good impression of you."

He threw back his head and roared with laughter. "I begin to understand," he said, "how you acquired the sobriquet Lady Hel!"

Lady Hel merely allowed her brows to arch, a singularly sweet smile barely curving her lips.

He took the exceedingly unsubtle hint, however, and made no more attempts to thank her. Instead he said, "I've some difficulty understanding just how you managed to rescue my daughter. I fear," he added a trifle ruefully, "that she cannot be brought to tell a coherent tale."

Between them, Lady Helena and Miss Stoner told him all each knew, the younger lady filling in those parts Lady Hel could not tell.

"Ah!" said Mr. Stoner at the end of it. "Then it is Lord Sanger I must thank."

"It is not," said Sanger from the doorway where he'd listened to the last bits.

Mr. Stoner turned in his chair, his back stiff. "Lord Sanger?"

"It is. One thanks the general who plans the battle and only secondarily, the men who fight it!"

"I have always thought that a trifle unfair," said Lady Helena. "It is the men who go into danger, after all."

"But the danger would be far greater if they'd no leader," objected Sanger.

"Then," said Lady Helena, "I suppose one might thank a good general." Her head tipped to one side. "It has always seemed to me, however, that there are a great many bad ones, who do *not* think of the men who must die, but only of achieving some goal?"

"You, however, worried a great deal about the dangers, did you not, my dear?" retorted Sanger. He chuckled when her cheeks glowed with more color. "So, by your own words, you, our general, must be thanked."

Miss Stoner, bemused, looked from one to the other, not quite certain what had passed between her heroine and her rescuer. Mr. Stoner, however, was no slowtop. He laughed softly.

"Lady Helena, Lord Sanger, you two have very obviously made a wonderful match of it. I could wish we were of a class with each other so that I could know you better, but we are not."

"Why should that be a problem? When his lordship and I are settled at Sanger-Monkton, we will invite you to join a small party who will appreciate you for yourself alone, Mr. Stoner."

Blushing with pleasure, Mr. Stoner insisted that was not necessary but that he'd be highly honored by such an invitation. And then, just when Lady Hel was certain she had made a grave error, he smiled, said that he had said far too much and added, "I truly must leave now. If you'd be so good, my lady . . . ?"

Helena took the hint and rang for a footman. Then she and Sanger left Mr. Stoner alone with his daughter so they might exchange a few more words in privacy.

"You would not believe what I discovered this morning at the Treweses'. How that woman can put things into disarray so quickly I do not know!" said Lady Helena to Sanger as they strolled slowly toward the front hall where Mr. Stoner would soon join them, "I will be very glad when it is over."

"When you may think of other things?"

"Yes. Our wedding, for instance." Lady Helena cast Simon a sideways look, biting her lip. Rather hesitantly, she asked, "Are you still of a mind to delay it?"

Unaware of the fears roused by his anger over the roof and Lady Helena's newly discovered love for him, Sanger merely smiled. "I should, but, at the moment, I'm again of a mind to bring the date forward. Of course, give us a day or two to rub each other the wrong way and who knows what I will think?"

"As you attempted just now with all your talk of generals and fighting men?"

"Oh no. That was no attempt at upsetting you!"

Helena cast him a look pregnant with suspicion.

"But, my dear, surely you understood!"

"I can see no reason why you should be so modest about the part you played!"

"My lady," he said with mock horror, "I could not allow Mr. Stoner to think I'd any great role in the rescue!"

"But you did."

"*Not,*" he insisted. "My dear—" His expression grew comical. "He might try to foist that brat off on me if he thought I'd had, hmm, *too much to do with her!*"

Lady Helena recognized the justice in that, but, on a teasing note, merely added, "It isn't fair he think you'd no great place in her rescue."

"Lady Hel, you become a bore!"

She cast him a look of mock horror. "No!"

"Yes."

"Well," she said, "we can't have that. How may we assure ourselves I do not become a bore?"

His eyes drifted over her face, his gaze settling on her mouth. "I'm sure I'll think of ways to assure it, my lady," he said softly.

Lady Helena, too, could think of ways of assuring it. She wondered just how soon she'd have the right to try some of them!

Nine

The first thing to go wrong with the fête was the weather. After many fine days, this one dawned wet and chilly, the cloud cover hanging low and set to stay. Helena took one look out the windows when Allie drew the drapery and turned over, pulling the covers up over her ears.

"None of that, now," huffed her maid, tugging them down. "You don't think a little wet will stop that Lady Trewes, do you?"

Helena sighed. Lady Trewes had become as bored with her house party as her guests. She wanted it over and everyone gone and Allie was correct. She'd not allow damp, or even a few drops of rain, to interfere!

"At least there will be a pair of large tents," mused Helena. "We can huddle under one or the other." She sighed. "Except for the children running their races and playing their games. I'd better suggest the housekeeper supply a large pile of towels with which to dry them off."

If Lady Trewes *had* thought to cancel the fête, Lord Trewes would have objected. He, too, wished to see an end to the party. He'd entered not only Big Red but a two-year-old and his favorite steeplechaser in the Doncaster races and wished to be gone from home himself. He told Lord Sanger of the entries in a sly fashion almost bound to raise curiosity among those who overheard them.

Sanger was not pleased, but there was nothing he could

do. He lifted his mobile brow and calmly replied, "I'll have to see about laying that bet on Big Red, then, will I not?"

"Mine, too," said Lady Helena who, with her protégé, happened to be standing nearby.

"Yours, Lady Hel?" asked Lord Trewes. "Women do not bet on races."

"Of course we do not! That would be totally unladylike, would it not? But I like that animal. I have good feelings about him. *Lord Sanger* will put an extra hundred guineas on him to win," she finished with a touch of mockery. She shrugged. "That is all I meant."

There were chuckles from the men, a sniff from Lady Hingly-Tumpton, and a giggle from Miss Stoner who, meeting that moralist's glaring eyes, instantly attempted to wipe the smile from her face. Lady Hingly-Tumpton, pleased to have cowed at least one of the chits, allowed a sour smile to twist her lips before she marched off to find Lady Humboldt with whom she could exclaim over Lady Helena's latest wild doings.

The rain held off until the children's games were over, which was a blessing. Another was that the kitchens managed to supply the food exactly as Lady Helena and the housekeeper had planned and the only contretemps was when Lady Trewes demanded answers to why certain dishes had not appeared.

Lady Hel used every ounce of tact she could to convince her hostess that that lady herself had canceled the more difficult menu in favor of one more suitable to al fresco dining and before long Lady Trewes was preening herself on her excellent planning.

Lady Hel rolled her eyes and made herself ready to untangle the next knot. That occurred not long after, when two boys, chasing after each other, tripped over a tent rope pulling the stake. A few screams when the canvas drooped, some laughter, one stolen kiss where the canvas hid a young couple who wished to wed but had been informed by their parents that they were too young.

That problem and other more minor incidents were quickly fixed. There was, after all, no *major* complication—much to the disappointment of some guests, as Lord Sanger had predicted.

The day finally ended, of course, as all end. Lord Sanger rode beside the carriage returning Lady Helena and Miss Stoner to the Cooper-Wainwrights'. A pistol sat in a saddle holster, and Miss Stoner's footman-cum-guard came riding beside the coachman, who drove with his blunderbuss across his knees. And of course, Rod Cole, unarmed but watchful.

Nothing occurred to mar the peace of the ride, but, Sanger's every sense, which had been honed while in the military, was on high alert. So it wasn't surprising that, within a small spinney, he noticed the sort of movement a restless horse makes. He almost turned off to check if it were not Mr. Woodhall lurking there, but decided it was better to do nothing which might endanger Helena or her charge.

Instead, once the ladies were safely home at the Cooper-Wainwrights', he returned by the same route and, carefully entering the spinney, checked for prints in the rain-softened soil. He found exactly what he expected, signs an animal had stood there for some time. He stared thoughtfully at the disturbed earth before remounting.

A grim look hung about his mouth and in his eyes as he returned to the Cooper-Wainwright estate. He avoided the house, going directly to the stables where he found Rod Cole. He walked the groom off into a nearby paddock away from any ears turned their direction.

"I've not known your mistress as long you have, Rod, but I know her well enough to guess she'll not be happy if I insist she be guarded day and night."

"She'd immediately begin dreaming up ways to evade

the men set to watch her," said the groom promptly, and then, a trifle apologetically, added, "She don't like being hemmed in, you see?"

"I see." Sanger described what he'd found. "I suspect Woodhall wants revenge, Rod. He's not the sort to come after you or myself. We might fight back, but Lady Helena . . . Frankly, I'm afraid for her very life."

The groom nodded thoughtfully. "The snake's a cornered rat now. He'll try to chew his way out of the trap."

"I think he did his chewing when he kidnapped Miss Stoner. Losing her to us will have turned the rat into a mad dog and we know how vicious mad dogs can be."

"I don't have a gun," said Rod, "but General Porson is still here—keeping an eye on Lady Catherine, you know. He might find me one."

Sanger nodded agreement, but was still thinking of the danger. "In my opinion Woodhall is most likely to attack when she's riding. Blast and bedamned to the man! Rod, it'll be bloody difficult to protect her when she goes back and forth between here and Sanger-Monkton."

"At least we'll need waste no more worry on the little Stoner," said Rod with a touch of irony. "She's to leave tomorrow. Her father sent his carriage, a driver, two guards and four outriders, all well armed. I doubt *she'll* have any trouble."

Sanger grinned. "Yes, there is no need for further concern about Miss Stoner. But I must do something about Lady Helena." His hand rose to his chin and he rubbed it again and again, the day's growth of beard making a soft raspy noise. "Rod, have you managed to spend an evening or two in any of the local taverns?"

"Once or twice," the groom admitted, tipping a look toward Sanger that was full of curiosity.

"Did you meet any ex-soldiers?"

"Sent home because they've lost a limb or with a weak chest maybe? That the sort you mean?"

"Hmm."

"I've seen three at the Blue Boar and some others at the Cricket."

"What sort of men, Rod?"

Rod frowned. "Didn't pay too much attention. Kept to themselves, rather. I'd guess reasonably good men down on their luck, maybe?"

"I wish I were not so damnably strapped for funds. One can buy loyalty, if one can afford it. Still, I can pay an honest wage. Do you think . . . ?"

Rod pondered the unspoken question. "Want me to see what I can find out about them? The barmaids'll know the locals."

"We must see the general, first. Then . . . Rod, if you find they are good men, tell them I'll find them work. Permanent work. Not just the patrol I need until the danger is past."

"A patrol . . . a good notion, that. They'll see to it no one lurks where Lady Hel will be riding. She doesn't need to know a thing about it."

"We'll not go so far as to keep her completely in the dark. She, too, must be on her guard, after all. She'll know you carry a gun, but I agree: I don't think I'll tell her about our patrol."

"I'll look out the men this evening."

"If you will send them to Sanger-Monkton I can make plans and see about arming them." Sanger frowned. "No, that won't do. I've a problem there. My predecessors emptied the gun room of anything which will still shoot and I doubt the men are trained to swords, which, in any case, only work if you are within arm's reach of your enemy!"

"Perhaps General Porson . . . ?"

"I'd better talk to him. I can tell him you are to be armed." Sanger eyed the groom. "Er . . . Rod . . ."

"Do I know how to shoot?" asked Rod, grinning widely.

"Do you?" asked Sanger bluntly.

"Grew up with Lady Hel, didn't I?" The young man grinned again. "We both learned under Lord Chabsley's huntsman. Lady Helena was generous that way. When we were small we played together and explored. When we got older she made me learn the things she learned. Her father didn't like my sneaking in to her lessons, so she taught me as she learned her letters." Rod grinned. "She threw a temper tantrum to beat all tantrums when I refused to learn to dance from the prissy dancing master Lady Catherine hired."

It was a very long speech for the groom and revealed his affection for Lady Helena. And yet Sanger heard nothing in the lad's voice of which he need be jealous—unless it was the other man's many years with the woman he was learning to love. Perhaps, as was sometimes the case when they were raised together from early childhood, servant and mistress were more like brother and sister than anything else.

"Come," he said, "I'll see to getting you a gun."

Rod retrieved Sanger's horse from where he'd tied it, and led the way through the maze of buildings behind the mansion. He left the animal near the kitchen garden and they approached the house. The dinner bell had not yet rung so Sanger sent a message in to General Porson, asking that the man join him in the back garden. There he explained his fears.

"You mean to arm discharged soldiers?" asked the general, his brows lowering over his eyes.

"That's my plan," said Sanger, "At least, I'd like to, but have no way of acquiring guns."

"Don't know if that's a good idea. Restless sorts. Not happy."

"I wouldn't be happy either if I were disabled doing my duty and then thrown on the trash pile and expected to stay nicely out of sight!"

Porson glowered. "Put that way it sounds pretty bad, but

the men know what to expect when they go into the army. Don't see why they whine when the worst happens. And don't know as if I'd trust 'em with guns."

"You fear Jacobites?" A muscle jumped in Sanger's jaw. Since leaving the army he'd heard many among the *ton* express fears of a revolution such as occurred some decades earlier in France. Far too many were of an age to vividly recall that horror.

As a result Parliament had instituted some harsh laws. It seemed to Sanger that that merely exacerbated the problems, but he couldn't seem to make anyone else see it that way. He drew in a deep breath and tried once more, finishing, ". . . And I mean to find work for these men once we know Lady Helena is safe. I'm certain there will be something they can do to earn their living if only I put my mind to it."

"Makes some sense, but still . . . don't know if I want to see guns in the hands of ex-soldiers," retorted the general stubbornly.

Sanger sighed. "General, have you any better notion of how I may protect my lady? One to which she will *agree?* I'd *like* to surround her with guards whenever she sets foot outside, but she'd never allow it."

The general paced along the path between neat rows of vegetables, swinging his cane ahead with every other step, placing the tip, and moving forward. It was a precise action, a habit begun long ago. Perhaps the man had been one of the more foppish officers, thought Sanger with a smile, one of those who always traveled with trunks of uniforms and a valet and his own wine . . . He'd known that sort in the Peninsula.

Finally General Porson stopped. Staring straight ahead, he swore softly.

"Can't think of anything, can you?" asked Sanger sympathetically, barely hiding humor which would be unappreciated by the general.

"Wench needs a cane taken to her backside!"

"If so, it should have been done years ago," said Sanger gently. "Now we must deal with the woman she is."

"I'll see to finding arms for your blasted patrol, but," added the general, biting off his words, "on your head be it if we're all murdered in our beds!"

"Yes, my responsibility and mine alone. I cannot thank you enough, and I believe you'll find Lady Catherine appreciative as well—"

That notion gave General Porson's thoughts a happier turn.

"—but please, whatever you do, do not let Lady Helena know what we're up to. If she discovers it, *she* is far more likely to murder us then is my patrol!"

The general gave a bark of laughter. "We'll say she's at least as likely to! You won't convince me those men aren't dangerous!"

Sanger sighed. It was rather difficult to argue the point when he'd yet to meet the men. "Don't, however, hide that you are finding a gun for Lady Helena's groom."

Lord Sanger had another few words with Rod and rode home to Sanger-Monkton where decent if not elegant quarters had been arranged for him in the caretaker's rooms.

Lady Helena was nobody's fool. When she discovered Rod was to be armed, she insisted she too be given a gun. She was forced, however, to ask her host to organize a shooting match before General Porson would agree to it. When he ceremoniously handed her a pistol and the shot and powder to go with it, he also, quite generously, told her he wouldn't have scorned having her in one of the squares in his regiment. He was more blunt with Rod. "Good man," he exclaimed. "Why aren't you in the army?"

"Because," Lady Helena answered for her groom, "the Cole men are bred to working in the Chabsley stables and *have* been for generations. It would never occur to anyone but you, General, that they should do anything else!"

No one pointed out to Lady Helena that Rod was *not* working in the Chabsley stables. No one dared remind her she was no longer Lady Helena Woodhall of Chabsley Manor, but merely Lady Helena Woodhall of nowhere in particular. So Rod wasn't from anywhere either. If anyone had dared do so, she'd merely have raised both brows, thinking such a suggestion beneath comment.

Besides, the real point was that Coles worked for Woodhalls and that remained the truth.

Lady Hel had a few words to say to Lord Sanger when they met, later that day, at Sanger-Monkton. They mainly had to do with his making plans without consulting her, but she ended her mild tirade with appreciation that he cared enough to worry!

"And do you not worry?" he asked, his concern writ large in his expression.

Her smile faded. "I know my cousin. I know he's vindictive. Worse yet, his situation has deteriorated. A rather terrible little man came to see Grandmother yesterday. He wanted Thurmand. When we couldn't help him, he demanded money. When we informed him we were not responsible for Thurmand's debts, he made threats."

"Against you and your grandmother?"

"Against Thurmand. So you see, not only will my cousin wish to retaliate for the harm he perceives I did him, he must do so from hiding, which he'll not like. He must be beside himself!"

"If I knew where your cousin had gone to earth—" Simon spoke with an edge to his voice. "—I'd be tempted to guide that fellow there myself!"

"I'd help you," said Lady Helena promptly. For a moment she put a hand on his arm, but then turned away and changed the subject. "Simon, have you any notion where the Mansanger muniment room is located? I searched for it the last time I was here but couldn't find it."

"You want the family papers? Why?"

"I went to the priest hole to get the statue of the lady to give to Grandmother and, curious, I opened the casket with that strange urn. Just to see if I could discover something we hadn't noticed, a paper explaining it or some such thing. Simon, did you notice it isn't really a trunk, but a container carved from a single piece of wood? The wood was halved and the inside is carved out so that exceedingly ugly vessel fits snugly. Why did someone go to so much trouble for the thing? I hunted for the records to see if I could discover the reason."

"I suppose I hadn't noticed they were missing—" He rubbed his chin. "—because my own family didn't have extensive records. But, now you raise the point, I've seen none and there should be documents going back to . . . well, at least, before Elizabeth. Maybe farther!"

"I will ask Grandmother."

"An excellent notion. She knew about the priest hole, so she may also know where my family's history is stored away! By the way, *did* you take her the statue?"

Helena's cheeks reddened. "I got interested in the urn and forgot!"

"I've been invited to dinner this evening. Why don't I bring it?"

"That would be better. It is, after all, yours, Simon."

"But without you two it would have remained hidden there." Simon draped an arm around her shoulders and they continued talking as they strolled through the rooms toward the library. "I suppose someone at some future date might wish to remodel the old portions of the house and if they'd torn out walls they'd have discovered it."

"Don't suggest you'll have descendants with so little feeling for history!"

"Or that *our* descendants will be so lacking in taste?" he corrected her. He chuckled when she blushed but forbore from further teasing. "I believe it unfair to burden future generations with demands they maintain what is no longer maintainable."

"Why would they not be able to keep this place up? Once we've restored it, there will be only maintenance to do."

"Helena, have you any notion what that involves in a place as old and rambling as this one is?"

"I very likely know better than you do," she retorted.

There might have been scorn or pride or at least a touch of irony in that, but actually, as Sanger realized before he became affronted, it was no more than a simple statement. He tightened his hold on her, pulling her closer for a moment, and then relaxed it again. "Ah," he said, "but what did you actually have to do with keeping Chabsley in good shape?"

"When I was sixteen my grandmother handed over its management. Of course it was only five years." Her lids drooped slightly over her eyes and the corners of her mouth tipped down very slightly.

"You still miss your father so much?"

"One recovers. It is only that he . . . understood me?"

Sanger chuckled. "What you really mean is that he is the only man you've ever known who would give you your head and laugh as you went your length?"

She smiled. "I don't think it was ever quite so bad as that. But he did encourage me in some of my demands for freedom and he did protect me, I suppose, from the consequences. Grandmother has had the very devil of a time since he died, convincing me I must put limits on my behavior."

"Will you think me very hen-hearted if I ask that you maintain some limits?"

Her smile broadened. "I am not so wild as I once was, Simon."

He pretended to shudder. "I will admit I am glad of *that* and tell you I have a very great admiration for your father."

"Why?"

"That he survived your youth, of course."

Helena pretended to pummel him and the tussle led to far more interesting behavior. Only Simon's strong will allowed him to set her firmly away before they'd gone too far.

"Behave, wench," he growled.

"I'm not certain I want to behave," she said, her eyes saying still more than her words as a heated look passed over him.

"You'll have to," he said, a muscle working in his jaw. "I'm damned if I'll debauch you." She blushed and he apologized for the crudity, finishing in a far softer voice. "When we come together, Helena, it must be for all the right reasons."

Helena sighed. "Should I apologize?"

"Why? Because we are attracted to each other and occasionally manifest that attraction as is meant to happen? The problem is merely that we must keep those expressions of, hmm, affection within bounds!"

"Then," she said on a dry note, "I think we'd better move or I may throw myself at you again."

They moved. "Here we are." Simon went alone into the priest's hole to get the box containing the statue. Helena almost followed, when it seem to take him forever, but then he returned. "You are correct that the casket was designed especially for the urn. I wonder why the family valued it so highly."

"We'll ask Grandmother. Perhaps she knows, and if not then she may know where to find your history. I can search it."

"It might be a very long and boring job of work," he warned.

"To the contrary, I will enjoy it immensely. My governess introduced me to the Chabsley papers when teaching me something of our history. I found the records fascinating. Oh, I admit ancient deeds and account books quickly become boring, but the diaries and journals—some of them bring the past to life in ways you can't imagine. We've one written during a year when the plague was rampant. The horrors the lady describes are not to be believed and then there is a simple statement that her son has come down with it, the page blank except for those few words."

Sanger waited a moment but she didn't go on. "Well?"

"Nothing. That is it. There is no more."

"And," he said softly, "that is, perhaps, the greatest horror of all?"

She gave him a wondering look. "You are the only one to whom I've told the story who has understood that. I've wondered if the boy died and she lost heart for her journal or if she took the sickness from him and also died. There is no record. Such times are ones of chaos. There is nothing more. Some years later, new records begin in an entirely different hand—a very bad one!—and no more journals for some decades."

"So you would know how to study my family record if we can find it."

They strolled back the way they'd come, joining Rod at the back door where he had tied Lady Helena's horse to the back of Sanger's curricle. Rod was already mounted on his own excellent hack.

The two men exchanged a look and Rod nodded. Helena narrowed her eyes, wondering what they meant by it, but, for the moment, put the question aside. She would need Rod on his own if she were to press him for explanations. After reviewing the next few days she swore under her breath. The next morning, early, they were off to the races at Doncaster and there would be no time when she could get her groom alone. Lady Helena tucked away the thought she must not forget to interrogate him. She was not about to have him keeping secrets from her and certainly not secrets with Sanger!

As they drove toward the Cooper-Wainwrights', she noted a man with only one hand riding along a ridge some way above and to the side of the road. She'd seen him before. A military-looking man, she'd thought then, and watching him now, agreed with that assessment. She'd also, once or twice, seen a man who limped rather badly strolling along the route she'd ridden. Both men were armed.

"Sanger," she asked, suddenly reaching a conclusion she felt foolish for not reaching sooner, "have you set out guards to protect me? Does Rod know all about it?"

"Why should I do that?" he asked, ignoring the last question.

"Because you are worried Thurmand will, once again, wish to do me an injury."

"You are wrong," he said placidly.

"He will not wish to harm me?"

"As before, he will wish to *kill* you."

It took her a moment to assimilate his words. "Kill me." She swallowed, hard. "As he wished to do before he learned he'd not inherit from me."

"But now it is because he wants revenge."

"That *had* occurred to me. General Porson gave me a pistol."

"Which you leave in your saddle holster! It will do you no good if Woodhall finds you in the house."

She cast him a startled look. "Surely, there are too many people around and about . . ."

"All of whom are busy in one way or another. There are many ways he could get in."

"Damn—"

Sanger hid a quick grin at the unladylike expletive.

"I have enjoyed my days at Sanger-Monkton, making plans and overseeing the cleaning and repairs!"

"I would have you alive and able to enjoy them once they are done, Helena," he said. "With me." Although speaking gently Sanger felt a hole in his middle at the thought she might yet die and he'd lose her, that they would *not* live together at Sanger-Monkton. "Helena . . ."

She interrupted. "Yet you did not warn me to be alert!"

"I got you the pistol. I didn't know until today that you weren't keeping it by you." He glanced down at her. "Now I do know, I am warning you, am I not?" He debated making her angry. Ah well, in for a penny . . . "Besides," he admitted, "Rod is watching over you."

His words confirmed that Rod had plotted with Sanger and kept it from her. Lady Helena used her whole repertory of swear words and phrases, including the new one she'd learned the night they'd rescued Miss Stoner. When she paused for breath Sanger handed her the reins and clapped softly before taking them back again.

Helena laughed. She couldn't help it. In the face of Sanger's gentle mockery her anger faded and humor revived. Also the tug to her emotions his presence always induced, something which had become so welcome she felt bereft when he was not near.

She drew in a deep breath, putting those feelings back in the corner of her mind where they lived. "I am a fool to resent that you care enough to see to my safety, but old habits die hard, Sanger. I have always been of an overly independent nature. At least, the high sticklers say I am overly independent. I, of course, do not agree."

"It would be a bad thing in you if you were not also intelligent enough that you realize there are times you need help." The entrance to the Cooper-Wainwrights' came into view. "Ah. We've arrived. Lady Cooper-Wainwright is very kind to have a room kept for me where I may leave my better clothes for occasions such as this."

"You stay the night, do you not?"

"Tonight I do. We make an early start tomorrow."

"I hope Big Red does at least as well as I think he will."

"I merely hope he wins!"

"Oh, he'll do *that*. Rod looked over the other entries in his race and was exceedingly scornful of their history."

"I see."

She noted his sudden withdrawal. "What have I said?" she asked.

"That Trewes entered Red in a race he is certain to win but which will give the horse no reputation for having done so."

"If that is his plan, Trewes is a fool. Red will come in so far ahead of the rest of the pack that nothing else will be talked of!"

Sanger's mood lightened at her half serious, half humorous analysis. *"Of course*. Why did I not think of that?"

"I don't know. Why did you not?"

"I haven't a notion. You are very good for me, did you know that?"

"I try," she said quietly.

There was something in her voice that had Sanger glancing at her, curious at what she really meant. Unfortunately, there was no time just then, to probe. Sanger tucked his curiosity away to bring out when he could speak to her with no interruptions.

Ten

Lord Cooper-Wainwright's coachman stopped so that the open carriage faced the shallow valley in which the races were to run. Lord Sanger, Lady Helena at his side, pulled his curricle in beside it. The men instantly descended and went to the back where they conferred.

"Sanger," called Lady Helena, when it looked as if he and Wainwright were about to walk off.

Simon returned to her side and she handed him a small purse and wasn't at all surprised when her grandmother tossed another his way. Sanger, who had frowned very slightly as he reached for Lady Helena's purse, laughed. "I cannot scold a lady when her mentor joins her folly! Very well, ladies. I will place your bets when I lay my own."

He bowed and returned to where Lord Cooper-Wainwright impatiently awaited him. Because of delays that morning, they'd barely enough time before the race to do their business and return to the carriages.

While they were absent, Lady Helena did her best to trace the course. It was, she thought, not a particularly difficult one, but had its tricky spots. There was, for instance, a tight turn followed almost immediately by a jump over a stone wall. She wondered how well Big Red handled surprises of that sort. There were a few places where the course passed through woods or a spinney. She hoped race officials were posted to prevent any of the nastier tricks sometimes played on horse or rider where no one could see.

"Is everything all right?" she asked Sanger when he rejoined the women.

"Quite."

The word was terse and Sanger's brow ridged with a combination of worry and hope and anticipation and . . .

Helena couldn't read every emotion which slipped across his features, disappeared, only to be replaced by some other as a new thought passed through his mind. Between them, hidden by their clothes, she covered his hand which, white-knuckled, clutched the edge of the seat between them. He spread two fingers, caught several of hers between them, and held her in that odd clasp as the entries lined up for the start of Big Red's race.

The race itself was an anticlimax. As Lady Helena had predicted, Big Red won it handily.

Too handily? she wondered. She saw a man approach Lord Trewes as he stood proudly beside Red and watched them speak. Obviously the stranger said something which upset Trewes, who shook his head, then shook it again more vigorously. Helena wished she knew what was going on.

"Simon?"

"I don't know. Wainwright?"

"I *believe* it is Jason Lord," said His Lordship hesitantly.

"Who is Jason Lord?" asked Simon, never taking his eyes from the scene below.

"Lord? Owns racing stables here and in Ireland. I've heard he likes to challenge new talent, matching it to one of his unknowns."

"Trewes looks like nothing so much as a snared rabbit," suggested Lady Catherine bitingly.

Helena agreed. She watched Lord Trewes mop his brow, shake his head . . . turn away only to have his arm caught. A rabbit cornered by a fox who was about to pounce!

"Trewes is a cautious man," said Martin Wainwright, his voice dry as the dust raised by the horses in the race which had just begun. "He prefers a sure thing until he's tested a horse in every possible situation. Throwing Big Red into a private race against unknown competition is not his style."

They watched Trewes glance warily from face to face of the men surrounding himself and Lord. He appeared to collapse in on himself as he nodded. Once. A roar of approval went up from those surrounding the two owners. Lord bowed. As he turned away from Trewes, Lady Helena noticed his tight little smile of satisfaction. She also saw him glance toward a wizened little man, very likely a retired groom, and nod once.

"Simon, Big Red must be watched every minute!" she said, her tone sharp with concern.

"Why?"

She told him what she'd seen and her suspicions.

Simon nodded. "Thank you, Helena. I'll see to it. Rod?" he called, and he and the groom, followed by Lord Cooper-Wainwright and his coachman, all of whom had overheard Helena express her fear, headed down the path to the valley. Helena never took her eyes off Big Red, watching everyone who approached anywhere near, but, at the time Sanger arrived at the animal's side, she was almost certain no one had attempted anything of a nasty nature.

Word traveled quickly among the race-goers. Big Red was to run a private race first thing in the morning against a newcomer from the Galloway Lord Stables. Helena recalled her father saying that Jason Lord thought it a great joke to dedicate a good horse to Lord Galloway if the horse was bred in the Galloway Lord stables.

Trewes was not a happy man. As Wainwright said, Trewes had quite a different method of introducing a horse into the racing community. Facing off with another excellent animal right at the start was *not* the way he did things. He considered telling anyone who would listen that Red had strained a hock and then take the animal home. At once.

But Sanger spoke quickly and at length and finally convinced Trewes to allow the race to go forward . . . and then nearly undid all his good work by insisting the horse be guarded closely between now and race time!

"Lord wouldn't . . ." Trewes began.

"I didn't say *he* would," interrupted Sanger. "A private race draws excessive betting. Some idiot may wish to assure his bet is good. That is all."

He'd no intention of telling Trewes that Lady Helena had seen a silent message pass between Mr. Lord and a man who might once have been a jockey. There was no proof anything underhanded was planned and, although he was not yet called its king, Lord was too big a man in the racing world for a novice like Sanger or a lightweight like Trewes to accuse him of fixing a race! Privately, however, Sanger asked Lord Cooper-Wainwright what was known of the racing ethics of the man who wished to be king of racing and made no bones about it. Wainwright didn't know.

"If you don't mind," Sanger to Trewes, "I'll help guard Red."

"And if I do mind?" asked Trewes bitterly.

"I will help to guard him anyway," said Sanger and grinned.

"Bah. Nonsense. But if you want a sleepless night for no good reason, then who am I to interfere?" Trewes turned on his heel and left, not even giving his groom orders.

"Where are the supplies you brought?" Sanger asked the groom.

Sanger and Rod secured Red's food in a locked chest and Rod went off to clean a bucket and bring in water he knew was pure. Sanger helped Lord Trewes's groom rub Red down and secure him in a loose box which had no entry from any direction but the divided door at which someone would stand guard.

"My lord?" asked the Treweses' groom, diffidently.

"Hmm?"

"You think we'll have a problem?"

"I hope not. I will, however, feel a lot happier if we take special care. You!" he interrupted himself, approaching a little man sidling closer to Red's stall than necessary. "Off with you."

"Just wan' ta see 'im."

"You'll see him tomorrow when he races. Take yourself off and don't come back," ordered Simon. The sneak crept away, sending a scowl Simon's way as he went out the double doors at the end of the alley between the boxes.

Simon stared after him. He wished he'd asked Lady Helena for a description of the man to whom Lord had given the nod. And he wished he had more help. But he didn't. So, having done everything possible, he settled himself on an upturned bucket to toss dice for ha'penny points with Trewes's groom.

The night held two alarms. The first occasion something flew over Lord Sanger's head and in through the open half door to the stall. Sanger had only moments to prevent Red from eating what proved to be a doctored apple. On the second occasion, Simon heard an exceedingly soft rasping sound from the back of the stall. He cautioned the coachman who also heard it, went into Red's stall, soothed the restless animal and crept to the back. There he waited. Finally a chunk of wood fell away and Simon pressed himself to the side where he'd not be seen.

For a moment nothing happened and then he heard a soft crooning voice, a sing-song sound barely audible within the stall. Big Red heard it, however, and was curious. He turned and snuffled briefly at the hole, backing up when a hand was thrust under his nose. Simon caught the wrist, dumped the contents and moved between Red and whatever it was. Red was not pleased and butted Sanger hard enough he very nearly released the struggling hand.

"I've caught our sneak," said Sanger.

Rod came into the stall, laughed softly when he saw how Sanger had trapped the man and then, taking the Cooper-Wainwright coachman with him, went and took the man in charge.

They marched the fellow into the stable where, having cleaned up the tainted oats, Sanger awaited him. The apple and the oats were set on the top of the upturned bucket. When, struggling between his captors, the man was dragged before him, Sanger stared at him, rubbing his chin. Finally he picked up the apple and thrust it toward the little man's face. "Eat."

The fellow jerked away to one sided "No!"

"Eat."

"Don't make me!" Sweat popped out on the man's ashen face.

"Why should I not make you?"

"It's . . . It's . . ." The fellow's body suddenly stiffened, his eyes widening in what looked like surprise, and then he slumped between Rod and the coachman.

Everyone had heard the shot. Sanger moved first, racing to the door . . . but it was pitch black outside, and, except for what might have been the snap of a stick some distance away, there was no evidence anyone had been there. Sanger sighed. It had never occurred to him that the situation would get this far out of hand. He turned back.

"Rod, you'll have to find the constable and a magistrate. I haven't a notion where to find either, so perhaps you should begin by waking Lord Trewes, who has a room above the tap room at the Little Digger. You might try throwing stones at his windows. I'd prefer it if we managed to prevent the whole world knowing what has happened."

A muscle jumped in his jaw. "Suddenly, I very much want to see this race is run." His eyes narrowed. *Run honestly.*

The Treweses' groom, embarrassed at having cast up his accounts, diffidently asked what he could do to help.

"Think you could stay awake the rest of the night?"

"Of course I can," said the groom stoutly.

"Then I think you'll help most if you and the coachman guard that hole in the outer wall. There will be enough activity in here I don't believe we'll have more trouble *inside.*"

Simon also decided he'd ride Red himself. Trewes would object that Simon was too large, that his extra weight would disadvantage Red, but Simon had ridden the horse during his early training. A lot. They knew each other, the little tricks which must be avoided or which aided.

Blast it! He'd ride if he had to buy Red back from Trewes, and he'd do it even if it meant borrowing from Helena! Red *would* win the race Jason Lord had forced on Trewes. Sanger relaxed. At least, he'd do what *he* could to see Red won. There was always the possibility, of course, Lord had the better horse.

Sanger chuckled softly at the scorn he heard in his mind at the notion there *was* no horse better than Red. Which was nonsense. Red was outstanding, but that didn't mean he couldn't be beaten.

A man, his graying hair tied back with a black ribbon in an old-fashioned queue, bustled into the stable and interrupted Simon's thoughts. "Now then," he grumbled. "What's all this, then? You Lord Sanger, then?"

Sanger forced his mind to dealing with the magistrate. He explained about the private race, about his fears such a race might lead to someone making a bet he decided later was more than he could afford to lose, and his fear there might be tampering to assure the right horse won. He explained how he had volunteered to see nothing happened to Red. Then he pointed out the apple, the little pile of oats, the hole in the back wall and how he'd caught the man's wrist.

And finally, soberly, how he'd begun to interrogate the man when, suddenly, a shot had rung out. "The poor fellow died instantly," finished Sanger.

"Tried to catch the marksman?"

"By the time I got outside there was no one in sight. I may have heard a stick crack under an incautious foot, but I'm not even certain in what direction. You know how difficult it is to pinpoint sound at night."

"Hurumph." The magistrate eyed Sanger. "Military man, hmm?"

"I was."

"Seem to recall reading in dispatches about a Mansanger of whom Wellington seems to think highly."

"I'm told my name has appeared in dispatches, but not, of course, for some time. I had to sell out when I inherited the title and I was invalided home several months before that."

"Now I remember." The magistrate snapped his fingers. "Caught a ball rescuing some idiotic vain hope, carrying it over the top. Never approved those vain hope strategies. Now you tell me whether you couldn't have . . ." The magistrate noted how the blood flowed into Sanger's neck and up into his ears. He looked around and noticed the wide-eyed interest in those listening. "Embarrassing you. Apologize," he said gruffly. "Besides, got a murder to see to." He toed the body. "Not that I can see what's to be done. Inquest, of course. Death at the hands of a man or men unknown bound to be the verdict." He sighed gustily—and then yawned widely.

"I doubt very much you'll find any proof to connect anyone to the actual shooting." Sanger thought of telling the magistrate that Lady Helena had seen Lord signal this creature, but then Lady Helena would be called to testify to what she'd seen pass between the dead man and Lord—

and that was out of the question. He mustn't do or say anything which would bring Lady Helena to the gentleman's attention. Ladies should never be put in a position of such public notoriety!

Which meant he must, somehow, keep Lady Helena from doing or saying anything *to bring herself* to the magistrate's attention! He'd better ask Lady Catherine's help—he suppressed a wry grin—or, perhaps her advice. It was bad enough that Helena's cousin seemed determined, in her words, to do her an injury. He feared that rousing Mr. Lord's anger, a man he judged far more competent than Thurmand ever could be, would result in disaster!

The possibility shook him more deeply than he'd expected. The longer he knew Helena the more aware he grew that he couldn't bear to lose her. He had had nightmares that she would take up his original suggestion and do the rational thing: she'd break their engagement and he'd spend the rest of his life regretting it. Worrying about that possibility and doing his best to make it impossible that Thurmand get close to Helena was more than enough. He didn't need Jason Lord complicating things.

The magistrate spoke with the race officials and, surprising everyone including Mr. Lord and Lord Trewes, an announcement was made to the effect the private race would be run on the inner oval in full view of everyone and that spotters would be placed along the course. Any shenanigans in the running of the race would mean instant expulsion from every race course in England.

"What the . . . !" Jason Lord glared at Trewes, but Lord Trewes was obviously in shock himself. Lord glanced around, saw the gray-haired man with the queue watching him and trod over to his side. "What has happened? Why are we being treated like a pair of criminals?"

"A man died last night. He'd tried, twice, to tamper with one of the horses."

"Died? There was a fight?"

"He was shot in the back after he was caught in his second attempt to tamper." The magistrate never took his eyes from Lord's but Jason Lord, if guilty, had himself well in hand and there was nothing to see.

In fact, Sanger, watching closely, was convinced Lord knew nothing about the night's adventures. He frowned, wondering who *had* been involved . . . because if it weren't Lord, then there was still another villain and there was no clue at all to whom that might be. Or perhaps, as he'd suggested to the magistrate, someone who had bet more than he could afford to lose . . . but would such a one *kill*?

Simon decided there was nothing he could do. Before a race, Sanger had an old habit of discussing the matter with his mount and now he went to Red, catching his bridle and bringing the horse's head down. He had a serious discussion with Red who seemed to nod his head occasionally in agreement and, once, shook it. Sanger tipped his head, thought for a moment and spoke again.

People watching wore wide grins—except for the little old jockey up on Lord's horse who frowned.

"Got it all straight?" asked Mr. Lord, grinning wickedly. He'd shrugged off his irritation and accepted the official's verdict after learning there'd been a problem in the night. "Hear you're to ride Big Red. Well, can't say I'll object. Big man for Big Red! But won't do the horse no good, carrying the extra weight, will it?"

"That's what I told him," grumbled Trewes. "Won't be my fault if Red loses. It'll be *his*."

"That's right. Find someone or something to blame in advance," said Lord in a falsely soothing tone.

"Damn you!" Trewes turned on his heel and marched off.

Jason Lord shrugged. "If I didn't like that horse, I'd not

have challenged Trewes. He's a fool, but he's got a horse there I wish were mine. Ah! I see they are signaling that we are to bring out our mounts. Ready, Gramps?" he asked the groom who grinned at him, several gaps revealing long-lost teeth. Lord shook his head. "Don't know why I continue to let you ride, you old geezer, you!"

In a surprisingly deep voice the little man perched atop the Lord horse responded, " 'Cause I keep on winnin', that's why."

"But not today," said Simon, mounting Red. "Red and I discussed it and he says he'll have no problem running the legs off your beast."

Jason Lord's jockey cackled. "Oh, a right one, you be. Good luck to you. You'll be needing it!"

Sanger reran the man's words through his head, listening for a threat. He heard none and smiled. "The same back at you!" he said, grinning.

They walked their mounts across to the oval. Simon looked up to where Helena would be sitting in the Cooper-Wainwright carriage with her grandmother and Lady Cooper-Wainwright. He let his eyes trail along the row of densely packed carriages and caught sight of a waving parasol. He nodded.

"I don't believe there were so many here yesterday," he said, taking a second look at the crowd.

"Every man in the county, if he didn't already own a horse, must have stolen one to get here," said Lord from where he led his horse and jockey. "I've always wondered how word of a private race travels so far so fast."

"The same way servants know everything before we do. And if you figure that one out, Wellington would like to hear the way of it. Getting word where it is needed as quickly as possible is his major problem!"

"Ah! I did hear you were an army man before you inherited. Miss it?"

"Occasionally, but I'm mostly much too busy to have time to miss anything."

"With your own stables?" asked Lord casually.

Sanger chuckled. "Not a stupid man, are you? I've been trying to keep that under wraps until a horse proves himself."

Lord nodded. "You can raise stud fees sky high if the sire produces a winner. Think you have one there, do you?"

Sanger chuckled again. "You said yourself you wished Red were yours!"

"Slip of the tongue," said Lord, tongue firmly in cheek. "Well, here we are. May the best horse win." He took off his hat and slapped it against his groom's back. Then he looked at Sanger. "You talk to your beast. I give my groom a swat on his behind. We're all a bunch of superstitious idiots." He nodded to the race official who approached the suddenly restless horses. "They are all yours," he said and walked off.

Two minutes later the race began.

Lady Helena rose to her feet. "He didn't say he was racing! Why is he racing?"

Lady Catherine tugged at her granddaughter's skirts. "What are you ranting on about?"

"Sanger. He's racing Red."

"He's riding?" asked the dowager, sharply. "Why?"

"Because he's a fool," said Lord Trewes, coming up to the carriage just then. "If he loses me that race I'll take him to court! How dare he demand to ride Big Red. How dare he take over control of my stables last night? How dare he . . ." He blinked. "Why are you looking at me like that?" he asked Lady Catherine.

"You are a fool." Her Ladyship turned back and focused her glass on the course. "At the moment it looks like a tie between them. Not a nose difference."

"It does?" asked Trewes and, not asking permission,

climbed onto the crowded coach next to the Cooper-Wainwrights' carriage. The young men atop the coach objected, but subsided when Trewes spit out that he owned the red gelding everyone was watching. Grousing only a bit, they made room for him.

Trewes was finally able to look across the valley to where the two horses paced each other. "Why doesn't he whip the creature in?"

"Too far yet," said a knowing young man. "Wind him if he pushes him too soon."

"Lot you know," muttered Trewes. "He's falling behind!"

"No he isn't," said another. "See?"

The two horses traded places for a small lead again and again. Each time Red fell back a pace, Trewes would hold his head and groan. It became a game with the young men to groan with him and then to give a loud heigh-ho when the horses reversed their positions. The pair reached the curve at the end, came around it . . . and then the true race began.

Sanger leaned into Red's neck whispering unnecessary words of encouragement, but it seemed Red had taken his rival in dislike and wasn't about to let the creature in front of him. In fact, it was almost as if Big Red realized they'd come to the last furlong because he suddenly lengthened his stride and, to those watching, seemed float across the finish line a good neck ahead of his opponent.

Trewes sat down hard on one of the temporary benches the young men had fastened atop the coach. His mouth gaped open and he stared into the valley. "He won."

"Handily," said one of the young men cheerfully. "Told you he'd win," he said to a friend who was cursing softly. "Told you I've an eye for a horse," he gloated.

"Oh shut up," said the friend. "Still say Lord always has the winner."

Trewes nodded. "Always."

"We'll say *almost* always from now on!" said the young man gloatingly. Obviously, *he'd* bet on Big Red.

Helena, from her carriage overheard most of what passed between Trewes and the lads. "Bet on Lord's horse, Lord Trewes?" she asked, her voice far too innocent-sounding to be true.

Lady Catherine glanced at her sharply, then looked up to where Trewes looked sick as a dog. She leaned back in her seat, covered her mouth with her hand, and laughed softly. Passing a quick glance at Trewes who still sat slumped, gazing blindly ahead of himself, she chuckled more loudly. "Trewes," she called and he jumped, turning to look down at the dowager. "Had you not better take yourself down to the winner's circle?"

"Winner's . . . circle?" He blinked again. "Winner's circle! Oh yes. Of course."

"Maybe," said Lady Catherine evilly, "what you win in the racing purse will make up for what you bet on Lord's horse."

"Make up for . . . ?" He shook his head, seemed to catch himself and scowling at Lady Catherine, growled, "You just keep your nose out of my business."

"Oh, quite gladly," said Lady Catherine, convinced she was right and Trewes would lose money on the race. If word got around he'd bet on his rival's horse he'd become a laughingstock. Catherine debated sowing the word when she heard a young man on the neighboring carriage make just that guess.

"No!" said another. "You'd never bet against your own horse. It isn't done."

"Oh, I dunno. I've heard of cases where a man has fixed a race *against* his own horse and bets heavily on another," mused still another.

"Remember yesterday? Lord Trewes didn't wish to race against Lord's horse? He made that obvious to the meanest observer. Perhaps he hedged his bet with Lord by laying another bet."

"Very likely. Maybe he'll have more faith in his own stock now."

"I doubt it. That big, rangy, red gelding is not his usual style of animal at all," said the knowing young man. "Besides, word gets around he bet against his own horse, he'll never have the nerve to enter another race!"

"That'd be a shame. Wonder if *mon père* would cough up the possibles and let me buy that Big Red," said another.

"Too late in the quarter for us to find enough amongst us we could go partners," said still another glumly. "At least, my pockets are to let until I get my next quarter's allowance."

Lady Helena, who had been listening while keeping her eyes on Sanger, turned her attention fully to the valley. The horses and owners were near the winner's circle. She watched Lord approach and her eyes widened when Jason Lord ignored Trewes and went to Simon holding out his hand. She wished she could hear what was being said, but the sudden quiet and then the wave of noise gave her a clue.

"I fear Jason Lord just revealed Simon's secret," she guessed.

"What secret?" asked Lady Catherine.

"His only asset before he inherited the title was a stable his father left him. Simon hoped he could establish its reputation *before* admitting to ownership. Stud fees and that sort of thing," she added when Lady Catherine frowned.

"And you think Jason Lord just let the rabbit out of the trap?"

"I'm almost certain of it. See?"

She indicated the men crowding around Simon who looked hot and harassed. She watched Jason Lord's mouth tip up at one side and his eyes narrow in amusement. She watched Trewes scowl and, hands fisted into his sides, glare at anyone who looked his way. Angry at everyone, his lordship almost fumbled the small bag of coins casually tossed his way by Jason Lord, who turned to his own animal before he even determined if Trewes caught it. Lord led his horse, still topped by the diminutive jockey, away to the stable.

"Always thought Lord a rascal," mused Lady Catherine. "An amusing rascal, of course."

"I doubt if Simon thinks him all that amusing!" retorted Lady Helena, who was upset that her fiancé's plans were overturned.

"You know, Hel," said Catherine, ignoring her granddaughter, "I wouldn't be at all surprised if, in future, those two didn't become the best of friends. Rivals when they've horses racing, of course, but otherwise? No, not surprised at all."

Eleven

"Why don't you train your horses and race them yourself?" asked Cooper-Wainwright when he and Sanger finally had a moment to themselves.

"Too chancy. I don't want anything to do with all that."

"But you'll breed horses someone else can race?"

Sanger grinned. "Never said I was a logical soul, did I?"

"Can't say you ever did. Of course I haven't known you all that long." Wainwright's brows arched.

The expression drew a chuckle from Sanger followed by a yawn. "I'm about to fall asleep on my feet. Must be getting old. I can remember times in the army when I got no more than snatches of sleep for several days and I could still function in top form."

"Yes, but then what happened when all the excitement was over?" asked Wainwright shrewdly.

"Hmm. I remember. I'd sleep hours. When do you mean to leave?"

"I'd like to see the first two races this afternoon but then I'll start home. That is, I will if it is all right with Lady Catherine and Lady Hel."

Lord Sanger yawned again. "I'll remember, in future, to allow someone else to be responsible for all-night vigils."

"You sat up with Big Red?" asked Cooper-Wainwright. "I knew you meant to have him guarded, but I didn't know you had it in your head to do it yourself."

"I'd reason to suspect trouble. I didn't like leaving un-
trained men to deal with it."

"Was there trouble?"

Sanger sobered. He stopped and when Wainwright did
as well, softly told him what had happened the night before. "We would like to keep it quiet, but I don't know if
that's possible." Sanger frowned, recalling Helena's obser-
vations the day before. "I'd better have a few words with
my lady before finding a bed."

More tired than he liked to admit, Sanger returned to
the carriage, and Lady Helena leaned over the edge. "You
will recall seeing Lord nod to a man you described as a
retired jockey?" he asked.

"Yes. The man rode Lord's horse today." Her brows
arched. "A little old I'd have thought."

Relief flooded Sanger that the dead man was someone
other than Lord's man and that Lady Hel needn't be involved. "He isn't a young man, but he's a very good jockey.
Helena, there was trouble last night. I just want you to
know it didn't involve that particular jockey."

"You are certain?"

Sanger recalled their prisoner sagging between Rod and
the coachman. *"Quite certain."* He yawned a jaw-cracking
yawn.

"You didn't sleep last night," accused Lady Helena.

"No, I didn't." Sanger was prompt to use the opening
to escape before his lady demanded a round tale of the
night's alarms. "I will, if you'll excuse me, find my bed for
a few hours. I believe we are to have a picnic later? I will
rejoin you then." He reached for her hand and drew it to
his lips, his gaze holding hers. " 'Til then, my lady," he
said softly and, before she could say a word, he walked
away.

Garbled stories of the death made the rounds long before
Lord Sanger rejoined their party and, although Cooper-
Wainwright did what he could by relating the true tale, Lady

Helena wasn't really happy until she, once again, had Sanger where she could see him. Realizing how deeply she needed to see him safe and well, made her unhappy all over again. It would be hell married to this man, loving him when he didn't love her!

Their picnic was interrupted by those who insisted Sanger tell, again and again, his version of what had happened. Only when the racing officials announced that the first race of the afternoon would begin in fifteen minutes did the crowd around the Cooper-Wainwright party thin out and finally disappear.

Sanger, who had managed, pretty well, to keep his temper while interrogated by one person after another, lost it when Trewes appeared pooh-poohing that there had been any problem at all. His voice low and but biting, Sanger asked, "A dead man is no problem?"

"A groom down on his luck," blustered Trewes. "Very likely all for the best, you know. Man'd probably starve to death come winter . . ." His eye widened in alarm when Sanger rose slowly to his full height, his body tensed. "Oh, come now," blustered Trewes, stepping back once and then again, "you know I speak the truth!"

"No man deserves to be shot in the back. *No man.* If you had ever been at war, had seen the cruelty of death again and again, experienced the carnage, the blood, the screams of pain, both man and horse, the . . ."

Cooper-Wainwright put his hand on Sanger's shoulder. "Ladies present," he muttered.

"Yes." Sanger shut his mouth tightly for the space of half a moment. "Of course," he added and forced himself to relax. "Trewes, you offered me hospitality when I needed it and for that I am under an obligation to you—"

"Also owe me a tour of your stables," inserted Trewes, who had relaxed when Cooper-Wainwright calmed Sanger.

"—but you came as close as that—" He held a finger and thumb up, very nearly touching. "—to telling what you promised to keep secret. Your groom guessed it, so I'd imagine others did as well. Therefore," he finished coldly, "we are even. There will be no tour."

"Hey now!"

"No man deserves to be shot in the back," repeated Sanger, his eyes narrowed. "No man deserves to die like a mad dog put down. Do not ever again pretend there was no problem last night or I'll—" Sanger's brows drew in at the thought. "—begin to wonder whose hand held the gun." His eyes on Trewes, his hand went to his chin and he rubbed it several times as he did when thinking. "Hmm."

"Here now," said Trewes, once again alarmed, "don't go thinking what ain't true. Was in my bed until that man of yours got me up."

Sanger's brow arched. "I don't believe I accused you, Trewes."

But Trewes obviously felt otherwise. "Wish I'd never set eyes on you or on that Big Red. Wish I'd never met you."

Cooper-Wainwright tipped his head. "Bet against your own horse, Trewes? Not the thing, you know. Not the thing at all."

"Didn't want him raced."

"Yes," said his lordship. "Just how badly did you not want him raced?"

"Here now!" Trewes swung back to Sanger. "See? Now there'll be all sorts of suspicions going round and about. Slander! I'll sue you for slander!"

"Nothing will go beyond this circle if you keep your voice down," said Sanger calmly.

Without proof he could not accuse Trewes before the magistrate. Nevertheless, he'd guess that, although Trewes hadn't had his own hand in it, it was his hirelings and that they'd gone farther than his lordship had meant them to do. He'd believe to his dying day that Trewes had done his best to tamper with his own horse. With Big Red!

"I don't suppose you'd like to sell Red back to me, would you?"

Trewes drew himself up and his sly self-possession returned. "Can't."

"Sold him to Jason Lord, did you?" asked Sanger.

Trewes lost his momentary gain. His eyes bugged out. "How the devil did you guess that?"

Sanger eyed the man. "Because you are clear as glass, Trewes. One knows how you'll react in any situation. You had Big Red's racing career planned out, did you not, to the last win? And then Lord upset it all. There was nothing for it but to get rid of Red."

"Don't see that," argued Trewes. "Could have changed my plans."

"Not when Red ran and won a race against one of Lord's coming animals. He proved himself too good. You'd have had to enter him in races where he'd have met real challenge. Oh, enough of this. I wish to see this race. Have a good day, Trewes—if you can." Sanger bowed and turned away, joining Lady Catherine and Lady Helena in the open carriage.

Trewes looked after Sanger a trifle fearfully. "What'd he mean by it? What'd he mean?"

"I haven't a notion," said Cooper-Wainwright in a what appeared a friendly tone, "but I'll tell you this, Trewes, in future, I believe I'll avoid betting on races in which you've a horse running." He also bowed and turned away.

Trewes looked around himself, assured himself no one had overheard their discussion, and, assuring himself the two men would never discuss mere suspicions with anyone else, regained his self-possession and strutted off to rejoin his own party.

Lady Catherine had a few words to say about their progress home. "I feel as if we've our own private army."

"It does seem rather excessive, does it not? Three riders with guns, a guard beside the driver and a blunderbuss at the driver's feet. I wonder they didn't hand us pistols to put in our reticules."

"Probably didn't think of it," said Lady Catherine, proving she knew nothing of the gift her granddaughter had received. "Shall I suggest it?"

"Please do," said Lady Hel, although she already carried a pistol. Then she remembered. "There is something I keep meaning to ask you."

"Hmm." Lady Catherine allowed herself a sly grin. "Didn't think we'd have this talk until just before your wedding!"

"Don't be nonsensical. We had *that* talk after I first witnessed a mare being bred. No, what I wish to ask is whether you knew of a muniment room at Sanger-Monkton. We can find no family papers."

"None?" Lady Catherine frowned. "Now that's surprising. There was a very well-organized repository. In fact, I based the organization of the Woodhall and, later, the Rolandson collections on what I saw at Sanger-Monkton."

"So where were they?"

"Why, in that room off which one finds the priest hole, of course."

Helena sighed. "That room is bare of everything but a table."

"Why would anyone remove old documents?"

"I'm more interested in *where* they took them than *why,*" said Helena.

"I recall how interested you were in the Woodhall papers. Do you mean to study Lord Sanger's history as thoroughly?"

"If I can find it. Grandmother, can you think of anywhere they might be? Any further secrets about Sanger-Monkton which might not be included in the architect's plans?"

Lady Catherine frowned. "There were rumors," she said after a moment, "of a tunnel. Also of secret passages, but the only one we knew of was from the priest hole upstairs to the master suite. Not exactly a passage so much as a connection, if you see what I mean?"

"And leading down?"

"Down? What do you mean down?"

"The ladder going up also goes down."

"In my day," said Lady Catherine, firmly, "it only went *up.*"

"Hmm."

"Now, don't you go exploring on your own!"

"No. I'll have Rod there if not Sanger, but I think I should see where that ladder goes."

"Likely be dangerous after all these years," warned Lady Catherine.

"That's possible. I wonder if there was once a trap door or some such thing covering the hole in the floor and that is why you thought the ladder only led upwards."

"Yes, and now I think of it, there was space within the walls upstairs where your papers might have been stored. To avoid an odd shape to the dressing rooms on either side there was a narrow passage between the walls. Quite enough space one might pile papers and journals and old account books, and what have you, into it."

"I don't suppose you recall how to get into that space from the master suite, do you?"

Lady Catherine chuckled. "Had no reason to learn! The Lord Sanger of that era was quite happily wedded to a very beautiful woman. The rest of us would have envied her if she hadn't also been the nicest creature you've ever met!"

"Do you know if there was entry from only the one side or was there an opening into both rooms?"

"I believe," said Lady Catherine after a moment, "that it was from both sides, but wouldn't swear to it."

"I've never before seen more than a hidden room, a

priest hole. If there are other passages, I wonder where they'd be."

"The Sanger-Monkton passage was very likely put in when the house was first built. The world was not exactly safe during Henry's reign, so it isn't surprising a house built during Elizabeth's studied to protect the family. I haven't a notion where the Mansanger family stood in those days. Either politically or with respect to religion."

"If I find the family papers, perhaps I'll find out. Henry's break with Rome caused an infernal number of problems, did it not?"

The next day Lady Helena went straight to the Sanger-Monkton library and, after lighting the lamp, entered the passage. For the first time, she went to the end where the ladder was attached to the wall. Only because she was looking for it did she see the trap door leaning against the back wall. Pressing one hand to the side wall, she leaned forward, caught the edge and pulled. The trap moved an inch or so on its hinges accompanied by a loud squeal. She yanked and it moved another fraction of an inch. She could get it closed no further.

Rod had no better luck. "I'll find the oil, my lady."

Helena removed to the library where she searched the shelves, hoping that something remained besides ancient collections of sermons and tomes written in Greek or Latin. She found one book in French, but of such an old form she had to struggle to read the first paragraph. Still, the subject appealed and she set it aside.

The oil worked a minor miracle, but not instantly. It took Roderick over an hour of gentle effort before the hinges worked smoothly. Then, before he reported to Lady Helena that he'd finished, he tested the ladder to see that the rungs were safe. He knew very well she meant to climb them!

And she did.

"Eureka! Rod, I do believe they are here," she called down, her voice muffled. "At least *something.*"

"You take care. Don't fall!"

She could barely contain her excitement. "Rod, can you bring that lantern up here?"

Lady Helena waited for Rod to climb up and set the lantern on the passage floor. They peered at the dusty, cobweb-hung papers and, silently, Lady Helena groaned. She hadn't expected quite so many, although she supposed she should have done. The dull gleam of metal caught her eye and she lifted the lantern so she could see better.

"A hinge! There's a door here, Rod. I wonder if it will open."

A popping-ripping sound startled her when she pushed against the panel but she persevered and it opened. The tearing sound was the wallpaper some previous mistress had hung in the dressing room beyond. She moved into the room, checked the torn paper which had hidden the secret of the passage, then shrugged. After all, she meant to redo these rooms, which would one day be her own.

"We'll carry all this into the parlor beyond the bedroom, Rod. There will be room to sort it and organize it. I hope it wasn't too badly disarranged when it was moved up here, or that may prove an impossible task."

She was relieved to discover that some care had been taken not to disturb the organization, although moving them again complicated that problem a trifle. Still, she had her records now. And she meant to discover the meaning of the urn. Or else.

As day followed day, it began to seem it would be "or else." Helena learned a great deal, skimming old diaries and journals, but she found nothing which gave a clue to the relic. There wasn't even a mention. However that might be, after a day's research, she would regale Simon with tales of his ancestors, some of which had him laughing and some sober and then again something that would make him proud to be of the Mansanger line.

"But is it worth it, my dear?" he asked one day when she looked particularly hot and disheveled.

The endearment, among the very few he'd given her, startled Helena. She felt a frisson of pleasure, a warmth, and recalled he'd asked a question. "Worth it? Oh, you mean my studying your history? I am enjoying it a great deal, Simon. Unless you wish me to stop prying into your family's past I will continue my studies."

"I only worry you are spending a great deal too much time indoors and not getting sufficient exercise. In fact," he said, adopting a high tone, "I believe I shall order you to break up each day by taking a ride with me directly after lunch." He grinned at her. "You may admire how I progress with *my* side of our efforts." He caught her eye and his smile softened. "Besides," he added more softly, "I miss you."

She didn't need more than the slight widening of his arms as invitation to go into them and felt exceedingly upset when he, obviously reluctantly, set her away. *One of these days!* she thought, wanting, needing, knowing only in theory what it was she wanted and needed, but determined that he would, at some point, lose that iron control and she *would* know.

"You said things progressed," she said. "They are here in the house, as well. Only a few of the floors still needed sanding and refinishing. There is painting to be finished and then—" She sighed. "—I'll have done all I can do until I go to London."

Going to London was becoming imperative. She needed to study pattern books and visit warehouses. She knew it, but she could not bring herself to break off her studies. Or for that matter, leave Simon! She kept putting it off.

New servants worked throughout the house. Each morning, Helena set their tasks, which included scrubbing and polishing and, having discovered one young man knew the trade, painting. Her hired workmen who had finished with the roof worked ahead of the servants on the floors and paneling, replacing what needed replacing, sanding and revarnishing. Helena prayed the weather would hold until that last bit was finished. There was nothing worse than varnish which would not dry! And, in between answering questions and checking the work, she continued her search of the family archives.

Finally she found a clue.

At last. At least Lady Helena believed the reference referred to the casket. It was only mentioned in passing but in the context of a religious ceremony, a reminder that eight young and sturdy workers must be chosen for the Progress. There was no further explanation. Still, it was a clue. For the next few hours she searched still older records for periods near the same spring date of the ceremony. She found nothing more.

Discouraged, she stared thoughtfully at the remaining papers, wondering how she might speed up her search. A notion wiggled into her mind and she checked the date. Looking up to tell Rod she was going down to the library, she found her constant and armed companion had fallen asleep. She smiled and shrugged . . . and left him to his rest.

She took the quickest route to the library, going down the ladder and through the passage. In her rush, she left open the secret entrance and hurried to the shelves which she'd idly searched several weeks earlier, taking the ancient French history home with her to read at night.

"Aha!" she said, finding the heavy oversized tome for which she searched.

She moved it to the table, opened it and sighed in disappointment. The book, as expected, given the title, listed the saints . . . but not by their day. The saints were listed alphabetically. She would have a great deal of reading to

do to find which had his day on the date she'd discovered
in the journal she'd been reading. Worse, there might be
more than one!

After scanning the page, she reached to turn another
of the oversized pages . . . and a creak of wood startled
her. Her head came up. She listened . . . nothing but the
sound of birds singing beyond the open windows. In the
silence she finished turning the page. Then the soft shuf-
fling of heel against wood caught her ear. She turned.

. . . just as a shot rang out.

A burning sensation streaked across her back and shoulder. In the doorway, almost unrecognizable, stood her
cousin. His hands shook as he attempted to reload. Helena
looked from him to the windows, to the anteroom, which
was merely a big closet, except . . . the priest hole!

She ran for it, slamming the closet door behind her. As
she raced into the secret passage she heard her cousin
cursing. Quickly, suppressing a scream as the open wound
burned all across her back, sobbing in frustration and fear,
she opened the trapdoor. Retracing her steps she hid herself in the priest hole. Slumped in the dark, half lying
across the urn's wooden chest, she waited. And waited.
Perspiration beaded her brow, ran down the side of her
face. Her back hurt, every smallest movement agony.

She heard nearly silent footsteps as Thurmand entered
the hidden passage. Then silence . . . what was he doing?
Would he find her? Did he, too, know of the priest hole?

His steps returned to the outer room. The pain in her
shoulder increased when she raised herself slightly, but
she barely noticed, her every sense straining to hear, to
interpret. Her heart raced when a fine line of light brightened the bottom of the door. The lamp. Thurmand had
gone to light the lamp. Surely he'd find the ladder. Yes,
he'd see the ladder.

Would he go up? Or down? Why had she never gone
down? What was down there? Or would he find her hiding

place. She was trapped here. What if he found her? Her thoughts racing in a dozen directions, she forgot and twisted to look directly at the door. Staggering pain exploded along the line of her wound. She felt dizzy with it.

Helena forced herself to concentrate . . . heard nothing.

What was he doing? Helena wished she dared look. She wished she hadn't left her reticule upstairs when she'd come down. If she'd had her pistol she might have shot Thurmand and then she wouldn't be crouched here like a rat in a trap, her back hurting so badly she wished to scream. But she didn't dare. Oh, if only she had shot Thurmand!

Except . . .

Could she have shot him? Even knowing he wished to kill her, could she have pointed a gun at him and pulled the trigger? Helena leaned her arms farther over the chest and lay her head on them, admitting it was unlikely. Perhaps it was as well she'd not had the gun with her?

And then the dizziness passed beyond dizzy to a black hole into which she seemed to fall . . . fall . . . fall . . .

Somewhere, distantly, Rod's voice roused her slightly. She tried to rise . . . but then it seemed too much effort was required to get up and discover why he wanted her, what problem needed a solution, or question an answer.

Later. She'd do it later. She closed her eyes and put her head back down.

Simon dropped his reins and grabbed Rod's shoulders. "What do you mean she's disappeared? That you think she may be ahead of a dirt fall in the tunnel? Under it, maybe? What tunnel? Man, if you don't . . ." Simon realized he was shaking Rod and opened his hands.

The panicked groom fell to his knees, hanging his head. He was dirty, exhausted, and afraid that Lady Helena was

dead. And now he had to face deserved anger from Lord
Sanger.

"I failed her . . . my fault . . ." he muttered.

"Roderick Cole, you make no sense. On your feet!"

Simon's parade ground roar drew Roderick up as if he
were on strings and although he trembled, he stayed on
his feet.

"Report. Quickly now."

"I was a fool. She told me to see if the polishing was
going well in the main stairwell and I went off. When I
came back I fell asleep. Once I woke and she wasn't at her
papers and I thought . . ." He grew red, his eyes flickering
to the side. "I thought . . ."

"I can guess what you thought. A call of nature," said
Sanger. "Go on."

"I . . . and . . . I . . ." Rod's face crumpled up and it
looked as if he'd cry, his eyes pleading for understanding.

"You slept. Boring duty often leads a man to do that.
Especially if the room is hot and close." Simon was doing
his best to control himself but he was wild to know what
had happened, what he faced.

And he decided that, at the very least, they could be
returning to Sanger-Monkton as Rod finished his tale!

He got them both mounted and side by side. "What
happened next?"

"I woke to find Woodhall in the room with me. I don't
know how he got there. Truly. It isn't possible he could
have entered the house with everyone round and about.
But there he was, looking like a wild man in a traveling
fair, his hair all no how and his eyes wild and his clothes
so dirty and torn and . . . and well, you wouldn't believe
how filthy he was . . ." Rod looked his amazement.

"Don't stop." The more Rod told the more fearful Simon became. What had happened to Hel? Where was she?
Was she hurt? Frightened? Was she all safe . . . or not?

Simon did something he never did: He laid has crop against his horse's rump.

Rod managed to keep him in sight, yelling the rest of his story in panting bits. "I stood up. I leveled my pistol at him. He saw me. He . . . howled."

Simon arrived at the terrace outside the library and dismounted.

"Howled," repeated Rod, joining him. "Like a dog." A touch of fear entered Rod's eyes. "I never heard anything like it and—" He grimaced. "—I guess I lowered my pistol and he ran back into the bedroom. I followed. But . . ." He looked down, up. Manfully, he admitted. "I was afraid. I took a quick peek into the dressing room and the panel was open. I saw him disappearing down the ladder into the passage . . . except he didn't stop!"

"Didn't stop?" Simon stepped through the open window. He wondered if that was how Woodhall had entered the house.

"He went right on down," said Rod at his back. "You know. Into the basements. You forbade Lady Helena to explore until you could be with her?"

"You followed."

Rod gulped, his skin turning white. "Yes. The lamp was lit and on the floor and I held it as far down the hole as I could. Wished I'd a lantern, but didn't so, well, I didn't see anything, so I followed. I managed to get down to the bottom, carrying the lamp, and, nearby, discovered bricks on the floor and a brick-lined tunnel heading off into nowhere."

"Yes, Lady Catherine mentioned a tunnel and other secret passages. Come on, lad. Give me the rest." Simon didn't like Rod's color. "What did you find?"

"I went in, thinking maybe Thurmand was chasing Lady Helena."

"Yes?" asked Simon.

"Got maybe fifteen, twenty feet on and suddenly a rumbling noise and dust and dirt boiling around. The roof came down, Lord Sanger. There was a cave-in."

"And you're afraid Lady Helena was caught by it?"

"Yes," whispered Rod.

"The air was clear when you first entered the tunnel?"

"Yes."

"And you heard the fall?"

"Yes."

"Unless there was an end just there and she was trapped? But she'd time, either to come back or go on, had she not, while Woodhall was upstairs? I'd guess she wasn't there. You needn't fear she's under that dirt."

"I hope the bastard's there and dead!"

Roderick spoke with a viciousness Sanger had never heard. For his own reasons, he, too, hoped the man was dead. If he were, they could bury him with decent ceremony and forget him. If not, then there would be scandal. Thurmand would either stand his trial or he'd be incarcerated somewhere, a confirmed madman. Either would give the gossips food to feast on for some time to come!

"The question," mused Sanger, "is whether *Woodhall* is under it or beyond and following her down the tunnel."

"The real question is what has become of Lady Hel," insisted Rod, and Simon didn't deny it.

Simon leant over the table, looking at the book he suspected Helena had been consulting. *A book listing the saints?* he asked himself, confused. Some particular research? She found something, perhaps in the papers and was attempting to check it?

Rod, anxious and wanting action, but not knowing what to do, roamed the room, his eyes skittering here and there. "Oh, my God!"

"What?"

Roderick touched the shattered wood of a bookcase shelf. He took out his knife and probed the wood.

"What have you found?"

As Simon came up beside him, Roderick turned, handing His Lordship the lead ball he'd pried from the shelf. The two men stared at each other, then Simon, his skin prickling, turned slowly. "The angle of the shot comes from that doorway," he decided. "It would have passed over the table."

"Where Lady Hel was sitting?"

"I think it likely. Now, if a madman shot at me, what would I do?"

Half dazed, Rod looked around.

"I'd head for the secret room and into the passage," said Simon, acting on the words. He entered the anteroom and stopped. Glistening in the light coming through the door were dark spots of . . . blood? He knelt, touched one. It was still tacky.

"The bastard hit her. He hit her! I'll kill him." Simon moved on but at the secret door to the passage, stopped again. *His Helena was somewhere, hurt, bleeding, in pain . . . perhaps dead?* "Rod, why didn't she close this door, give herself time to escape . . . or was he too near?"

The two men slid sideways through the narrow entrance and stared at the open trap door which, the last he'd been in the passage, had been closed.

"Why open the trap?" asked Simon.

"Make Woodhall think she went down?"

"Except he went up and found you."

"And *then* he went down!" replied the groom.

"So," said Simon, fretting, "did Helena go up or did she go down?"

"Neither," whispered Lady Helena from where she leaned into the far wall. "Neither . . ." she repeated and slid slowly, gently, to the floor.

Twelve

Lady Helena opened her eyes. Lazily she looked around. *Such plain surroundings.*

"How odd," she murmured. She closed her eyes and tried to roll onto her side—only to gasp with pain.

"No, my love. Don't move."

Her eyes snapped open. She stared straight up into Lord Sanger's concerned face. "What . . ."

"You don't recall?" He touched her forehead lightly, lingeringly.

"Thirsty," she decided.

"I'm not surprised," he said. Blood from the furrow the bullet drilled across her back had soaked her gown down into her skirt. It had been something of a job cleaning her and caring for the wound. Now, very carefully, he slid an arm low under her shoulders and lifted her. He held a glass of cool water to her lips but allowed her to drink no more than a sip.

"More."

"Soon. You don't remember being hurt?"

"Hurt . . ." Suddenly Helena's eyes widened and a fearful look entered them. She turned her head fretfully, her eyes darting here and there. "Thurmand!"

"He's gone."

It seemed the easiest explanation. Sanger hoped it was true. If Woodhall had been beyond the fall of brick and dirt that blocked the tunnel, if he'd found the end of it and escaped, then the cursed man might reappear at any moment. Far better if he were trapped under the collapsed ceiling.

"Rod went for a doctor and your grandmother."

And, thought Sanger, looking at her with sad eyes, *when they arrive they'll make me leave you, my love. I don't want to.*

The realization that he'd come within a inch, *literally,* of losing her, losing his dear love, had shaken Simon to his roots. The bullet grazed a path along her back and shoulder which suggested that, if she'd been at only a slightly different angle, it would, at the very least, have shattered her spinal cord. As it was, before they'd found her, she'd lost more blood than he liked to think of. She was weak as a cat. If an infection set in . . .

His heart pounded violently.

. . . he could still lose her. He couldn't bear to think of it. The thought of leaving her side was equally unbearable, but it must be done. That tunnel must be emptied of dirt until they knew with absolute certainty whether Thurmand Woodhall had or had not been caught by it.

The foreman was already organizing the preliminary work. He'd crossed their path as Simon carried Helena to his bed and been alerted. The good Scotsman was seeing to the necessary boards to shore up the ceiling, and shovels and buckets for carrying away rubble.

Softly Simon swore at the unknown and secretive ancestor who had removed the tunnel from the plans so that they couldn't simply go to the other end and enter from that point! Or perhaps it had never been written down in the first place?

"Thirsty," insisted Helena.

He helped her drink and again allowed her less than she wished. He set aside the glass and turned back to lay her onto her pillows.

Lady Catherine bustled in. For half a moment the dowa-

ger wondered if she were viewing a seduction—but only
for that moment. Then she assessed her granddaughter's
condition, saw it was serious and, closing her eyes, said a
brief prayer.

"Thirsty," insisted Helena still again, weakly catching at
Sanger's hand.

"You can have more in a bit," he soothed, and catching
sight of movement, turned. "Ah. Your grandmother has
arrived."

"I've brought our maids and a footman," said Lady
Catherine, her gaze never leaving the bed. "Roderick went
on for the doctor. Do you know where my . . . grandson
has gotten to?" she finished, her voice breaking. Suddenly
she looked every one of her years.

"There is a possibility he is dead. I'm sorry if I speak too
bluntly, but—" Sanger glanced down at Helena. "—frankly,
I hope so! Now you are here I must discover what, if anything, has happened to him."

Lady Catherine caught his sleeve. "One moment before
you go. Thurmand shot Helena?"

"Yes. I cleaned the crease and I poured some damn fine
brandy over it before covering it. She lost a fair amount
of blood, but if there is no infection, she'll recover soon
enough."

"Infection." Lady Catherine, looking *more* than her age,
sighed. "Yes, that is always the problem, is it not?"

"Can you . . . ?" Sanger glanced from Lady Catherine
to Helena and back.

"My lord," said the dowager, rallying, "in my day, I've
nursed very nearly every problem that lays man, woman,
or child low. A simple gunshot? I can manage that . . . *and*
my granddaughter."

"I thought you could," said Sanger. He stared down at
Helena. "I don't want to leave her," he said, abruptly.

"My lord, you are not a man to put off a duty. Go."

The revealing muscle jumped in Simon's jaw, jumped

again. If Woodhall was *not* under that cave-in, he was still a danger to Lady Helena. That must be determined. Unfortunately, the work was far too dangerous and the result far too important to leave it unsupervised.

Without another word Simon leaned over Helena, kissed her brow, and then, quickly, left the small bedroom.

Her eyes fluttered open. "Thirsty . . . Simon . . . ?"

"He had to leave. I'll help you, Hel."

"Grandmother . . . ?"

"I'm here, my dear."

"Simon . . ."

"He must discover what happened to that jackanapes."

"Thurmand!"

Helena struggled and was hastily restrained.

"He shot me! Thurmand shot *me.*"

Lady Catherine chuckled. There was a watery sound to it, but it was a laugh. "My dear, you sound thoroughly outraged." She slumped into the chair by the bed. "Blast and bedamned." She stifled a sob. "It is all my fault, Hel. *I'm so sorry.*"

Something, perhaps her fear of Thurmand, perhaps pain, cleared Helena's head. She frowned. "Nonsense. You didn't put a gun in his hand and tell him to shoot me!"

"No. I merely told him the truth when he found me in the Cooper-Wainwright gardens one day." Lady Catherine sighed deeply. "I think he meant to ask for money, but I told him his history before he could say more than a word or two."

"So he knows he's not, by blood, a Woodhall. So?"

"Helena, he turned so white I thought he'd faint. And then he stared right through me. He said no, kept on chanting it. No, no, no."

"What did he do?"

"He ran off saying no over and over."

"So you think he went mad and decided to kill me because he isn't a Woodhall?"

"He was so very proud of our blood lines, Helena." The dowager sounded tired, old. "I did that, too."

"No," said Helena firmly. "That was his mother's doing. I think she tried very hard to make it impossible for him to believe he could be anything else, assuming he ever heard rumors about her."

"But there was no hesitation. He believed me. Instantly."

"Grandmother, his mother still has that same footman."

"Oh." After a moment she added, "I didn't know."

"It is an on-dit that doesn't die, because she flaunts the man whenever she comes to town. Which, thank heaven, isn't often now." Helena tried to move, and bit back an exclamation. Several swearwords she shouldn't have used passed her lips.

"She's better?" asked Rod, sticking his head in the door.

"It sounds like it," said Lady Catherine dryly, recovering her poise at the intrusion. "Is the doctor here?"

"If this oaf will remove himself from the doorway," said a testy voice, "perhaps I may be allowed to see my patient!"

Rod, his face reddening, moved into the tiny bedroom and into the far corner. He cast a worried look toward Helena who winked at him. At that proof she was very much herself, he relaxed.

The doctor stepped to her side and Lady Helena turned her attention to him, studying him even as he studied her. "Well, my lady," he said still more testily. "Seen enough, have you?"

"I don't know, do I?"

He chuckled. "Won't have just any old doctor poking and prying into your hurts, is that it, my lady?"

"Yes."

"Hmm." He folded his arms. "Fair enough. So what do we do?"

"What do *you* mean to do?"

"First I must look at the wound. Can't tell what's to be done 'til I see it, can I?"

Helena thought about that. "I find I cannot roll over. I'll need help turning."

"I'll turn her," said Rod eagerly and came to her side.

"Better, maybe, if she merely sits up," suggested the doctor and, by that decision, won Helena's trust.

With help she leaned forward over Rod's strong arm. The doctor bared her back, studied the crease, which was glazing over, the seepage drying into a fragile glistening coating.

"Hmm. What was done to this?"

"Lord Sanger cleaned it," said Rod. "Then he poured brandy over it, saving a small tot for each of us to drink. I don't know about him but I needed it."

"Where'd the man learn to do that?"

"I'd guess while in the Peninsula, Dr. Stollard," said Lady Catherine quietly.

"Seems to have worked. Waste of good brandy, though. Use gin next time?"

Helena laughed weakly. "I hope there isn't a next time," she said.

"Oh well . . . always cuts and bruises, you know. Doesn't need to be a pistol shot. Who shot at you?" asked the doctor casually.

"She doesn't know," said Lady Catherine firmly, cutting off anything Helena might or might not be about to say.

Rod's mouth dropped open. Carefully, he closed it.

The doctor shook his head. "Nasty business, people going around shooting at other people." As he spoke he laid a strip of clean linen over the wound and then laid on a bandage.

"Very nasty," agreed Lady Catherine, giving the man no gossipy information he might pass on to others when he made his rounds. "You may lay Lady Helena back now, Rod, and then perhaps—" She glared at him. "—you should go help Lord Sanger?"

Rod understood Lady Catherine wished to be rid of him.

He also realized that Lord Sanger was working on the tunnel and he, as much as anyone, wished to be assured that there was no further danger to Lady Helena, that Woodhall was dead and not, once again, in hiding. He left the room quietly and quickly.

His face the picture of curiosity, the doctor watched the groom go. "No one knows anything, is that it?" he asked.

"Exactly."

"Been a rash of minor thefts in the area," said the doctor. "A chicken and a few tarts cooling on a window ledge. That sort of thing."

"Sounds like gypsies," said Lady Catherine.

"Hmm. Always useful to have the gypsies to blame," said the doctor, tying the last knot to the bandage. He patted it and then placed his hand on Helena's forehead. After a moment he stood up, turning to Lady Catherine. "Trouble is," he said politely, "no one's seen hide nor hair of any gypsies."

"So?" asked Lady Catherine. When the doctor said no more, she added, "The constable will have to search for another culprit, will he not?"

"Hmm. So he will."

"I am established at the Cooper-Wainwrights'. You may send your bill there."

"Here now!" When he feared for his patient, the doctor lost all interest in what he considered a mystery. He looked from Lady Helena to Lady Catherine. "Don't you go moving my patient! Not 'til that wound heals more'n it is now."

"No. I have observed that every time a sore opens, the danger of infection is greater. We'll not move Lady Helena for some days."

"Ah! In that case I'll come by here tomorrow. You behave, my lady," he said, shaking a finger at Lady Helena. "I've heard about you, I have!"

"What it is to have a reputation," murmured Helena as

the man left. She yawned. "Thirsty," she said, rather peevishly . . . and once she'd drunk, fell asleep.

"Are we ready?" asked Lord Sanger, looking at the pile of lumber and posts the men had brought to the basement under the library. "I want no more accidents. The roof must be shored up as we go. Rod says it is over twenty feet to the cave-in, so we've a good-sized job ahead of us."

"I'll just check the roof between here and the cave-in," said the foreman and, a knowing look in his eye, added, "Perhaps, if you want to go see to your lady?"

Sanger was torn. "I'll discover what the doctor had to say," he decided and headed for the ladder. He'd grasped it and was about to climb when feet appeared at the top. He stood back.

"Ah, Rod. The doctor has come?"

"He's bandaged her. Lady Catherine said I'm to make myself useful."

"Ask what you can do, Rod. We'll need every hand."

Simon took the steps quickly and strode through the house to the kitchens and into the small apartment which had been cleaned for his use. He rapped softly at the doorjamb, catching Lady Catherine's attention. She rose to her feet, her finger to her mouth, and pushed him gently back into the kitchen.

"The doctor has gone?"

"Hmm. Quite impressed with your nursing abilities."

"One quickly learns how one can help when you've wounded men all around you. That was nothing." Simon waved away the compliment. "Did the doctor say . . . Did he know . . . ?"

"Assuming no infection, she'll be up and around in a few days."

"So quickly?"

"Lady Hel heals remarkably quickly. She always has."

"No fever?"

"Not yet. With luck there will be none."

"Can I see her?"

"She's sleeping."

"I'll be quiet."

Lady Catherine studied him. "You love her."

"Yes."

"Tell her—" Her ladyship grinned. "Oh, not right now, of course, but *tell* her. A woman needs to know she's loved, my lord."

"I only realized it when I came so close to losing her."

"Tell her that, too."

"But," he said on a sigh, "not now."

"Come." Lady Catherine beckoned. "See for yourself she only sleeps."

As they entered the small bedroom, Simon heard Helena's voice. "Thirsty!"

He chuckled softly at the imperious if querulous tone and, lifting her, helped her drink.

Her eyes snapped open as he set her back. "Simon?"

"I'm here."

"Good." Her eyes closed.

"I can't stay. I only came to see how you are."

But she was already back to sleep.

Staring down at her, Simon sighed. "I must go. You will send for me if she wants me?"

"She'll sleep for some time now. I doctored her water with just a touch of the poppy, you see."

He turned sharply. "Is that wise?"

"You don't approve of the use of laudanum?"

He frowned. "I don't suppose a very little will hurt."

"That is all I ever dose a patient with. Just a bit to relax one. I firmly believe sleep is a cure to most ills."

He hesitated another moment, staring at his love. "Well . . . send for me when she wakes."

"I'll do that."

Still he didn't go. Finally, casting a harried look at Lady Catherine, he bent and, again, kissed Helena. This time on her cheek.

When he returned to the basement, he found men moving the wood into the tunnel. Just as he was about to take a hand himself, the foreman appeared. "What have you done?" Sanger asked.

"I tested the roof and it's firm for as far as I went. We don't need to shore up the first bit."

"How far in do you have faith in it holding?"

"Likely a full twenty feet."

"Then begin the shoring at fifteen. I'll not take chances with the men's lives."

"Verra good, my lord."

Several hours passed, but the work actually progressed more quickly than Sanger had thought possible. The supports were in place all the way to the first signs of the cave-in, and he'd gone into the tunnel with the foreman to decide how to proceed when, muffled by dirt and fallen brick, the two men heard the distinctive sound of a pistol shot. They looked at each other.

"A signal? A call for help?" asked the foreman after a moment's hesitation.

"Or despair?" suggested Sanger, softly. They looked at each other. "If I thought I were trapped and would starve to death . . ."

"My God," breathed the foreman. The Scotsman shrugged and appeared to put aside all thought of what might be found at the other end. "We must form a line, like for putting out a fire? Two men filling buckets and the others passing them back. Maybe a cart near that outside basement door so we won't have to shovel up a pile later?"

The work began. It was slow, the men forming new and more serious supports for the weakened roof as they moved forward, until they reached a point where, before they could get to it, there was a sudden new fall. Fading daylight could be glimpsed through the dust. The foreman moved the bucket operation out of doors and the work went more quickly.

Still, when a man with a shovel uncovered a booted foot, it was very nearly dark. He shouted, and Sanger, who had been above hauling buckets along with the men, came to the edge of the pit.

"What is it?" he called.

"A boot, my lord. Think maybe we found him, my lord."

Sanger scrambled down the dirt, pushing some ahead of him. The workman brushed it away and Sanger knelt. He worked the boot off the foot and touched skin which was already cold, the ankle stiffening. He stood slowly, looking down at the blue-white flesh.

"Dead, my lord?" asked the workman a trifle unsteadily.

"I believe so, but we must be careful from here on. In case he is alive, you know?" Simon looked from the foreman to the workmen.

"Yes sir," said the foreman.

The men nodded solemnly.

Gradually, Thurmand Woodhall's body came clear, the feet and legs, then the lower trunk with one hand laying at his side, and finally his back and shoulders, his other arm bent upward.

Simon was in the pit when they carefully brushed dirt from Woodhall's shattered head. There was sudden retching, a workman pushing back and finding a bucket over which he leaned, casting up his accounts.

"Sorry," said the man unsteadily. "Never seen the like."

"I'll finish," said Simon grimly. He had, all too often, "seen the like" in battle. It was something he'd hoped he'd never see again.

He removed what dirt he could from the shattered head and gently removed the pistol from Thurmand's gently curved fingers. The foreman lowered a wide board and Simon lifted the body to it. He asked for something with which he might cover it. Then he guided it as it was raised to ground level.

Simon felt pity that Woodhall had shot himself, unaware help was on the way. Or perhaps, the man had heard them working, had known rescue would mean he'd be taken before a magistrate?

Whatever the case, Simon breathed a prayer of thankfulness he no longer need fear for Helena's life. Then he remembered Lady Catherine, and that she must be told her grandson was dead. He didn't look forward to it.

As it turned out, it was not so very difficult after all. Lady Catherine was in the kitchen, nodded when he appeared and turned back to where she was hacking up a chicken from which she meant to make broth. Mrs. Bradden, who did Simon's cooking and cleaning, stood at the other side of the table chopping vegetables.

When Simon, standing behind the dowager, pointed at her ladyship, at what she was doing and frowned, the servant pouted. Sullenly, she said, "Ask the saint if I didn't tell her it wasn't fitten', Her Ladyship a'working in my kitchen!"

Lady Catherine laughed. "So you did. It is *not* Mrs. Bradden's fault, Sanger. I've never been good at twiddling my thumbs. I need to be busy. I insisted she allow me to help." The dowager deftly cut off a wing. "Tell me how your work progresses?"

"We've found him," said Simon quietly.

Lady Catherine's hands stilled. "He's dead."

"Yes."

"Thank God." Very gently, she laid down her knife. Slowly she turned from the table. Carefully she straightened. "Take me to him," she ordered, wiping her hands on a damp rag.

"He isn't a pretty sight, my lady."

"Death, however it comes, is never pretty. Take me to my grandson."

Simon knew Lady Helena would prefer he protect her grandmother from what the dowager demanded to see. He, however, had greater faith in her ladyship's courage and strength of mind and led the way to a building with double-thick brick walls. It had been used as a cool-house in the days when winter ice was stored in a hollowed-out space below it. Even with no ice, the thick walls meant the inside remained cooler than most places at this time of year. The men had laid Woodhall on an old table.

"Tell me what to expect," she said, holding his hand when he'd have uncovered the body.

"He was trapped, my lady. He had a gun. Before he could know help was coming"—Sanger had decided this was the better of his theories with which to burden her ladyship— "he worked his arm up so he could get the gun to his head and then did what I'd have done in his situation."

"So his head . . . his face?"

"Only a bit of his face is damaged. One side and back of his head."

"I can imagine." Once again Lady Catherine forced her spine into a column as stiff as a poker. She nodded.

Lord Sanger had had the wits to place Lady Catherine on the side of the table which revealed as little as possible of the horror. She stared at her grandson for a long moment. Then, kissing her fingers, she placed them on his undamaged cheek, holding them there for another long moment.

"Whatever you became as an adult, Thurmand," she murmured, "you gave me great joy when you were a boy. May you finally find peace, lad."

She ducked outside quickly. Her hands tightly clasped before her, Lady Catherine stared over the dark lawn. One of the newly acquired sheep baaed softly. A cricket thrrrrwpted. An owl floated silently by, hunting.

"He must be taken to Chabsley, of course," she said, her voice slightly muffled.

"I'll arrange for his removal, my lady," said Sanger quietly.

"Hel must be at the funeral."

"Must be?"

"There will be scandal enough. I would keep tongues from wagging more than necessary."

"She cannot travel."

"She can and will. But not tomorrow and very likely not the next day. I must return to the Cooper-Wainwrights' and write letters informing those who may wish to attend. But before I do those, I'll write his mother's vicar who must break the news to her."

"And Lady Helena?"

"Her maid and mine will see to her," said the dowager absently.

Then she lost the starch holding her stiffly erect. Lord Sanger caught her and turned her into his arms. She cried into his shoulder. Some minutes later Lady Catherine pushed away and searched for a handkerchief.

"I must go," she said abruptly.

He knew he should escort her, but, since she'd not thought to give the order that he leave Sanger-Monkton while Lady Helena lay under its roof, he decided he'd not do it. If he went with her to the Cooper-Wainwrights' he'd be taking the chance that the notion crossed someone's mind and he'd no desire to argue about where he'd sleep that night—but it wasn't at the Cooper-Wainwrights'! He could not be easy leaving Lady Helena to the maids. He'd see to his love himself.

The funeral was sparsely attended, the official first

mourner, Thurmand Woodhall's mother. Mrs. Woodhall threw the first clods of dirt into her son's grave and turned away. Helena, standing across from her, saw her reach a hand to her footman who stood only a step or two beyond her. He, thought Helena, looked far more haggard than Thurmand's mother, and she presumed he knew it was his son they'd just buried.

As they rode together to the house, Mrs. Woodhall informed Lady Catherine that she meant to leave England as soon as it could be arranged. She would go to America.

"Where you mean to remarry?"

"I don't know. Marriage is a big step, after all."

"So it is."

Mrs. Woodhall glanced at Lady Catherine and scowled. *"You* needn't sneer. You weren't married at far too young an age to a . . . a brute who wanted absolutely nothing from you but an heir."

"I was younger than you when I first wed," said Lady Catherine quietly. "The difference, I suppose, is that I, too, wanted to bear our son. And our other children."

Lady Woodhall bit her lip, but her chin rose a notch. "Gerald has been everything to me."

"Then wed him," snapped the dowager, but, less harshly, added, "When you reach America, of course."

"Perhaps I will."

Lady Catherine adroitly removed herself and Lady Helena from the funeral party before Lord Chabsley's butler announced that the funeral meats were served. Mrs. Woodhall, as chief mourner, could, for the first and last time, play at being hostess at Chabsley Manor.

"Now," said Lady Catherine, a day or two later, "explain to me what it is I am to look for." She stared at the tome listing the saints. It still lay open on the library table.

"That date I gave you. I believe it must be a saint's day."

Lady Catherine's jaw dropped. She closed her mouth, staring at her granddaughter. Then she asked, "You think the casket contains the relics of a saint?"

"Well, there's a priest hole here, which indicates the family was Catholic. And there is, I'm told, the remains of an abbey only a few miles distant."

"You are guessing relics might have be brought from there?"

"Removed here for protection when Cromwell was on the rampage. Or, more likely, it was done still earlier, when Henry ordered the dissolution of the monasteries. We think the abbey was founded by the Mansanger family, so very likely the family felt a sense of ownership of the bones and took them away?"

"Your imagination was affected by your wound," said Lady Catherine with a bit of a bite to her tone. Then, casually, "I wonder if I can think of someone who will know the history of that abbey."

"You promised you'd help search for my saint."

Lady Catherine smiled. "You are exceedingly possessive of a saint who may not exist!"

Helena chuckled. "You would say I've taken a thread and made up a whole yard of cloth from it, would you not!"

"I'd have said that very thing." Lady Catherine nudged the book with one finger. "I'll not waste my time with that. I've recalled a priest who is something of a scholar. It will be far more expedient to visit him."

Lady Helena bit her lip, glancing back toward the well-hidden priest hole. "Grandmother . . ."

"I will merely have developed a sudden interest in the history of the abbey ruins. I'll not reveal the existence of a saint's relics. Especially since I can't believe that's what you've found!"

"The wooden casket is ancient and was designed especially for the urn it contains. The urn is very heavy and sealed in such a way I don't believe one could open it without damaging the vessel beyond repair."

Lady Catherine mulled that information. "You have had it out of the casket?" she asked.

"No. I tried lifting it once, but couldn't manage it. It was too heavy. You can see how it is sealed, however. At least, you can see part of the seal! The other half lies hidden in the bottom half of the casket. It looks as if the urn had been dipped in molten metal so that there is no longer an opening."

"Dipped." Lady Catherine straightened at those words and stared blankly at her granddaughter. "Where is Lord Sanger?"

"Here," he said, just then stepping over the window sill from the terrace. "Has something more happened?"

"Lord Sanger, I want your escort for Lady Hel and myself to Cirencester. Today, if possible."

"Why?"

"I've had a thought." She shook her head. "No, I'll not give voice to the utter nonsense which is in my head. Nevertheless," she added slowly, "it is certainly a possibility."

"*What* is a possibility?"

Lady Catherine glanced up and grinned a mischievous grin that reminded Simon of his love. "You'll know," she said, "if and only if we find proof I've not become mad as a hatter."

When they arrived in Cirencester, they had no difficulty finding the priest, a Father Cartney. He was an older man, very nearly Lady Catherine's age. He'd very pink skin and a drift of soft white hair which floated about his head whenever he moved. He welcomed them to his small house, which sat next to an equally small church. "Do come in," he said. "I will find my housekeeper and she'll make us tea," he added, once he'd seen them seated in his parlor.

When everyone had been served not only tea but warm scones slathered with clotted cream and berry jam, he smiled. "Now," he said, folding his hands into a prayerful attitude, "tell me why I am so honored," he suggested, looking from Lord Sanger to Lady Helena and back again.

"We wish to know about a certain ruined abbey lying somewhat north of here."

The man lost some of his ebullience, looking again from one to the other. "Oh, dear," he said softly. "I had thought you'd come to arrange a wedding." He spoke wistfully. "I do love the sacrament of marriage, you see." But then his impish smile reappeared. "The abbey, you say. If you are Lord Sanger, sir, then you must refer to the ruins, or perhaps one should say, the remains lying on your land. It was, of course, pulled down, stone from stone, after Henry broke with Rome. I visited it once. There wasn't so much as a partial wall standing, merely flagged areas rapidly disappearing under the grass and, if you dig for them, foundation stones buried under the sod. So, what is it you wish to know?"

"Can you tell us when it was founded, by whom, and if it protected the relics of any saints?"

The priest blinked. "It was founded by the first Lord Sanger, of course, at the birth of his first son."

"My ancestors? Then they *were* Catholic?" asked Sanger.

The priest's brows arched. "But of course they were. They were Norman and came to England with the Conqueror. William the Bastard, you know. The title and original lands and other honors were granted to your ancestor with the proviso he build a castle, defense against raiders from Wales. As you must know, the Welsh were never conquered."

"A castle." It was Sanger's turn for arched brows. "I know of no castle."

"I believe it was little more than earthen works, a hill fort with a small keep."

"Ah. There is a Forge Hill, an oddly symmetrical rise of

land where there are no other hills. Perhaps it was, once, Fort Hill?"

"An excellent guess," approved the priest. "Now, I believe you had other questions? Ah, yes. The relics of saints." His eyes narrowed. "Is it permitted that I ask why you wish to know?"

"I think not," said Lady Catherine, laying a hand on Sanger's wrist.

The priest was silent for a moment, his gaze resting thoughtfully on Lady Catherine who stared back blandly. Then, quietly, he spoke. "I cannot, offhand, recall the saint's name. I can search for it if you wish it. Assuming I've the right tale, the first abbot brought this saint's relics from France. Every spring the reliquary was placed on a platform and carried around the borders of the Sanger manor and into the village. Each household had the opportunity to touch the cords falling from the corners of the cover and ask a boon of the saint. It is said the saint often granted the wishes of those who worshipped at the abbey chapel. Henry changed that, of course. But your people remained Catholic even in the face of difficulties. And then—" One could read the distaste in the priest's face. "—Cromwell."

"The reliquary disappeared?"

The priest shrugged, but his eyes narrowed. "One must suppose that Henry's men destroyed it."

"And if they did not?" asked Lady Helena softly.

The man rose to his feet. "My lady," he said earnestly, "if you know where the relics are, please do not keep it a secret. They must be cared for properly, must be given the honor due them."

When Lady Catherine raised her hand, he stopped speaking. "Sir, if the relics were returned to the care of Catholics who value them, must the *reliquary* also be returned?"

Confusion crumpled his old face, lines appearing which

had not formerly been revealed. "I . . . don't understand."

"I believe the relics are holy to you. Is the reliquary also considered holy?" explained Her Ladyship.

"You would say you'd like to return the contents and keep the casket?" asked the priest in a confused tone.

"Yes."

He first blinked and, his features returning to normal, he chuckled. "Well. That is plain enough."

"Someone had better tell me what is going on," said a bewildered Lord Sanger. "Helena, what have you discovered?"

"Only a single clue," she said. "That eight strong and sturdy young men must be chosen for the annual Progress."

"And you, Lady Catherine?"

"I am told the urn is very, very heavy. So heavy my granddaughter cannot lift it from the casket."

Sanger stared from one to the other. "Heavy. But it is tin or pewter? Ah! Perhaps it is lead. But a lead urn?"

"Dipped!" Lady Helena's eyes widened. "I told you it was as if it had been dipped," she said. "Was it merely *coated* with a lesser metal? Oh dear . . . surely not!"

"And if coated," asked Lady Catherine, a significant note in her voice, "what does the base metal cover?"

"I see," said the priest. He glanced at Sanger, who was obviously astounded. The young man had had no part in this visit although gossip said the new Lord Sanger needed every penny he could raise. "I think I see. It is your considered opinion, my lady, that the Mansanger family deserves a reward for keeping the relics safe. Do I understand you, Lady Catherine?"

"You do."

"But . . ."

"Lord Sanger," snapped Lady Catherine, "shut your mouth."

"I will not," he said in a firm tone. "You suggest the casket contains a gold urn which in turn holds the bones and ashes of a saint. If that is so, then it must be returned to where it belongs, except how does one know where it belongs?"

Sanger stared from one to another and finally returned his gaze to the priest's face.

"If it were possible," Sanger said slowly, "that one might communicate with France, then perhaps it should be returned to the abbey from which it originally came, but with the war . . ." He shrugged.

"Good lad," said the priest, grinning broadly.

"You would simply hand over the gold which would free you forever from debt?" asked Lady Catherine.

"I am not a thief, Lady Catherine."

"I am not suggesting you are. I agree you must return the relics. I am not convinced you need give back the reliquary."

Sanger drew in a breath and let it out through pursed lips. He stared at nothing at all. Lady Helena reached toward him and he grasped her hand tightly. "I have made my decision. You, sir, must contact whomever you believe appropriate, tell them the tale we have told you, and ask that someone search available records, that they make whatever tests are necessary. They must prove that what I have in my possession are indeed the relics of a saint. Or not, as the case may be. If you decide that is what I have, then we must decide what is to be done with them."

"Grr," growled Lady Catherine. "I wash my hands of you, you foolish boy!"

"As you once washed your hands of Lady Helena?" he asked lightly. "I hope it goes no worse with me than it did with her!"

Lady Catherine could not hold to her temper. She shook her head, smiling. "Rogue. I had thought my granddaughter might lead you a merry dance, but I see she must be on guard that you do not lead her one!''

The priest eagerly offered to write the proper letters and Sanger escorted the women back to the Cooper-Wainwrights'. Everyone had agreed to keep their speculations and discoveries secret until they knew what the end would be.

But Lady Helena, privately, decided she'd a boon to ask of the saint, if saint it was. She was Church of England, of course, and nothing was likely to come of it, but surely it couldn't hurt to ask if something might not be done to help Lord Sanger in his current difficulties!

Thirteen

Lady Catherine glared her famous glare. Lady Helena had just announced that she and Sanger meant to have the banns read and would wed in little over a month.

The news had not set well with the dowager. "There hasn't even been an announcement ball!" said Lady Catherine. She stared down her aristocratic nose.

Helena cast her grandmother an exasperated look. "One could say, we had that at the Treweses'," she suggested, tongue in cheek. "And, as to bride's clothes and linens and that nonsense, I must soon spend more time than I wish in London choosing paper and carpets and other items for Sanger-Monkton. I can do that more conveniently as Sanger's lady then as his betrothed. I might as well order a new wardrobe and linens at the same time."

"You are expected to embroider your linens with your new crest or perhaps, in your case, merely a monogram," said Lady Catherine on a sly note.

Helena relaxed. If her grandmother had begun teasing, all would be well. "If any of my linens bear embroidery it will not be I who does it—as you well know. Grandmother, I am getting tired of the long ride to and from Sanger-Monkton each day. I would live there and may not do so until Lord Sanger and I are wed."

"Is that the only reason you wish to wed?" asked her grandmother on an even slyer note.

"Grandmother!"

"Well?"

An unusually contemplative expression settled over Lady Helena's features. "I believe," she reluctantly admitted, "that I've fallen in love with him. I regret it, but I do not know what I can do about it. I suppose that bears on my wish to wed, but more important from Lord Sanger's point of view, I am convinced there is information in his family record which *must* be found before a decision is reached concerning those relics. Managing the work and jaunting back and forth takes far too much of my time."

"You are convinced they are relics?"

"Oh yes. Several times I've heard people who grew up on the estate say one should *ask the saint* about something."

"Yes," said Lady Catherine, thoughtfully, "I myself heard Lord Sanger's cook say it when you were wounded."

"I've queried the older tenants, asking if they know how the expression arose, but they simply insist it has always been said. It suggests, however, that Father Cartney had the right tale, does it not? The relics were carried around the estate and anyone could ask a boon. It is easy to see how that expression *one should ask the saint* became part of local lore, is it not?" She eyed her grandmother and abruptly returned to the earlier subject. "Please do not forbid the banns."

"You will continue to nag at me until I allow it, will you not?"

"You know I will," said Lady Helena and sighed a very small sigh at what she believed a failing on her part. "Once I get a thing settled in my head, it is very difficult to change it."

"And you have settled it that you will marry at once?"

"Simon and I both wish it," said Lady Helena.

"What sort of wedding will it be, with everyone looking at your waistline and counting the months?"

"You and I know that is not the reason I would wed."

"You haven't told him you love him."

"No."

"You should."

Helena moved to the window. Her back to her grand-mother, she spoke in a thoughtful tone. "There are, I think, three reactions he might have to such unwanted news and I like none of them. He might simply ignore my admission, which would be best, of course. Or he might pity me, and that I could not bear. Lastly—" Lady Helena frowned, the frown deepening as she considered, "—and, perhaps, the worst? He might *use* the knowledge to my disadvantage. No. Not the worst," she decided. "Pity would be far worse."

"But, believing he might behave in such a contemptible manner you would wed him anyway?"

"Yes."

"There is a possibility you've not mentioned," said Lady Catherine, her eyes narrowed. She waited for Helena to ask what she'd forgotten, but Hel disobliged her, ignoring her. The dowager spoke sharply. "He *might,* you know, tell you he loves you, too."

"I cannot think there is the least possibility of that. He didn't *wish* to wed me. He is resigned, but . . ." She shook her head. "No. It is not possible."

"Nevertheless, you should tell him."

"No."

"I am aware you believe your emotions are not to be paraded before every wit and wastrel of the *ton,* but you are behaving in a most ridiculous manner if you think they've no place in a marriage."

"I will not burden him with the knowledge!"

"Fool." Lady Catherine eyed her granddaughter, chewing on her lip. "I've decided. Helena, I will allow the wedding only when I've Lord Sanger's promise he'll not touch you, carnally, for two full months after the vows are taken!"

"Grandmother!" After a moment it was Helena's turn

to try for a sly note. "We are both of age. We do not actually need your permission."

"But you want my blessing," retorted Lady Catherine promptly.

Helena grimaced. "Yes. We do."

"I, my dear child, can be just as stubborn, not to say pig-headed, as *you.*" Lady Catherine folded her arms and glared.

"So you can." Helena sighed in exasperation. "I will have Lord Sanger attend you this evening before dinner," she added sourly.

"Alone," said Lady Catherine, achieving the last word— which she could not always manage when arguing with her granddaughter.

At the news of the wedding, the rumor concerning Lady Helena's waistline hatched—mostly by people *not* invited to the wedding—and took wing, but the new countess didn't allow it to concern her.

The wedding itself, held in London a month later, was small but perfect. Those favored with an invitation agreed the bride was beautiful in her high-necked russet gown, and the groom as handsome as any groom could be in a dark blue Bath cloth coat, his cravat tied in the stark style known as the Oriental. The wedding breakfast was as tasty as ever was and the wine of the very best quality. Some, in fact, whispered that the champagne must have been smuggled in. That particular rumor died when the butler brought up a few more very dusty bottles from Lady Catherine's cellar, where she'd hoarded them for just this occasion.

The pair left their wedding breakfast after speaking with each of their guests. Lady Catherine saw them to the door and drew Lord Sanger aside.

"You will remember your promise," she said sternly, her gaze fixed on Lord Sanger's.

"Perhaps," said Lady Helena acidly, "you should come with us as chaperone."

"It crossed my mind," said her ladyship blandly.

Lady Helena's mouth dropped and her eyes widened. Very gently Lord Sanger pressed her jaw back in place. "She is teasing you, wife. She knows I will obey her. After all—" A twist to his features gave him a rather devilish look. "—even if we must wait another two months, it is sooner than we'd originally expected to wed!"

Lady Helena did not soften. "Grandmother had no right to extract such a promise from you!"

Sanger's features sobered and he grasped the hand Lady Catherine extended toward her granddaughter. "She only wishes to protect you, my dear."

"There has been gossip about me for years and very likely it will always be so. They may say what they please."

"They might say what they pleased about Lady Helena Woodhall, but not," said Lord Sanger, "about my countess."

Helena's eyes widened. "You mean to be a stern husband?"

"I mean to protect you. From yourself if need be."

"Bah." She scowled. "I had thought you understood my need for independence."

"I do," he said softly. "I merely wish you to learn wisdom. There are times one may indulge one's whims and times one may not. Come, love. Your grandmother wishes a private word with me. Await me in the carriage?"

Lady Helena looked from her grandmother to her husband. "If I must." She turned on her heel and he followed her through the door.

At the carriage he held out his hand and, after only a brief hesitation, as she wondered if she'd made a serious error, Helena placed hers in it. He squeezed it reassuringly once he'd handed her into the coach and returned to Lady Catherine.

"Lord Sanger . . ." began Lady Catherine and, surprisingly, her voice failed her.

"My lady?"

She drew in a deep breath and tried again. "You have not told her. Told her that you . . . ?" Again, quite out of character, she didn't finish.

"That I love her?" He said it for her. "No. I've not yet told her."

"Tell her."

He smiled but there was a touch of pain in it. "When I think it proper, I will tell her."

"Coward."

"If you wish me to keep my promise," said Sanger, his voice cold, "do not force this particular issue."

"Ah." Enlightenment brought a smile to Lady Catherine's features. "I see. Allowing love to enter into your relationship would complicate the problem of keeping your promise you not touch her, would it not?"

"It would!"

"Fool."

"You forced the promise."

Lady Catherine sighed. "Yes. As you guessed, I, too, would protect her. The gossip is already far worse than she knows and, if she gave birth to your first child even a day too soon, it would harm her dreadfully!"

The newly married couple were no sooner closed into the carriage together then Simon pulled Helena into his arms. For the first time, he kissed her with all the passion of which he was capable, kissed her as she'd longed to be kissed. But that was all he did. Kiss her.

It took every ounce of her self-control not to demand more of him, but Lady Helena managed to content herself

with nothing more than kisses—although she was pleased
to discover that he was very generous with those.

While in London awaiting their wedding day, Helena
had ordered wallpapers and carpets. She'd also chosen
some necessary new furniture which was to be sent on as
soon as she wrote she was ready for it. And she'd found
material from which some much-needed drapery would
be made.

Even though she no longer had a long ride each day,
overseeing the work left less time than she liked for her
search. As she finished each pile of documents, they were
removed to the small room off the library and onto free-
standing shelves designed for their reception: Helena refused to cover the walls with shelving. Despite her difficulty
in originally locating one single plum, she rather liked the
ornate carving.

Although it was taking much longer than she'd hoped,
she *was* reaching the end. In ancient times a century's
worth of documents were fewer than a decade's in later
centuries—and she'd discovered nothing but stray remarks, none of which could be considered proof of anything.

She began to despair and every so often went into the
priest's hole to sit beside the casket. Sometimes she
opened it and laid her hand on the cool gray metal—but
never did she ask the boon she'd threatened, once, to ask.
Somehow, when she actually sat there and thought of saying the words, the notion felt . . . wrong.

She was there one day when Simon came to find her.
"I've a letter from our friendly priest," he said, settling
onto the floor beside her.

"What does he say?"

"We are to be honored by a visit."

"Tomorrow?" she asked sharply.

"It may be a few weeks yet. Father Cartney will come
himself, along with a bishop and a representative from the

original French monastery. He's just had word out of France, you see."

"But I've found nothing. *Nothing!*"

"What did you hope to find?"

"I don't know. But something."

"You've time yet."

"Do I?" She paused. "Simon, is it ridiculous to feel there is something you truly need to know *before* those men, with their own interests, arrive?"

"Hmm. Ridiculous, no. Perhaps serving *your* ends instead of *theirs?*" He touched the urn. Suddenly he rested his hand firmly against it. "Helena," he asked slowly, "have you ever had this thing out of its casket?"

"I once tried, but I cannot manage it."

"Let us see what I can do."

"Why?"

"You have your irrational feeling," he said on a wry chuckle, "and I have mine."

He stood and fitted his hands along the edges of the urn, but there seemed no way to get a good hold. He felt the wood along the edge of the urn, trying to find some place where he could insert his fingers. Suddenly a bit wobbled slightly.

"Aha! I thought there must be a way."

He pried out a triangular-shaped age-blackened chunk of wood and felt along the other side, finding a matching piece. With those removed he could get his hands beneath the urn and lift it away from where it nestled. Setting it aside, he felt around in the depression and, once again, gave an exclamation of success.

Helena leaned nearer. "What is it?" she asked a trifle breathlessly.

"What I'd hoped to find. It is stiff with age and will shatter if we are not very very careful!" Tenderly, Simon lifted out a square of folded vellum which had taken on the shape of the urn. It was tied with tattered ribbon, faded to an uneven gray. An official seal, broken and compressed all out of recognition, still hung from it.

"Let us take this into the library where we can see what it is we've found."

Helena trailed at his heels and then, impatient, watched as he laid the vellum down and attempted to unfold it. A chip fell off.

"There must be a way . . ." He frowned.

"If it were moistened?"

"But how? Simply wetting it will, I fear, damage it."

"Perhaps if we put it in the well house?"

"The damp. You think the vellum will soften if it absorbs moisture gradually?"

"I don't know, do I?"

They stared at each other. "Do we dare?" he asked.

"It is useless as it is." Another long moment passed. "Perhaps if I wrap it in a piece of linen first?"

"*Damp* linen?"

"Might that not be too much too quickly?"

"I wonder how long it will take."

"The sooner we begin, the sooner we shall see!"

The linen-wrapped vellum was placed on a shelf in the well house and everyone was warned it was not to be touched. Each day Lord Sanger and Lady Helena checked, and each day it seemed just the merest bit softer. Perhaps. But not nearly to a degree it could be unfolded.

"We aren't seeing what we wish to see, are we?" asked Helena anxiously on the fourth day.

Simon held her in front of him, his arms around her and his chin on her head as they stared at the packet. "I am sure it is beginning to soften. I just don't know how long it will take."

"I've reached the earliest years of estate history, Simon, which is only bits and pieces. There's not much left and still I've found nothing. At least, I don't think I have. I fear my Latin isn't up to the job."

"Hmm. Perhaps this evening I can help you."

That evening they sat in Helena's sitting room. She had reached a period when *everything* was in Latin and, for some days, Lady Helena had been able to do no more than identify papers that were *not* relevant to her search. She handed over those where she'd been unable to determine the contents and told Simon to see what he could do.

"Lord love me," he muttered when he paused sometime later to drink from the wine set at his elbow. He looked across to where he insisted his wife sit, far enough away so he wasn't tempted to lay aside the papers, lay *her* down and . . . Lord, how beautiful she was.

"What is it? What have you found?"

Simon blinked. "Oh! What I've found is that my Latin is exceedingly rusty from long disuse! This is *work*, Hel! I'd almost rather be back facing French guns!"

It was one of those rare occasions he used her nickname and she smiled to hear it. "At least you have enough Latin there to rust. What very little I learned is barely enough to determine leases from sales of land and purchase agreements, which have anything to do with our search—until I find the establishment of the abbey which I've yet to locate. Back to work, my lord. Perhaps the work itself will oil your rusty memory!"

It was a thought which proved true. The more he read, the more he recalled and, finally, Lady Helena heard what she'd been waiting for.

"This may be of interest," he said slowly rising to his feet, his eyes never leaving the thin sheet of vellum in his hand. "If I haven't misread this, it is an agreement between the first Abbot and the first Lord Sanger."

"But what sort of agreement?"

"There is something about the use for the life of the abbey of the ceremonial urn . . . that the abbey undertakes to keep it safe for the family."

"For the life of the abbey . . . Safe *for the family?*"

They stared at each other.

"But how," asked Helena, "could Lord Sanger have given the use of the urn to the abbey if the abbot brought the relics here from France inside it?"

Simon rubbed at his jaw. "When I lifted the urn and tipped it to set it on the floor—did you hear something move inside it?"

"A sort of clink?"

"Hmm. *Not,* I believe, the noise ashes or bones might make. Would you not agree?"

"My impression was that it was more like metal against metal. So . . . ?"

"So, do you think it possible that the original reliquary was inserted inside the urn and sealed there?"

"Would not Lord Sanger have *given* the urn to the abbey for the purpose?"

"As I remember my history lessons, even *after* William announced he'd conquered England, the times were dangerous. Although small wars and raids were common, nearly everyone respected the possessions of religious houses. If the urn were something the first Sanger valued highly, perhaps he sent it there to be safe."

"So . . . Simon, we *must* unfold and translate that vellum that was with the urn!" She got up and moved to his side, placing her hand on his shoulder. "What if it hasn't softened before those men arrive?"

His hand covered hers. "Why are you so worried?"

"Because, despite you insisting you will give it back, I do not believe the urn is theirs!"

His jaw firmed and a muscle jumped. He, too, rose to his feet, moving away from her touch. "Helena, I will not keep that which is not mine!"

Helena's hands formed fists. "We've clues, now, that it *is!* Oh, not the relics or reliquary, but you suggested those may be *inside* the urn, did you not? And that paper you just translated—for the life of the abbey, safe for the family—that is not phrasing which implies a gift!"

"I am not so certain of my translation that I may agree or disagree. Perhaps I have read what I wish to read?"

Helena sighed. "We've a bit more to search. With my luck the last item I look at will be the one we want! Also, there is a sort of journal which I cannot read." She pointed to a thin volume bound in cracked leather.

Simon brightened. "A journal! Now that should be more interesting than dry old papers dealing with how many men have given allegiance to the Sanger banner and may be counted on to go into battle!"

"Is *that* what the list of names is all about?" asked Helena, picking up a sheet of vellum. "I thought perhaps it was a roll of monks at the abbey or some such thing. Ah well, you have been very good and gotten through a great deal." She handed him the journal. "Here is your reward."

"Reward she says." He caught her wrist, pulling her into his embrace. He kissed her. "Now that," he said softly, "is what I call a reward." Moments later, upon opening the journal, he growled, "A reward, you called it?" He glanced up, amusement revealed in the creases deepening around his eyes. "Helena, not only is it Latin, but in exceedingly bad handwriting! I don't know if I *can* decipher it."

"Try," she muttered, already poring over another sheet on which crabbed writing detailed, she discovered, the purchase of the land on which the abbey had stood, ceding the acreage to the abbey. She set it aside.

"Reward," he said again in a disgusted tone, thinking of the *reward* he *wished* he were getting. Lord, would the two months never pass? How long? Another five weeks, two days, and however few minutes he could manage!

The elfin priest from Cirencester arrived unexpectedly a full two weeks later, with a French monk and a high-ranking English Catholic bishop accompanying him. Helena sent a groom to find Sanger, who'd gone to discuss, again, crop rotation with a tenant reluctant to try new ideas.

"It is very difficult. Travel, I mean," explained Father Cartney earnestly when Lord Sanger returned to Sanger-Monkton. "Bishop Trantor traveled into Portugal on an army supply ship. From there he still had difficulty reaching the founding monastery in France, but reach it he did. Ah! The return! Not only himself, but Frère Vincent! So very difficult."

"He exaggerates," said the monk in soft French. "It was merely a question of discovering where one might hire a smuggler."

"I believe that might be an adventure all in itself," responded Simon, his French rough, but polite and comprehensible. "The, hmm, *gentlemen,* as they like to be called, are known to be reluctant to have people know of their existence."

The Frenchman shrugged. "It is enough that it was arranged. We have brought proof," he finished in an insinuating tone that, somehow, also managed to sound impatient. He'd been clutching a packet against his chest and now brought it to the table. There, he unwrapped layers of oiled cloth. Next he broke the several seals laid over cords tied around a thin metal container, keeping it tightly sealed. Then, with difficulty, he pried the two halves of the container apart and with careful fingers gently withdrew a thin stack of ancient vellum.

The writing was, surprisingly, in old French rather than Latin. Lord Sanger looked at Lady Helena and grimaced. "Can you decipher it?" he asked.

"I am more than merely adequate in modern French, I believe," she said, speaking in fluent and unaccented tones, "but this may be more difficult for me than your rusty Latin was for you! Luckily, I have been entertaining myself by reading a very old history of France and the practice may be a help in my efforts here."

She bent over the papers the monk spread along the table. The first was obviously *not* the initial letter of what must have been a lengthy correspondence between the first Lord Sanger and the then abbot of the French monastery. She said as much to the monk who looked surprised that a woman had made such a discovery and then, perhaps, not too happy she'd done so.

"The very first letters were not thought important," he said abruptly. When Lady Helena continued to stare at him he turned his eyes away and, quite plausibly added, "Until something began to be settled, they were irrelevant."

Helena decided she did not trust the fellow. She turned to the bishop who, his eyes narrowed slightly, also watched the Frenchman. There was the faintest of frown lines between his brows. Helena relaxed. This one, she thought, could be trusted!

Lord Sanger brought her a chair and she settled in to study the detailed agreement between the abbot and Simon's ancestor. "Aha!" she finally said. She said it very softly, but the four men, who had adjourned with a bottle of wine to the far end of the library, heard her and lifted their heads.

Simon came to her side. A hand on her shoulder, he asked, "What is it?"

"It's about the saint and a description of the reliquary."

"Tell us."

"A gold casket—" She glanced up. "It is quite small, I believe, but I cannot translate the exact size." Simon nodded and she continued. "Forty diamonds and a hundred pearls the size of early peas set into the sides and the top, four sapphires, cut *en cabochon*, set in the top in a diamond, and a ruby, also *en cabochon*, centered in that. Also red gold worked in relief, forming cartouches on the side panels. Shall I translate the pictures the relief work make?"

"Not just yet. Does it say how the reliquary will be transported?"

Helena bent to her work. "In a wooden casket which is . . ." She paused. "Simon, *more* figures. *You* tell me how large it is."

Simon did a quick calculation, muttered some dimensions and smiled. "Not nearly so large as our casket."

"What?" exclaimed the Frenchman. "Have I come on a . . . a what do you say? A wild duck chase?"

"I believe your journey is not a wild *goose* chase. We must merely determine exactly what is yours and what is not," said Helena.

"I do not understand. The relics must return to their home."

"We do not argue that," said Simon.

"And *will* not argue that," inserted Helena. "But we will not give up what is *not* yours."

The Frenchman, looking offended, turned on his heel and faced the high churchman. "I will not speak with a female. It is not proper."

"And I will not be left out of anything which is important to my husband," said Helena just as firmly. "We do not deny we've a problem. Simply, it must be settled honorably and justly."

Simon, surprised but pleased by her vehemence, took her hand, lifted it to his lips. He wasn't at all astonished, however, when she ignored his action, never taking her eyes from the monk.

"I must have the relics! They have a long history of . . ." Frère Vincent suddenly closed his mouth into a tight line.

Helena eyed the Frenchman, wondering what he'd not said. "Have we said you will *not* have the relics?" she asked. "It might be nice if they made one last procession around the estate as was done each year they rested at the Abbey, but—"

The monk shook his head vehemently.

"—we'll not insist."

The monk's mouth pressed into a hard firm line, the lips very nearly disappearing. "I would see this chest which is large."

"When we've sorted though the relevant papers," said Helena quickly, grasping Simon's arm when, politely, he'd have gone for it. "We've some documents of our own to present, one of which—" She frowned. "—Well, we've not yet been able to read it."

"And how do you know it is important if you cannot read it?" asked the monk sourly.

"Because it was kept with the outer urn."

"*Outer* urn?" The monk frowned.

"It and a paper we have in our possession," explained Sanger, "suggest my ancestor sent a family possession to the Abbey, asking that it be kept safe for the family. We believe the original reliquary was inserted into our possession and that it must be removed before handing it over to you."

"If the reliquary is inside it, then the family must have given the protective urn to the abbey," said the monk before the churchman could speak.

"I think not," said Simon, catching and holding the monk's eyes. "I will ask our countrymen to read our documents before a decision is made."

"I, too, must read them!" insisted the monk.

"But only after they've been read by our English bishop and his priest."

"The reliquary is mine!"

"It is your abbey's," said the high churchman quietly and a trifle sternly. He turned to Simon. "May I see your documents please."

He read the first with far more ease than Simon had

originally done. ". . . for so long as the abbey exists. That seems clear enough. But what is it the abbey kept for the family? Can you prove that this item you wish to retain is this particular possession?"

"I think we can," said Sanger, "but not until we can read the thing! I don't know if we can yet unfold the vellum we found in the casket."

"I'll get it, Simon," said Helena. She returned with the vellum, which still retained the shape of the urn under which it had lain for centuries. "Simon, I think we should ask our guests to check that this came from the casket, since one of them seems to have an excessively suspicious nature—" She scowled at the monk. "Can you bring it out or should I call someone to help you?"

"The wooden casket alone is not all that heavy, Helena." He brought only the casket into the library. Helena carefully unwrapped the linen and laid the vellum into place. The high churchman nodded although she heard the Frenchman mutter that it was all a plot and why would they not simply give him what was his.

"Our problem, as you can see, is that the vellum is very old. It had dried out."

The churchman touched it, gently pressing it down against the table. "You did well to let it soften slowly. Many would have been impatient and the document ruined." With far more patience than Helena knew she had, the man began to separate the halves. The work was delicate and he did not rush it. Seeing it would take time, Helena went away, returning with a footman who carried a tray of refreshments. The monk, she noted, ate greedily, but the churchman merely shook his head, continuing his careful effort.

At long last he lifted one side away from the other, very gently tipping it. When a crack appeared at the fold he stopped. "If you would hold that lamp I believe I can now peer in."

Simon held the lamp. His hand shook slightly as he waited to hear what the churchman could read.

"There is a seal at the bottom. The ink has faded over the years, but I believe . . ." The man's hands shook and he took them away from the vellum, fearing he'd damage it. "Surely not!"

"Not what?"

"Not the Conqueror's mark!"

Except for the monk, who continued to mutter, everyone was silent, awed at the thought.

"You would suggest," said Father Cartney softly, "that the casket contained a gift from William the Conqueror to Lord Sanger's ancestor?"

"I believe that is what is recorded here," said the bishop, who had once again bent to his task.

"Then it is not surprising the family wished the abbey to see to its safety!" The priest's hands clasped. "A gift from William!"

"I still think whatever you had in this rough wooden casket was given to the abbey!" snarled the monk.

"You believe no such thing," said the bishop sternly. "We've enough information in these two documents to agree that the contents of this case belong to the Sanger family. We must, then, remove what you, Lord Sanger, believe to be inside and, if it proves to be the reliquary described in Frère Vincent's document, then that must be returned to the home abbey in France." He looked from Lord Sanger to Lady Helena and back to His Lordship. "Agreed?"

Simon and Helena looked at each other and then at the churchman. They nodded in unison and Simon sighed. "Now," he said, "we've, hmm, *merely* the problem of getting the urn open."

"And why is that a problem?" demanded the Frenchman, suspicious all over again.

The difficulties of opening the urn without damaging

it were considerable, but the process did prove what Lady Catherine had suspected from the instant she'd heard the tale. The urn itself, under the lead coating it, was solid gold. At some point it had been dipped in molten lead, the resulting ugly gray color very likely an additional safeguard against thievery—with the additional advantage that they sealed the saint's relics safely within.

Simon, as soon as they began working to free the relics, sent a message to Lady Catherine, but she and General Porson didn't arrive before the lead around the top had softened enough so that it could be dug away from the gold, and they weren't there when, very gently, the bishop reached into the urn and lifted out a small gold box covered in pearls, the uncut precious stones round moons of color.

A sigh ran around the room. No one spoke. Helena, drawn, laid her hand on the top and, silently if fervently, begged that her marriage to Simon be long and happy for the both of them. For a very long moment no one moved and then, lifting the casket from the bishop's hands, Helena moved gracefully to the French monk. She held it out to him.

The Frenchman hesitated. Then, grimacing, and very careful he not touch her, he took the casket and hugged it to his breast as he'd previously done the papers. His eyes closed and Helena thought he might be praying, which was the first thing she'd seen in the man to approve!

Frère Vincent carried the casket to the table, set it down and, after searching within his robes, pulled out a small leather pouch. He opened it. From it he took a key. The key fitted the tiny lock and turned easily—even after the centuries it had lain unopened.

Before lifting the lid the monk removed a crystal vial from the same pouch along with a tiny gold spoon. He lay those aside and then, again pausing for prayer, he lifted the lid.

Opening the vial he, with some difficulty, spooned a portion of the long-hardened ashes and a tiny sliver of bone into the crystal container. After a moment he placed the spoon in the casket. "Sacrilege to wipe it," he muttered. He screwed on the top to the vial. Ceremoniously, he carried it to the bishop and handed it to him.

"My abbot said I was to leave this with you. That something of the power of the saint should remain in England."

"I will send him my thanks," said the bishop, handling the crystal with reverence.

The casket was relocked and the key replaced in the pouch, which disappeared inside the monk's robes, and just then Lady Catherine and General Porson swept into the room, all curiosity as to what had happened.

The story was soon told. At the end Father Cartney smiled and nodded and said, "Well now, that wasn't so bad."

Lady Catherine looked from one disbelieving face to another and chuckled. "Like a child and its spring tonic? Not so bad once it is over?"

After the churchmen left, the others settled down for a much-needed interval of assimilation of the meaning of the urn and what Simon, suddenly enriched by the gold, might now do. They welcomed their tea, but the conversation among the four was, for reasons Lady Helena could not understand, vaguely uncomfortable.

Finally Lady Catherine, who had looked anxiously from one to the other again and again, glared at Simon. "You've not told her," said Her Ladyship, bitingly.

"No."

"Coward!"

"Very likely," said Simon, his voice exceedingly dry.

"Told me what?" asked Helena.

"And *you*—" Lady Catherine turned her glare on Helena. "—have not told *him.*"

Does she refer to the fact I love him? thought Lady Hel. She sent a quick sideways look toward Simon, her cheeks reddening.

"So?" Lady Catherine looked from one to the other.

"When it is time . . ." began Simon.

"And if I say *now* is the time?" demanded the dowager, imperiously.

"It is not a thing you can simply order done!" said Simon. For a moment his glance clashed with, and then brushed beyond Helena's.

"And what is your excuse, Hel?" Catherine's voice contained more than a touch of acid.

"You have said it, I believe," said Lady Helena pertly— but her heart pounded. "I am a coward."

"Bah! General Porson!" Rising to her feet, Lady Catherine told him, "Return me to the Cooper-Wainwrights'. I wash my hands of the two of them!"

Simon and Helena stared at each other, neither bothering to escort their guests from the room. In fact they barely knew the couple left.

"You've something to say to me?" asked Simon, expectantly, his gaze speculative.

"As I understood my grandmother," said Helena, hope rising in her breast for the very first time, *"you* have something to say to *me."*

"You first," suggested Simon after a moment. "It is only polite after all, the lady first."

"In this I think it would be more proper that I defer to my husband." Her brows arched.

Again silent, they stared at each other.

"I've a notion," said Helena. "Perhaps if we were to speak as one?"

"On the count of three?" he suggested, tension making his voice crack.

"One . . ." said Simon.

As they counted, they drew closer. Closer still.

"Two . . ." said Helena.

Their hands met and their gazes locked.

"Three—"

Two voices chimed together.

"—I love you."

They struggled to find each other's lips, clasp the other close, closer.

"About time!"

And they heard Lady Catherine's smug-sounding voice. They broke apart, turning to look at Helena's grandmother who stood in the library doorway grinning at them. Helena felt her cheeks redden, glanced at Simon and felt better that he, too, revealed embarrassment.

"I suggest," said the dowager, her triumphant smile much in evidence, "that we consider a full two months have passed." Lady Catherine nodded once, turned, and again left the two alone.

For which Simon and Helena devoutly thanked heaven above!

Dear Reader,

Lady Helena had her problems, did she not? I'm glad they were finally resolved and that Sanger grew more than merely resigned to their marriage.

My next book involves a different sort of problem. The war with France is finally over and my heroine is determined her army-mad brother will come home. The only problem is that no one at the Horse Guards will admit to knowing where he is, so Constance Mordaunt travels with her niece and nephew to London to discover the truth—and is mistaken for her brother's wife.

Her brother returns to England, but only after Constance takes her reputation in hand and dares accept the escort of Jack Durrant, Major Lord St. Aubyn, going into France to find him. As a married lady this is barely acceptable; when Jack discovers she's *not* married he offers the only possible solution, the protection of his name. They will, of course, tell those who met her in London and thought her Mordaunt's wife that she is his cousin's widow, thereby smothering any gossip that arises.

"The widowed Miss Mordaunt!" laughs Jack.

Mordaunt is convinced he must sell out of the army, so Constance no longer worries about the estate or her young relatives. *Now* she worries about saving Jack from his own honorable self and how she may convince him she really does *not* want to wed him. Since she *does*, that proves difficult.

Actually, of course, it proves impossible—but by then she's learned Jack loves her, so that's all right.

I hope you enjoy *The Widowed Miss Mordaunt,* which will be published in March 1999. And I hope you'll want to read my next book, too, which will be released in the fall.

Happy reading to all . . .

Cheerfully,

P.S. I enjoy hearing from my readers and can be reached at P.O. Box 1771, Rochester, MI 48308. I'll be certain to respond if you include a stamped, self-addressed envelope.

LOOK FOR THESE REGENCY ROMANCES